Man with an Axe

Man with an Axe

Jon A. Jackson

The Atlantic Monthly Press
New York

Published simultaneously in Canada
Printed in the United States of America

FIRST EDITION

Library of Congress Cataloging-in-Publication Data

Jackson, Jon A.
    Man with an axe / Jon A. Jackson.
       p.   cm.
    ISBN 0-87113-708-9
    I. Title.
    PS3560.A216M36   1998
    813'.54—dc21   97-34357

Design by Laura Hammond Hough

The Atlantic Monthly Press
841 Broadway
New York, NY 10003

98 99 00 01 10 9 8 7 6 5 4 3 2 1

For my father
Jabe Cook Jackson
1905–1997

Man with an Axe

Blues Going Up

July 30, 1975

"'T'ain't what you know," Tyrone's uncle Lonzo was wont to say, "it's what you don'." Sadly so, it's the single thing that we do not know that so often shapes how things go for us. Tyrone Addison knew and understood most everything about his true wife, Vera, but he didn't know everything—couldn't, mustn't know—and that was more or less fatal.

At this moment in the late afternoon of a summer day in the suburbs north of Detroit, Tyrone was determined to believe that they were driving to Machus' Red Fox Inn for drinks before an early dinner with his old friend Janney Jacobsen. It was something that he wanted to do, knew he should do, but in the way of such things he had to act as if it was all Vera's idea, that it was a terrific bore to him or even a great nuisance. "The same-o, same-o," as Uncle Lonzo liked to say—and Tyrone affected to see it that way.

"Every time things get tight," he said to Vera, speaking loudly over the noise of the elderly Volkswagen engine, "you think it's time to eat out. That don't make sense, girl. Shift! Shift the damn gear!"

"That's not fair," Vera said, shifting the laboring engine into third gear. But it was true: in moments of stress she had a tendency

3

to suggest a nice dinner, automatically. It had something to do with her childhood, perhaps; she didn't know. But she felt that eating well would make everything better. This dinner was different, but she knew that Tyrone wasn't just thinking of that. She knew he was harping on this to avoid saying something else, something that if said might not be so easy to unsay. It was much better for him to complain that when times got tough she was secretly glad, because she had money and he had none and now she could play the *Duchess,* which was a name Tyrone had for her when he was feeling put down, when he felt at a disadvantage. She was grateful that he didn't say it, that he chose rather to focus on a presumed tendency of hers to squander money on dining out, or her bad driving.

Here was the problem, simply put: Janney Jacobsen was Tyrone's friend, his admirer, and his sometime financial backer. If that had been all there was to it, that would be problem enough, but Janney was also in love with Vera. That is too simply put. In fact, although Vera went by the name of her true husband, Addison, she had married Jacobsen, a Dutch national, to provide him with American citizenship, and she was still legally married to him, years later. At the time of the marriage, Tyrone was playing sax in Phil Woods's band, which was touring Europe, and he had met Vera in Paris and Janney in Amsterdam. Janney was rich; he wanted to emigrate, but there was some complication that had to do with a youthful criminal escapade, long forgotten except by the U.S. Immigration and Naturalization Service. Janney would be allowed in as the spouse of an American citizen, and then he could devote himself to promoting his friend and musical idol, Tyrone Addison. So it was done, at Tyrone's urging.

This is the complication, and it's more complicated than that, but is not presently germane. The point is that Vera and Tyrone were on their way to meet Janney for an early dinner at the Red Fox, to discuss money for a recording project. Whether it meant that Janney got to sleep with Vera is not important, because the meeting did not take place.

"Well? Are we going to the restaurant or not? Turn! Damn, Duchess, can't you watch what you're doing?"

Vera angrily swung the van across the southbound lanes of Telegraph Road into the parking lot of the suburban restaurant and was instantly blinded. She was driving right into the waning sun and the glare off the filthy windshield badly obscured her vision. Tyrone, as ever, was wearing dark glasses, so he saw the man who burst out of the shrubbery.

"Stop!" Tyrone shrieked. "For godsakes, don't hit him!"

Vera stopped just in time. The man actually bumped against the bullnose of the Volkswagen van, but she hadn't hit him; it was the man's impetus that propelled him against the vehicle.

The man looked wild. He was stocky, in late middle age, and his eyes were wide and rolling. He was wearing a black, short-sleeved polo shirt and slacks. He angrily bashed a hefty leather briefcase at the nose of the van. It thumped solidly.

"Whyncha look where d'hell yer goin'?" he snarled. His voice was quite audible with the windows open and the engine silent, killed when Vera had slammed on the brakes.

Suddenly the man swiveled his head, peering into the foliage of the shrubbery that shielded the parking lot from the surrounding terrain, which included a suburban shopping area on one side, with its large parking lot, and on the other side some sparsely wooded acreage. It wasn't clear which direction the man had come from, perhaps from the restaurant itself, which was a modest brick building, with a contemporary low-profile structure but sporting some faux rustic half-timbered effects, which licensed this suburban eatery to proclaim itself an "inn."

Evidently, the man heard something that alarmed him more than being hit by a vehicle. He scampered around the side of the van and took hold of the sliding door handle. "Lemme in," he rasped. "Lemme the fuck in!" He slid the door open and hopped in, crouching on the mattress that covered the floor of the van. "Get goin'!" he demanded. "Go! Go, go, go!" He ducked down.

In a panic, Vera tried to start the engine but managed to flood it. Unfazed, Tyrone leaned over the seat and demanded, in his best jive style: "Hey! What the fuck you doin'? Who invited you, motherfucker? Get the fuck outta my damn car!"

The starter whizzed but the engine did not catch. Tyrone lifted his long-suffering eyes to the sky. "Jesus! Give it a rest, Duchess," he said wearily. He turned back to the man and in a semiwhitey voice of detached calmness, said: "Listen here, my man . . . what the hell you up to? Tell me that."

The man gestured with his briefcase, which he had partly open with his hand buried within. It was a threatening gesture, Tyrone felt. But he didn't like being threatened in his own car—or his wife's car—by some old white man who looked like a crazy Polack. "Whattayou, some kinda damn lawyer? You gon' sue? She didn't run into you, you ran into us. Whatchoo got in dere?" he demanded, slipping back into the spook act. "You tryna tell me you got a gun in dere? Show me yo' piece, mothafucka."

"What I got in here," the man rasped, his voice betraying desperation, "is a goddamn good reason for you to get the fuck goin'. So get the fuck goin'! Help the broad, f'chrissake!"

The car started. Vera looked at Tyrone. He nodded resignedly; she put it in gear and they coasted forward. They cruised through the parking lot. This lot surrounded the restaurant, except for the front, which faced Telegraph Road, and it was all but empty at this hour, too early to call evening. There were a couple of flashy cars, Cadillacs and Lincolns, and toward the remote fringes the humble Fords and Chevys of the staff. Vera stopped at the edge of the neighboring parking lot, but the man spoke up from the depths of the back.

"No, no, turn right. That's it. Turn. Go on out on Telegraph."

Vera turned onto Telegraph Road and began to drive south. She looked at Tyrone. He shrugged. "Man got a gun, Duchess. Guess we do what he wants. Hey! Old man! Old-man-with-a-gun! Where you wanta go?" Tyrone nodded his head then slightly, rhythmically, quietly mouthing the phrase, "Oman, omanwitta, omanwittagun, wittagun . . ."

"Anywheres, just keep goin'." The man scrambled toward the back and tried to look out, but the rear window was filthy, as always. There was fairly heavy traffic on Telegraph, particularly the northbound lanes. If the man was concerned about someone following, and clearly he was, there was no way of determining it. There were a few cars coming up behind them, but they were hardly identifiable through the dirt of the back window. "Get off Telegraph," the man rasped. "What's this comin' up, Thirteen Mile?" He peered through the windshield. "Turn left, turn left."

Vera turned left and they drove about five hundred yards before their passenger bade them to pull over. "Get off the friggin' road," he said. He actually said "friggin'," evidently in deference to the presence of Vera, as if he had only now realized that a woman was in company. They sat quietly on the side of the road as several cars turned off Telegraph and cruised past them. Only Tyrone absently nodded his head and muttered, "Oman, omanwitta, gunwittagun. . . . Tha's kinda cool, got its own little beat. E, C, B-flat, maybe. Hmmm."

Shortly it began to seem that no one had followed them. The man seemed to relax, a little anyway.

He looked his rescuers over carefully. What he saw was a pretty white woman, about twenty-five (in his aging eyes), with long blond hair, wearing a shapeless cotton dress that almost hid a busty figure and an essential slenderness. Some kind of hippie, he thought, and assumed that accounted for her friend, whom he saw as a black fellow wearing shades, slightly older, maybe as much as thirty. It looked to him like the black man was stoned, nodding his head and muttering.

The man had known a lot of black people in his sixty-two years and he had given up trying to estimate their ages. In fact, he had Tyrone's and Vera's ages almost exactly reversed, but he wouldn't have been surprised; he'd dealt with too many smooth-faced seventy-year-olds and gnarly-faced kids. He didn't think much of Tyrone, at first sight: a long face with thin lips and a ridiculous, wispy beard. He wore his hair long, not so much kinky as twisty, under a brocade or embroidered silk skullcap that had a tassel.

The man didn't care for the cap, although it was distinctive, because he didn't like blacks to be so assertive. And he didn't notice Tyrone's thin, aristocratic Ethiopian features. The black fellow had a good voice, the man thought: deep, articulate, well-modulated, sort of rhythmic somehow. But the nodding and muttering annoyed him.

What Tyrone saw was an old white man with a blunt, tough face and hair combed straight back, Polack fashion. Pure honky. An auto worker, Tyrone thought, except for the authoritative manner. That wasn't the way of a man who worked in a factory, but he was dressed like they all dress, in strange brownish-purplish-gray form-less slacks. He thought: Where do they get those pants, and does that color have an actual name? Black laced shop shoes with thick rubber soles, and a black short-sleeved polo shirt that had a little animal on the breast. What was it, a snake or something? No, an alligator.

The man was stocky and looked overweight at first, but then Tyrone noticed that he was really hard, muscular. He was intimidating with his little, hard blue eyes and his thin, mean mouth.

Vera thought his mouth looked humorous, like a man's who told jokes and laughed a lot; and the beady glitter of the eyes she saw as twinkles. He looked like Uncle Vance, a not very successful brother of her mother's, a man who had bankrupted two auto dealerships. There was something about him, though. He looked

8

familiar. And suddenly she realized who he was. It thrilled her. "Are you . . . ? Aren't you Jimmy Hoffa?"

"You got something against Hoffa?" the man said, but he seemed gratified to be recognized.

"No, no," Vera assured him.

Tyrone took off his glasses to get a better look and then said, "Somebody after you, Mr. Hoffa?"

Hoffa was making a face, seemingly to deny Tyrone's suggestion, when a large, gleaming maroon Cadillac turned off Telegraph and came along Thirteen Mile Road at a slow pace. "Jeeziss!" Hoffa exclaimed and flopped down in the back. The car cruised on past them.

"Who's after you?" Tyrone pursued.

"I don't know. Nobody," Hoffa said, rising barely enough to peer over the front seat at the stately progress of the Cadillac.

"You must know," Tyrone said, "'cause you reckanized that Caddy. Some gangsters on yo' case?"

"Whaddya talkin' about? I didn't see no gangsters."

"Look like gangsters to me," Tyrone said. He gazed dispassionately at Hoffa, then shrugged. "Ain't no business of mine. Man wants to pretend they ain't no gangsters on his case, that's cool with me. Well, nice meetin' y'all, Mr. Hoffa. Can we drop you some place?"

"Yanh, take me back to the restaurant. Okay?" Hoffa sounded much calmer, more polite. Perhaps it was the knowledge that they knew who he was. "Don't worry, I'll pay you for your trouble."

"Don't worry about it, man," Tyrone said, waving away Hoffa's hand, which was holding more than one bill. "But you sure you wanta go back there? I thought somebody was after you."

Hoffa withdrew his hand and seemed to ponder. "Yanh, yer right. I wasn't thinkin'. Sorry. Listen, how 'bout you find me a telephone? I'll call a buddy a mine. It won't take him ten minutes to get here, but I need for you to maybe stick around. Okay?"

"Sure, man, sure."

They drove farther east on Thirteen Mile, careful not to overtake the Cadillac, until they spotted a telephone booth. It stood on the edge of a paved expanse belonging to a gas station. Hoffa wouldn't get out. He was edgy again.

"Check it out for me, will ya?" he asked Tyrone.

Tyrone didn't complain, didn't even make a face, just clambered out of the front seat and stretched. It was still quite hot, a typical Detroit summer day, humid. The sun was angling down, but had a ways to go before dark. Tyrone rubbed his nose where his glasses had irritated the skin, then walked over to the phone. The door was open. He stepped inside but didn't close the door. He picked up the receiver and he got a hum, though not of course the dial tone that waited for a dime. He let the phone dangle and went back to the car and leaned in the window. "I need a dime. You want me to place the call for you?"

"That'd be great," Hoffa said eagerly, and provided a number along with a handful of change.

"That gonna be a toll charge?" Tyrone asked, looking at the change in his long, slender palm.

"Nah, I don't think so. You got anuff," Hoffa assured him. "Dial it. I got more if you need it."

Tyrone had just dialed the number, and it was ringing—not a toll call, after all—when a gleaming maroon Cadillac swept into the gas station and pulled up by the Volkswagen. He squinted through the dirty glass of the phone booth at it. It looked like the same Caddy that had spooked Hoffa earlier.

A heavy white man got out of the passenger side and approached the van, then stopped when he took in Tyrone. His right arm dangled straight down, a huge revolver in his hand, pointed at the ground casually. He seemed totally unconcerned about nearby traffic, or the possibility that customers of the gas station or the help might notice the revolver. He glanced at Vera, then at Tyrone, then back to the car. He walked over to the rear of the Cadillac and a dark-tinted window rolled smoothly down. A pale face shone in the interior. The man leaned to the window and spoke in an ordinary tone. Tyrone could hear him quite clearly.

"It's just a spade, boss. He got a white whore. You want me to . . . ?" He gestured slightly with the revolver. He leaned closer as the man inside spoke. Tyrone could not hear what was said, but his blood ran cold as the big man straightened up and turned to look at him, with his head tilted to listen to the voice within the car.

The man regarded Tyrone for a long moment, his face blank, mouth open tentatively, as if bemused. With his left hand he fingered the revolving chamber of the pistol, slowly turning it. The oiled clicks were quite audible. Then he nodded, as if to the speaker, and his lips curled in a strange smile. "You're in luck, Willie," the man called out, hefting the revolver meaningfully. "Hope you find a trick for her." The man cupped his hand under his crotch and tugged. He nodded toward Vera and then he got back into the car. It roared away.

"Hello? Hello?" a man's voice called distantly from the telephone. Tyrone lifted it shakily to his ear. "Is that you Jimmy? You there?" the man asked, anxiously. "F'chrissake, talk t'me!" Tyrone replaced the receiver and almost staggered back to the car, his legs felt so weak.

He got in the front seat and closed the door and leaned his head back against the headrest and closed his eyes. "Jesusfucking-christ," he breathed. "That motherfucker was about to . . ."

Vera leaned anxiously across the console, embracing him, saying, "Honey, honey, honey, don't, don't."

"Let's get the fuck outta here," came a muffled voice from the rear. They both turned and looked. Hoffa was crouched on the floor, under some blankets. "Get goin'. They might come back. Somebody mighta seen me get inta yer van. Drive!"

"Right, right," Vera said. She got the van started and they drove on east. They were almost calmed down when they saw the Cadillac parked on the westbound shoulder next to another big car.

The big man was out of the car talking and gesturing to another man. He had put the pistol away, but when he recognized the Volkswagen his left hand went to his crotch again and he laughed to the man next to him, pointing at them as they cruised by, his right hand imitating a gun and his mouth silently opening as if to say, "Pow!"

"Keep going, keep going," Hoffa said. "Don't slow down, but don't speed. I don't wanta see no cops."

Tyrone craned around. "Why not?"

"Cops got radios, numbnuts. Even if a cop ain't on the pad, they talk on the radios and other people got radios, too." Hoffa peeked out from the blanket. "And out here, buddy, I don't know who's on the pad."

Tyrone looked at the man cowering under a blanket. Then he looked at Vera. She was driving with great concentration, trying not to let on that she was about to flip out. She looked brave, he thought, but he could see she was scared shitless. Strangely enough, knowing she was scared made him feel stronger. He smiled encouragingly at her when she glanced at him.

"Just keep driving, sweetie," he said in as calm a voice as he could manage. He turned back to their passenger. "Hoffa. We have to let you out now. Not out here on the road, you understand, but on one of these side roads. You dig?"

"Not on your life, buddy," Hoffa said. He showed Tyrone the barrel of a nickel-plated revolver. "You drop me off out here and those birds'll be on me like crows on a roadkill possum."

Tyrone nodded his head. He supposed the man was right, though he had no idea why Jimmy Hoffa should be afraid of gangsters—wasn't he a gangster himself? But a lifetime of coping with gangsters in Detroit had left Tyrone with the feeling that their activities were as inexplicable and unpredictable as wild animals. It was better to give them a wide berth and not waste time figuring out what they were up to. "So what do you want to do?" he asked.

"Take me into the city," Hoffa said. "Where do you guys live?"

"The city's a long ways," Tyrone said. "We're living in a motel, right now, clear back in Highland Park." This was not true and he was glad that Vera did not react. Usually she was so stuffy about telling the absolute truth that she would not have let such a falsehood pass. "Must be some place we can drop you. 'Cause man, it ain't cool ridin' around out here like this."

Hoffa nodded. The thinking was sound, he felt. They were a conspicuous couple. With the men in the Cadillac that had actually protected him, but it didn't do to attract attention. A suburban cop might pull this van over for any excuse—a broken taillight, perhaps—and then search the van for drugs. The trouble was, he couldn't think of any place that would be safe. The men in the Caddy knew his ways too well, and they were vicious. He was worried about his wife, Jo, but he believed that while they would certainly be keeping an eye on the house, they wouldn't bother her. It was him they were after.

He shook his head. "I don't know."

Tyrone looked at him. "You don't know? You ain't got no place to go? Woman." He turned to Vera. "Shift!" She had pulled away from a light and, as often happened, had forgotten to shift into fourth gear.

"Listen, Jim," Tyrone said, turning back. "We can't be out here all night. You got any money? Lemme see." A hand grabbed his guts when Hoffa dumped out the briefcase: a pile of bills in neat little packets. "How much is that?" he asked, deeply impressed.

"That's a couple hunnert," Hoffa said, "less about fifty bucks."

"That's more than a couple hundred," Tyrone said.

"A couple hunnert thous'n," Hoffa said, almost smiling. "Sorry. I thought you'd see that. The point is, Henry, it don't mean shit if that Caddy comes after us again. I got this"—he brandished the revolver—"but I gotta admit, I ain't famous for no shootin'. I shoot with my mouth, as my old lady says. So if you can figure out some safe place for me and this bread here, Henry, I'm sure we can work out some kinda appropriate remuneration, if you get my drift."

"The name ain't Henry. It's . . . Ty-yyyaylor. An' this here is my wife, Alma." Tyrone had no idea where "Alma" had come from; it had just popped into his head. Vera glanced at him and grimaced. If he hadn't been so stressed he might have laughed. In fact, he was feeling so damn stressed that he was afraid that if he ever started laughing he'd make like a hyena and never quit.

"Taylor? Is that your first name or your last? Never mind. Okay, Taylor. Any ideas?"

Tyrone thought. "Well, we could go to my uncle Lonzo's, in the Thumb. Uncle Lonzo ain't there. But I know where the key is. Nobody be there. Nobody bother us."

"Your Uncle Lonzo lives up in the Thumb? Whereabouts?"

"It's a resort. A black resort. It's called Turtle Lake. You ever hear of it?"

Hoffa had heard of it. It was also called Nigger Heaven. It was one of a few such strictly Negro resorts in upstate Michigan. There was a larger Nigger Heaven farther over by the Lake Michigan shore, near Baldwin. But this Turtle Lake was older, closer to Detroit. It struck him as an absolutely ideal hideout. No Mob goon would dream of entering the gates of Nigger Heaven.

"You know a colored fella named Books?" Hoffa asked. "I don't remember his last name. Little guy, kind of dapper. He's a kind of fixer, a bagman. I think he's s'posta have a cabin on Turtle Lake."

"I know him," Tyrone said. "He's over the other side of the lake from Lonzo's, by the golf course."

"I don't want to see him," Hoffa said. "I don't want to see nobody. And I don' want Books to see me. Nobody sees Hoffa. Got it? And no phone calls. Got it? You don't tell nobody that Jimmy Hoffa is staying over to your uncle Lonzo's. I'll keep inna house. A couple days and this'll blow over and Hoffa'll be outta yer hair. And you'll have a coupla grand. That sound like a deal, Taylor?"

"A coupla grand! You gotta be shuckin', Jim. Ahmo lay my ass on the line for a coupla grand? Shee-it!"

"Awright," Hoffa responded readily, "make it ten grand."

"Twenny be more like it," Tyrone popped back.

"So, make it twenny," Hoffa easily agreed.

"Hey, it's a deal, Jim." Tyrone hoped that his voice didn't sound as false as Hoffa's. Once you'd seen two hundred grand, twenty big ones didn't look so big, all of a sudden, especially when you were just talking twenty, not holding twenty. "You get some sleep. It's at least an hour, maybe more on them back roads. You feelin' all right?"

"Tell ya the troot, Taylor, I'm kinda wheezy. You know? How you doin' for gas? When we get out a ways you can stop for gas." He handed Tyrone a couple of fifties. "Get me some Pepto, or Di-Gel, somethin' like that. I'll be all right. Just a little wheezy. Too much coffee or somethin'."

Tyrone nodded. Soon he was humming, staring into the darkness of the country road they'd turned onto and patting out an interesting rhythm on the dash. "Oman," he sang, softly, "omanwitta, gunwittagun." He reached over and squeezed Vera's leg and grinned at her. She smiled back, happy as a bird in a bush.

Suddenly she gasped, her face stricken. "Oh my God! We forgot Janney!"

"Jeesus!" Tyrone exclaimed. Obviously, he had just as completely forgotten the projected meeting. But almost immediately he was suffused with a certain gladness. As liberated as he might be, he had hated the idea of carrying his wife to a meeting with Janney that would almost certainly have involved her being, in a sense, "sold" to another man. "Oh, well," he said, blithely, "fuck it. Fuck Janney."

He glanced at his wife. She smiled and squeezed his hand. And they both felt very good.

1

Absent Head

*As to structure, my own form is narrative, which is not every
historian's, I may say—indeed, it is rather looked down on now
by the advanced academics, but I don't mind because no one
could possibly persuade me that telling a story is not the most
desirable thing a writer can do.*

Barbara Tuchman, "The Historian as Artist"

I agree, though I am no writer, nor a historian. I am a
detective. My name is Mulheisen. My initial impulse was to tell this
story in the form of a report, a crime report, but for reasons that I
hope will become plain, it seemed more appropriate to simply write
it up as a story. Maybe by the end of this narrative I'll know what to
do with it.

By now I have talked to just about everybody who was involved that is still available and I have thought about their versions
and this is what I have come up with. I think it is probably as close
to the truth as we are likely to come to about what happened to
Jimmy Hoffa, the former president of the International Brotherhood
of Teamsters, who disappeared from public view on July 30, 1975.

Though, after all, this is not just an account of the Hoffa
affair. Like every story, its true origins are hidden deep in the past.
When we stand in the present, confronted with this or that event,
and look back, only the most narrow-sighted can see a single or
even just a few paths dwindling into the distance. What any sensible person sees, I believe, is a network of paths and thorough-
fares, cutting across one another, spreading out further and further.
They've crossed here.

They've crossed here and now they start spreading out again. But if I had to pick one thread that led directly to this account, it would be a Sunday morning in March just past, when I was called to go to a scene on the Detroit River, where a body had been found.

Every winter, ship traffic on the upper Great Lakes ceases when it is no longer possible to maintain a channel through the ice. The closure starts at the Soo—the locks of Sault Sainte Marie— and there are always a few ships racing to beat the ice at the southern end of Lake Huron, make it across the relatively shallow Lake Saint Clair, through the throat (de troit), and thence into Lake Erie and on to the Saint Lawrence and the sea. And in the spring it goes in reverse. As Lake Saint Clair breaks up and clogs the throat, ships are already waiting in Lake Erie.

The ice as it comes down past Detroit can be quite a spectacular sight, depending on the brutality of the winter. This past winter it wasn't too bad, but the ice filled the river for days, bringing down with it all sorts of things. Like smashed docks, fragments of boats. And a well-preserved corpse, which was sprawled across a chunk that was forced into a channel and scared the hell out of some schoolkids who were flinging rocks.

As it happened, the body was discovered downstream from Windmill Point in Grosse Pointe and just into the Ninth Precinct, where I work. It was necessary for a detective to go, because this wasn't just a body, an accidental drowning perhaps. Unless the swimmer had decided that he could swim without hands. Or a head.

There wasn't much to detect. The body had been badly beaten up by the ice. It had gone into the water probably a couple of weeks before, according to Doc Brennan, at the Wayne County Morgue. Ice had complicated his estimation process. But he thought that the usual processes of water invading the cells of the corpse had not been too badly affected by cold and ice. Still, the corpse could have been deposited on ice and only entered the water when the lake broke up, assuming the body had been placed on the lake, rather than in the river below it. That is, the man could have been murdered—probably a fatal head injury—and the body placed on the lake ice and covered with snow, or perhaps deposited in a shallow ice grave.

It was a male, in good physical condition at demise, aged about twenty-five to possibly twenty-nine. Probably about six feet tall, probably weighing about 185 pounds. Well nourished. Not much physical exercise but young enough to resist the tendency to overweight that would surely have caught up to the fellow in another few years. The doctor said he'd do some tissue studies. He had a young lady in his service who was getting to be a whiz at detecting such things as dietary habits, physical activity, and the like, which could be useful indicators when you couldn't otherwise tell who the person was or where he came from.

So that's how it started, although I couldn't know it at the time. One almost never can detect the beginning, at the beginning. It was the beginning of an investigation, of course, but not necessarily into anything more than an unusually brutal attempt to thwart identification of a murder victim. As a detective, my hopes were slightly raised by the unusual: in the great morass of murders that urban police forces must contend with, the unusual sometimes gives us a chance. It suggests an imaginative murderer. An imaginative murderer is almost always caught.

I have to emphasize that it was only much later that I recognized this as the beginning. I didn't see it then, nor for a long time thereafter. For the most part I thought it began with the discovery of Grootka's notebooks, which I'll get to a minute. As you see, I'm trying to get this properly organized.

I repeat, I am no writer, but after this I make no apologies. The reader isn't interested in apologies, I realize. The reader just wants to hear the story. But when I first started out to "simply write it up," I quickly discovered that it isn't as easy as it looks if it's going to make sense. I have learned a few things, though, and I hope in the process I'll learn a few more so it won't be so painful for you, the reader.

First of all, I have the story as I got it from Grootka. He also was—he's long gone now—a detective, a mentor. He did not tell me this story firsthand, for some reason. He left me the story in some notebooks, though even there he didn't simply leave them to me. But I'll get into that later. I think it is important to hear him tell it. The only thing is, this is not exactly the way he wrote it. I had to edit it, although I've retained many of his peculiar usages to give the flavor of the original. I'll discuss that later, too.

Actually, notebook #2 was the first one to come to my attention, but it seems appropriate to open with book #1, even if I came upon it later. It was written in blue ink, in a nice hand, a remarkably legible, almost graceful script. I believe the style was known as the Palmer method, or something like that. Nice big rounded vowel forms, uniform loop tails on the *p, q, f,* and so on, with everything slanting the same way. It was how the nuns taught handwriting in the Catholic schools of Detroit. It was inscribed in dark blue ink with a fountain pen (another interesting touch), in a composition notebook with black-and-white marbled-effect pasteboard covers. I'd used notebooks like this in high school; I think they're called composition books. In the blank label space on the cover Grootka had written: "Every Good Boy Does Fine."

He had wonderfully acquired the script, but Grootka was one of those who could not spell. It's a problem for many, especially with the English language.

"You knoe the trubbel I yousta hav whith reports so I gess yul knoe how mutch I hait to rite this but I awweeze thawt I shud poot sumthin down in case it ever came down on you. Awltho wye the hell I shud waist my time werryin uhbowt yore but ime dammed if I knoe. Ackshally I awweaze wannid to rite a direy but I cudden figyur owt how to go at it. Deer direy seems like a dumm thing to rite. But then it accurd to me that I cuod juss rite it too you. And its funney but it seems rite. Innywaze this is abowt Jimmy Hoffa. The labor gye you know. Nun uv this cuod go in the files caws to minny innacent peepel wuod be hirt. (Yeh I know it sowns funny for me to be werreed abowt innacent peepel cawz I youzhally say that thear aint no innacent peepel but in this case thear is.)"

Well, that's an adequate sample of the orthography. I like the way he tries to be consistent, for example, with *cuod* and *wuod,* and he seems to have some idea that the spelling is odd in those kinds of words, but he doesn't quite know what the problem is (although, I should caution that it's never safe to assume anything with Grootka—he could well have deliberately misspelled words to make me labor over the text.) Sometimes he throws in a *g* or an *h,* but I guess he didn't like the effect because later he drops it. It's pretty painful to read, and the literal text is not essential to appreciate what he says, so I won't bother with it from here on out; one may take it as translated from the style quoted (although I can't resist tossing in some of his more creative variations).

"Maybe it won't matter," Grootka writes, "so you could just tear this up or burn it. It's up to you. As a matter of fact, I know what I'll do. I'll give it to Old Lady Newman [*Grootka's neighbor and landlady, the rabbi's widow—M.*] to keep and that way the only way you'll ever see it is if you ask her, which you would never do, obviously, unless you were investigating the Hoffa case, or maybe the whole shitaree has backed up on you and you need some help.

"Jesus, look at this! I already filled a whole page! If Sister Mary Herman could only see me now! This ain't like writing a term paper!

"But to get back to business, this is about Jimmy Hoffa, the Teamsters guy. What happened is that when Hoffa disappeared I didn't pay too much attention because it wasn't in Detroit, naturally. It was a suburban case. I figured we'd have some pieces of the puzzle to work out, as usual, but that it wasn't our business. The F.B.I. and the 'burbs could chew on this s.o.b. to their heart's content, because when they didn't find the body right away I figured they weren't ever going to find it, except by accident, because somebody took some pains to make sure that it wouldn't be found. You know me, Mul: I figured the s.o.b. was bagged and tossed inna trunk of an ayban [*abandoned car—M.*] and that even if we looked in all the aybans in Detroit, the chances were good that it woulda been crushed and smelted at Zug Island the day before. That's the way Carmine and the Fat Man do their hits when they don't want them found. Most of the time they want them found, to send a message. But what the hell's the message here? Jimmy Hoffa's a bad guy? Since when? The Mob loved this s.o.b. If I'd thought about it, I'd have seen that something funny was going on, but I didn't bother.

"Now I've got to backtrack," Grootka writes. But I see that his prose is even more complicated than I thought; the diction is pretty tangled. I'll try to give you a synopsis. He explains that some time earlier—I get the impression that it may have been more than just a few weeks or months, perhaps even a couple of years, say around 1972 or 1973—he had become acquainted with Tyrone Addison, the well-known jazz saxophonist. A friend of Addison's, whom Grootka doesn't identify, had called and asked him to help Addison because he'd been caught up in a marijuana investigation and he was basically innocent and besides he was a great musician. Cops constantly get requests from friends to help out other friends, and God knows Grootka was one of the most acquainted people in Detroit. Most of the guys usually make at least a pretense of helping, so Grootka looked into it and he says he got the guy out of it. "He wuz a compleat roob," in Grootka's words. (I confess I like the evocation of Izaak Walton's spelling here.) At any rate, Grootka apparently liked Addison and . . . well, let him explain (these passages are partially edited):

I used to play a sax at St. Olaf's, but I hadn't played in maybe forty years. But I always liked the sound, except I always wanted to play the big horn, the baritone, not the C-melody, which is what I got to play. So I got interested in Tyrone's music. Well, this is a little complicated. First I liked the stuff he was playing around town and on records. Tyrone was a real hard bopper. But after I got to know him I got into his new stuff, his Free stuff. It's very different music. It ain't like the old jazz. Okay, I ain't going into that now, but it's very serious music. I didn't think I could ever play like that, but Tyrone told me that I could play a lot better than I thought. All I had to do was try. He convinced me to take lessons from him. At first, he loaned me one of his saxes. But then I bought a used Selmer, on his recommendation—a Mark VI.

Mul, it was terrific! I can't tell you. It's amazing how hard it is at first, but then you kind of break through and it gets easy. But then it gets hard again. Then another breakthrough. And so on. Every time you learn something it gets easier, but then you realize that there's so much more to learn! So it's harder again. I kept thinking that I'd practice and learn for a year or two and then I'd play—you know, for other people. I don't know: a recital didn't seem like the right thing, but maybe I could play in the band with Tyrone, when he performed his "Nigger Heaven" concerto, which is this great Free piece he's been working on. I started learning the soprano sax part, because naturally, Tyrone would play the baritone part.

This went on for quite a while. Maybe a year. It was kind of a joke. I'd run into him at Klein's or someplace and it was: "Hey, Tyrone, when we gonna get together and practice? When's the concert?" That kind of thing. I learned my part, but I never did get to play it for Tyrone. Also, I never did really work out an improvisation [*"empravazhun" in the text—M.*] which the score asked [*"axed"—M.*] for.

Then Hoffa disappeared. I didn't pay a hell of a lot of attention. I kind of asked around, like you would, but my snitches didn't have crap on it. They had a bunch of rumors that the Fat Man and Carmine were behind it, but that rumor is an everyday thing, you

know. Even the weather is blamed on the Mob. The annual fish-fly
hatch in Saint Clair Shores even. A guy told me, "You notice how
the fish flies are worse than ever since the Fat Man moved out
there?" I'm not shitting you, Mul. But then another guy says that
the fish flies ain't hatching like they used to since the Fat Man
moved out to the lake. Yeah.

I hadn't seen Tyrone for a while but someone said he had
a gig in New York with Woody Shaw and Marcus Belgrave,
which seemed a little odd to me since they're both trumpet players. And then I saw Marcus was playing in town, over at Klein's, so
I stopped in there and Marcus said that was bullshit, that he wasn't
on that gig but Tyrone was supposed to be, only he didn't show. A
[woman] at the bar said Tyrone was "up at the lake," meaning that
resort up in the Thumb, Turtle Lake, which I heard they were
trying to change the name to Basie Lake, but then another bunch
wanted it called Lake Ellington, and then some group suggested
Lake Rosa Parks. In the meantime, everybody calls it Nigger
Heaven, but not to me, of course. I knew Books had a place up
there so I called and sure enough he was up there. I asked Books if
he'd seen Tyrone and he said I should talk to Lonzo Butterfield,
Tyrone's uncle, a bail bondsman. You remember him, Mul. A big
fat man, blacker than a boot.

I remembered Lonzo, all right. If Grootka says he was a big
fat man, you can bet he was big. I'd say he topped out at six and a
half feet, at least three hundred pounds. He'd been a legendary
basketball player in the rec league and an amazing handball player
out at Palmer Park and Belle Isle. He'd have been in his early forties then. Some guys are actually hard to look at. Lonzo was one: a
ferocious-looking man, very dark with skin that looked too tight,
as if it were inflated, almost like a swollen corpse. And he had these
jaundice-yellow eyes. He looked angry all the time. Very intimi-

dating. In conversation he appeared to have the I.Q. of, say, a mud puppy. Grootka had some interesting insights into Lonzo.

You want to watch yourself around Lonzo, Mul. He looks as subtle as a drop forge, so damn ugly he looks like his mother fed him with a slingshot, but he's always thinking, always something going on there. He acts stupid, I figure, because of his size—maybe when he was a kid he was always too big for his grade, and the other kids must of thought he was older than he was and when he didn't act it they figured he must be retarded, and then he figured out it was clever to seem dumb. People make mistakes around a dumb guy, say things they figure you won't get. But I rousted him at his pad once and I seen a few things, like music and books, that made me wonder. He never would let on to me, but I think maybe to you he might let a few smarts drop.

The thing is, people who really know him say he's a pussycat, even though he looks like the old heavyweight, what's his name, Sonny Liston. But I think that's bullshit. Lonzo's a pussycat the way a sabertooth tiger is a pussycat. Anyway, if Books says to go see him, I go see him. Lonzo says he don't know if Tyrone is up to the lake, but he'll let me know. And the next day he calls back and says, Naw, Tyrone ain't up there. He *was* up there, which he wasn't supposed to, 'cause he didn't ask first or some such shit, but he left. And naturally, old Lonzo can't resist being a tough ass, so he says it's none of my fucking business anyway and why don't I go piss up a rope.

So I'm thinking, Is Lonzo really dumb, or is he just playing to me thinking he's dumb? Or did he let something actually slip? I mean, what's the big deal? I was just asking about Tyrone, what he was doing these days. But you know how it is, Mul. A guy like Lonzo always thinks something heavy is going down. He can never figure it's just innocent interest.

This was an amusing thought: Grootka expressing innocent interest. I tried to imagine these two hard-asses having a simple conversation. Images of the scorpion and the snapping turtle came to mind.

Naturally, I decided to take a drive up there. [*Naturally!*— M.*] I could always go visit my old buddy Books. It's about ninety miles, not a bad drive. But it's July and hotter than hell. I was glad to be getting out of Detroit and looking forward to sitting in the shade by the lake, enjoying the cool breeze, maybe on Books's porch or something. I never been there, but I imagined what it was like. What do I know?

The lake is about three miles from the nearest town, which is one of these religious nut places. I think they're some kind of Haymish, or something, but the next town over, where I stopped to get instructions, called them "Hoots." [*In the text, Grootka refers to them as "Haymish," or "Hamish," apparently meaning Amish. In fact, they are a Hutterite sect.—M.*] The men wear beards and black clothes, the ladies wear these little net hats, and the kids wear Huck Finn straw hats. Everybody dresses like before World War I, with high-top lace-up boots. There were some horse-and-buggies around, but most of them are driving regular cars, and pretty big, new ones at that, like Buicks and Chryslers. They mostly raise potatoes and sugar beets, I was told.

Anyway, these folks are into the idea of whatchamacallit, group privacy, or, you know, social kinds of I don't know community things. Something like that. They kind of picked up on this deal about the black folks wanting a place where they could just be black folks, without a lot of fuckin' whiteys hanging around. So they sold them this big tract of land with a pond on it, which they now can't figure out if it should be Turtle Lake (which it was originally, or Turtle Pond) or Lake Rosa Parks, the woman who sat down on the Birmingham bus, who happens to live in Detroit now. For all I know, Mrs. Parks has a cottage herself on the lake. She's a big hero, you know. Well, it took some balls.

I guess the land was actually bought by some kind of group of investors, which I guess it was all Negroes, but I didn't look into it. And then they sold lots and put up a clubhouse and a golf course and a so-called casino, which was also a hotel and had a bar and bandstand. There were a bunch of other things that were going to be built but they ain't been built yet, which some of the people who bought in, like old Books, is pissed about. Books bought a lot on the lake and had a cottage built, which it was pretty nice, one of these summer cottage things, fir or something—cedar. It was red cedar, and it looked pretty nice. Mostly glass in front, looking out on the deck and then the little bitty yard and then the little dock, where he had a rowboat tied up. Only the lake had shrunk some. The dock didn't go out far enough. So the rope on the rowboat got longer and longer, so that the boat wouldn't be on the mud, and now the rope was about sixty feet long and you had to walk on these planks that Books laid on the mud to get out to the boat. But there wasn't any reason to get out to the boat, since the pond was full of weeds. You couldn't row in it anyway, and the only fish in it was these little bitty bullheads, which the kids would catch and then throw at each other and they were laying all over the place, stinking. Maybe they should call it Turd-el Lake, ha ha.

It was about as hot as Detroit. The country was low rolling hills, farmland, with these little woodlots here and there and old farmhouses with barns. I don't know nothing about farms, but it looked to me like some of these farms had gone belly up, or maybe a few of the farmers had done better than the others and had bought out some of their neighbors and let the old homesteads go to hell, or maybe it was the Haymish who done it. But there would be these old farmhouses here and there, with big trees in the yard and the grass all grown up and the lilacs, or whatever the bushes were, growing up wild over the porch. It was kind of gloomy.

The Negroes had I don't know how many acres, a few hundred, anyway, including the pond, but it was in a kind of a basin, surrounded by these low hills and there was only a few grown-up trees, except for a bunch of willows by the pond. So it was hot. Burning hot. And it was very bright in the sun. Hardly anybody about.

You drive in through this fancy stone gate. They had a fence around the place, only it was ornamental black iron for just a few paces, then it was just a regular farm fence, a post-and-wire fence like around a pasture. There was a guard at the stone gate, in a little outhouse, with a wooden lift-up barrier attached to the shithouse, painted with black stripes on white and a couple of orange reflectors. And this guy had a uniform and even a gun! But he had the shirt unbuttoned to his navel and he was wearing silver shades and a Tigers hat. Young guy. Kind of a pain in the ass. "Where you goin'? Who you gonna see?" That kind of shit. "They know you comin'? What's they numbah, I gon' call 'em." And you got to put up with that crap. Even the people who lived there, especially the young chicks. He gives them all a hard time. I found out from Books that most of the people most of the time take the back way, which it turns out is a pasture kind of gate way out on the back side, which is just left open and there is a little dirt road that leads back into the community center.

So I get past this shithead, anyway, by calling Books, and I drive down to the pond. Books's joint is about a block from the community center, which was a mistake, he tells me. The parties at the center can go on all night and get pretty loud.

I asked him what was the problem with the lake, 'cause I see it's getting farther away, plus the casino, which is across the pond, also has a dry dock, now, and theirs is pretty big. Books says it's a drought and also it turns out that the Haymish are using more water than they used to, for irrigation, so the little creek—I think he called it Jaxon Creek—is down to nothing. Plus they got some drainage problems. There was supposed to be a sewage-treatment plant, which they got a federal grant, but it wasn't put in right, or the drains weren't, and I think they tapped into the pond or the water table, or something, and at the moment they were using bottled water, couldn't use the tap water at all and you could only flush the toilet once a day, which in the heat was a real bitch. But some of the houses, the newer ones that were away from the pond and elevated, had their own wells and septic systems, so they were all right. And that's where Lonzo had his joint.

I went over to the casino with Books. It was just around the pond, maybe three or four city blocks away, but he insisted on driving. I thought it would be an interesting walk, hot though it was, but I guess he didn't want to be seen walking around with a white guy. Which I have to say, it was one of the few times I can remember thinkin', So this is what it's like to be a nigger. Only I'm the nigger. I can see the people there in the street, they come out of the little grocery store or the post office and they're lookin' at me driving by and they're thinkin', What's he doin' here? Which you get the point. But what the hell, how's Books gonna hide my white ass? I'm sure the minute I come through the gate the word was all over the joint.

At the casino, which is only a frame building built like a T, with the top of the T fronting the road and the long part running out toward the pond, which like I say has taken a hike, and there's this big deck all around the long part. There's a bandstand inside and a bar, a dance floor, and on one side they have these doors which are the walls, which they can take away in hot weather, so the whole thing is kind of open to the deck and the air. It wasn't bad. Pretty nice, in fact. The roof extends halfway out on the deck and it's cooler.

Off to one side there's a big excavation, which Books says is gonna be a public swimming pool, but it's run into some kind of snag and so nothing's happening for now, just a old dragline sitting there by a half-dug hole, which has some stagnant water in it and a couple of old tires and some soggy plywood.

But the casino was okay. They had some pretty good bands come in there. Tyrone played there, but he wasn't there now. I asked about him and I get this bullshit, Ain't seen him, Heard he was in New York, Got a gig in Chicago. Unh-hunh. They'd seen him. He was around. I didn't say nothing. I figured he'd show up if he wanted to. By now he would know I was there. I didn't give a shit. Anyway, it's so damn hot. It's about five o'clock by now, middle of the week. Nothin' happening anywhere. I'm happy to sit in the cool shade on one of these Adirondack wood lawn chairs, on the edge of the barroom and drink beer and smoke cigars and bullshit with the guys, which a number of them I knew from Motown. No point in mentioning all of them right now, but if it's important . . . [*Here he writes out a list of about thirty names, mostly known to me, of no apparent consequence.—M.*]

I'm trying to figure out what the hell is Lonzo's thing and basically it looks to me like this: Lonzo is running this whole zoo. He's the big cheese. I don't know who is behind all this and it don't matter. Mostly it's just what it looks like—working-class folks who bought a little something in the country, up on the lake, to put the wife and kids during the summer, get them out of the neighborhoods. But there's also a scam going down. There's dues, and there's numbers, drugs, probably all kinds of shit. But so what? As far as I could tell, there wasn't anything too heavy. It's just that the folks who bought in found that they weren't through paying and that things didn't go the way they expected them to. The sewer scam was just a part of it, but I think it was like everything else—there was a road tax but the roads didn't get paved, the streetlights didn't get installed and the bulbs weren't fixed when they got broken or shot out, and houses weren't secure in the off-season, although there was supposed to be a security force (the asshole at the gate, for instance).

The golf course was burning up (no water for irrigation, although there was supposed to be a project and fees had been assessed). But people went out and played. They had low expectations, I guess.

But what the hell . . . by early evening I was having a pretty good time. All the old ladies had been out barbecuing since mid-afternoon and you can smell the ribs and chicken and pork butts . . . oh, man! The ball game is on the TV, and some of the guys had come into the clubhouse with their instruments and were starting to play a few licks. [*He mentions some names, a bass player, a piano, a couple of horns and a drummer, but they weren't familiar to me.—M.*]

That's really nice, you know, maybe nothing better. A guy starts picking out some easy blues on the piano and pretty soon the bass takes it up and the drummer starts mixing it up a bit on the cymbals and the brushes, and then a trumpet starts noodling away. Yeah, on a hot evening when nothing else is going on, just an ordinary old summer night with a lot of frogs croaking and you're sitting around chewing on some ribs with real sauce, knocking back a few sweaty brews—there was a Stroh's distributor there, buying rounds—and maybe a shot of something hard now and then, puffing a stogie and swapping a lot of bullshit while the guys just play around on the horns . . . well, you can spend a hell of a lot of time doing that.

And about the time you forget what the hell you're there for, along comes ol' Lonzo, who I thought was back in Detroit. But I guess he jumped in the ol' Caddy and breezed up to Nigger Heaven to get away from the hot city streets. He rolls in with a couple-three of his stooges and they sprawl all over the place and it seems like we're all just having a gay ol' time, socking back the Stroh's. Except that I see Lonzo can't tear his eyes away from me and neither can his stooges. Man, they were giving me the heebie-jeebies.

But finally I noticed that the band had quit, some time ago. And just about everybody else except for Lonzo and Co. had split. And about that time I stood up and, I'll be goddamned, the fuckin' dock started rockin' and I sat right down, only I missed the fuckin' lawn chair and I flopped right on my ass and damn near fell into the fuckin' stinkin' mud! And ol' Lonzo, he's laughin' and tryin' to get me up and we both fell down, and we're laughin' like lunatics and I'll be damned if he didn't find a bottle of Jim Beam and him and me and Books decided to walk home.

It was a nice moon, almost full. The wind had come up and a lot of clouds were blowing by. It got quite a bit cooler. We had walked up on the ridge overlooking the settlement, or whatever you want to call it. And we drank the Jim Beam and by golly, Books got me to walk home. Hell of a time.

Whew, man! I had a hangover like, well, you just wish everybody would quit jumping and yelling and carrying on, or hell, why couldn't the world just stop? But a man has got to get up and face it, right? Anyway, the weather helped. It had turned colder than shit and a low deck of gray clouds had blown in. It was okay with me. Fuck a bunch of heat when you're hung over, eh Mul? A nice cold morning helps. I grabbed some coffee and got Books to borrow a sweater from a neighbor. I'd slept on the couch and I was a little achy. I wanted a walk. I strolled up the hill toward Lonzo's. It wasn't really a hill, more of a rise, out on the rim of the basin, which was a depression for the pond. The wind was still tossing the few trees that were around.

I got to Lonzo's, which we hadn't been able to get to the night before, being too damn drunk. I was wondering if me and Books had actually crawled home. I saw I was at Lonzo's, cause his big red Caddy convertible was parked out front. He had one of the few trees, a nice big one, very spreading, like the chestnut under the village smithy, or however the poem goes. I guess it must of been about seven or so. A couple of Lonzo's boys are sacked out in the

Caddy, with their coats pulled over their ears and their feet sticking over the side. It was too early for visiting and I was enjoying the fresh air, so I just walked on by, on out in the country and pretty soon I got up on the ridge where I could see off to the countryside. The Haymish were out working, like they do, haying or something, with tractors and equipment, off in the distance. I started back and I had to just stop and look.

A white woman came out of Lonzo's house, which was a sorta new place, a single-story cabin kind of place, with redwood or something for siding and a big deck, lots of tall windows. It looked like it had maybe three or four bedrooms, which made me wonder why the boys weren't allowed to sleep inside, but maybe they just didn't want to, except it was damn cold for sleeping outside. Course they were as drunk or drunker than we were, so maybe they just didn't make it inside.

Anyway, this white chick is a hell of a babe. Big set of knockers, blond, hell of an ass in tight jeans. She jumps into a VW van that's parked out back and goes tootin' off down the road and over the hill toward the back gate. I never saw any babe like that with Lonzo. The man would scare any normal woman out of her wits, he's so ugly. For all his money and his muscle, I never saw him with anything but a few scraggly little whores. This babe was a bombshell. And she looked kind of familiar, although I didn't get close enough to really see her face and I'm sure she didn't see me.

Here he runs out of space. He seems surprised. On the inside of the back cover he has scrawled: "See you in book two. Which reminds me: where can you find good Books? In the Library! Ha, ha! G." (Literally: "C U in book 2. Wich remines me. Wear can U fine good Books? In the Liberry! Haha! G.")

This was the text, but as I say, it wasn't the first segment that came to my attention. I've only put it here because it seemed like the sensible thing to do, to avoid confusion.

2

Blue Girl

A number of other events occurred at about this time that later I realized were interrelated. This is not coincidence, but it is not necessarily a conspiracy either. At the time, of course, I didn't remark it. Even before Grootka's narrative surfaced, somebody from the police department's Public Relations office called and asked me to entertain a young historian named Agge Allyson: actually, whoever it was said something like "chat her up, the usual." The idea was that I should consent to be interviewed by Ms. Allyson. So I agreed to go to lunch with her and suggested my favorite place, Pinky's, down on Jefferson.

The meeting went very well—she was on time and nice to look at—but there was an initial moment when it almost went awry. I was sure she was about to say, "I'm something of a detective myself." It's a line that detectives hear a lot. Often, I can see it coming, and it fills me with a horrible dread. Ms. Allyson was a fine-looking young woman and I didn't want her to say anything so banal, but how can you stop it? I fell back on a heartless remedy: a more deadly preemptive banality.

"You seem very young to be a historian," I said.

She had expressive brown eyes and I thought they widened in disappointment. We were sitting in the bar at Pinky's, a nice place, old wood and dark leather; the afternoon light from the street gives a very pleasant amber glow.

I tried to soften her dismay with one of my *little* smiles, a slight lift of the lips on the left. I'm aware that my smile can be intimidating, they don't call me Fang for nothing.

She graciously dealt with the banality by explaining that she wasn't a full-fledged historian, yet. She was engaged in a post-doctorate study, part of a general history of Detroit in the second half of the century. "My part, for which a grant has blessedly and unexpectedly materialized but which is not going to be enough money if I spend too long at it, is about the police. The police and the community."

I nodded, trying to be helpful. "Oh yes? What are some of the other . . . um, parts? Who's doing them? You know, the story of the auto industry, for instance," I added, when she frowned in puzzlement.

She said she didn't know, but she seemed a little surprised at herself for not having considered that. "I was just so relieved and happy to get a grant, I didn't inquire about the other aspects of the project."

"Sure," I said. It was quite understandable. "But didn't they give you any guidelines?"

I could see she felt a little defensive. I suppose she hadn't expected to have her project questioned. "I'm sure the foundation didn't feel that they could be too directive," she said. "The foundation director, Mr. Toscano, was helpful, but not overbearing. The idea, he said, was to give the grant recipient support, without unduly influencing my research or the report."

I shrugged, agreeably. "Still," I said, "'The Police and the Community,' isn't that a little vague?"

She almost winced. "I hope not. I want to focus on a personality. Mr. Toscano was very supportive of that approach. I prefer

34

history when it is seen through the eyes of a 'character'—most people do. You know—someone who has experienced the history. It helps to bring it alive."

"The police in different voices," I said, half aloud.

"I'm sorry?"

"It's a line from a novel," I said. "'He do the police in different voices.'" That wasn't cool, I realized. It sounded like a parody of black speech. "A Charles Dickens novel," I hastened to explain. "Joe the crossing sweeper, he reads the police reports in the paper in different voices, kind of a performance art."

"Oh?" she said, her face a study in neutrality. But then she smiled sweetly and said, "I think you'll find that it was *Our Mutual Friend,* not *Bleak House,* and it's Betty Higden who says it. As I recall, she's referring proudly to her teenaged foster child, Sloppy, who reads well. The novel has a subtheme of literacy."

"Does it?" I said. "I must have missed that. I'll check it out." I was sure that the novel was *Bleak House,* and the character Joe, but there was something about her self-assurance that undermined my own. At any rate, I was grateful that she had so skillfully finessed my near-gaffe. She was very sharp. And attractive—in fact, stunning. She reminded me a little of the great Detroit jazz pianist Geri Allen. The same bright look, the vitality and obvious intelligence. Sometimes you look at a young woman like this and you think: maybe they *can* save the city . . . the country . . . hell, the species. This one had left enough buttons undone on her blouse that I could see cleavage forever, right down to the brassiere clasp. Now, why would a woman do that, I wonder?

A more relevant question was why this dishy young historian wanted to talk to me. I'd been around the department for quite a while, but I couldn't pretend to be a "character," someone likely to make a historical narrative come alive. It was a mystery. But Public Relations has their hands full . . . you try to help, if it isn't too much bother. I asked her straight out how I could help.

"Well, everybody kept mentioning a Mr. Grootka," she said.

"Everybody? Grootka has been dead for—good Lord, going on five years! People are still talking about him?"

"Well, not everybody, maybe," she conceded, "but his name did come up more than anybody's. As soon as people caught on to what I was looking for it seems like they'd say, 'Aha! You ought to check out Grootka, if you want a character.' Grootka seemed to find me."

"I like that, 'He found you.' Even dead, Grootka is a better detective than any of us. I have to admit, he was a character. What can I tell you about Grootka?"

"What was Grootka's first name?" She had an ingratiating smile; I gave her the little smile in return.

"Grootka didn't have a first name, as far as I know."

"Everybody has a first name."

"What's yours?"

"Agge. As if it were *i-e,* but there's no *i.*"

"Aggie? Would that be short for Agatha?"

"Just Agge. Now, don't make a face. What's wrong with Agge?"

"Nothing. Agge's fine. In fact, I've never liked Agatha. It always reminds me of what's-her-name, who invented all those dippy detectives." I felt stupid. Time to change the subject. "You're the second person to mention Grootka to me today."

"Really? Well, you see? The same people who mentioned Grootka to me also said the guy to talk to was Mulheisen, that you used to work with him . . . you were his best friend."

"Grootka didn't exactly have best friends," I said, "but I was probably as close to him as anybody. I can tell you about Grootka, but. . . . What's the interest in Grootka? I mean for a historian? Grootka wasn't a particularly historic guy. Historically, I suppose you'd want to talk to some of those guys who were involved in . . . oh, I don't know . . . the Algiers Motel thing. You know, during the riots, in sixty-seven."

Before she could inquire, I hastened to say, "I wasn't on the force then. I was in school."

"Public school?"

"How kind of you," I said, almost retaliating with a Fang smile. "No, law school. I didn't like it. I went a couple of years. The most intensely boring two years of my life. I thought of going back, but now . . . it's too late. Grootka was on the force, sure, but what he did during the riots I don't know."

Good Lord, why was I babbling on? I shut up and tried to look indifferent. Maybe it was the unbuttoned shirt. It is very hard not to stare into an unbuttoned shirt when it is so well filled. Impossible, perhaps.

"If Grootka was your partner, surely you talked about the riots?"

I thought about it. I sipped at my coffee and discovered that it was cold. I signaled the bartender for another cup and gestured at the history girl. She looked puzzled. "Would you like more coffee?" I asked. "A drink? A beer? A little cognac?"

She settled for coffee, and I felt composed enough to tell her a quick little tale about Grootka.

"Grootka told me a lot about his life, his career," I said. "Mostly about the forties and fifties. He seemed nostalgic for that period. It was a better period. And it's funny, too"—it had just struck me—"I had a similar nostalgia." It had not previously occurred to me, this shared taste. Perhaps it accounted for our getting along as well as we did.

Agge Allyson alarmed me with her raised eyebrow. "Oh no." I was strangely eager to correct any misapprehension. "I'm not anything like that old. Grootka was much, much older than me. Twenty-five, thirty years, anyway. But it's odd . . . you see, my parents were fairly old when I was born. My mother was nearly forty, I think. She's eighty-some, now. My dad died, oh, twenty years or more ago. But growing up with them, with their outlook . . . even as a child I had a notion of the twenties and the thirties, a sense of familiarity. It was almost as if I'd experienced the period, because that was what my parents talked about. I knew about comic strips that hadn't been published in decades, big bands that had sunk into total obscurity long ago. Did you ever hear of the Ray McKinley–Will Bradley band? No? Or radio characters like Ish Kabibble or Joe Penner? Joe Penner said, 'Wanna buy a duck?' on the radio."

She laughed, a soft, gurgly laugh. It would convince any man that she found him genuinely amusing. The shirt rose and fell and I looked away.

"The forties and fifties were yesterday to my folks," I went on. "They had just happened. The twenties and thirties had a little more distance, but they weren't ancient history. Maybe"—I had a sudden thought—"maybe that's why I was always so interested in history. Like you."

She smiled encouragingly and asked what I meant.

"History is practically my main interest," I informed her. "After work, that is. I'm interested in Detroit history, Michigan history. Your project sounds intriguing," I said, "but I'm more interested in earlier periods, although I'm not caught up in this current craze for the Civil War. Are you? No? The Civil War is interesting, sure, but it's become kind of faddish. I'm more into Pontiac's Rebellion. Or, if we're talking recent history, the labor struggle. I'm interested in that. And the War of 1812! The naval action on the Lakes."

"Grootka," she said, with mock severity. "Postwar to the seventies. Don't get me sidetracked into discussing Pontiac. I did my thesis on Pontiac's Rebellion and the opening of western migration."

"Really?" Amazing. "This isn't some 'great man' theory, is it? I thought that was passé."

"No, no . . . although I'm not so dismissive of that notion as prevailing attitudes. . . . Obviously, unusually powerful or forceful individuals have an impact on events. But this is more a variation on the *Annalistes* . . . let's say *Annalistes avec personnalité:* find an illustrative individual or circumstance, not necessarily the famous and familiar one, and then . . . but what about Grootka?"

"Okay. Grootka." I paused for a moment, then dove in. "I have a picture of Grootka, a mental picture, of him striding down a street, a gun in each hand. Everybody scatters. Yeah, that's Grootka. Cool and unflappable. Just walking down the street, keeping the law." I laughed, to show her I wasn't serious. "He really wasn't like that, of course. But . . . sort of like that."

Shut, up. Gassing away like a shot Zeppelin. I looked at this chick. What was she about? Pontiac and the opening of the West? And now she wants to write history about Grootka? Nice shirt, though. But she can't figure out if she wants to show it or hide it. Are they all like that? Once in a while you meet one who doesn't seem to care. That one you better get close to. This one . . . who knows?

"'Keeping the law,'" Agge said. "What does that mean?"

I had to give this a little more thought. What did it mean? It was something about Grootka. The way he was.

"Was he intimidating?" she asked. She had velvety brown eyes, full dark lips.

"Grootka was very intimidating," I said. "Intimidation was his basic wardrobe, like the gray suit, the same red tie—he always wore the same tie, never untied it, just slipped it on and off. He liked to 'invade your space,' as they say these days. He'd stand very close to you, too close, and put his big face into yours. His breath wasn't bad, though usually there was a faint odor of booze—you could feel the heat of it. Obnoxious as hell."

"A big man?"

"Oh, yeah. About six-four, six-five, something like that. A big raw-boned man. He had a face . . ." Jeez, how could you describe that battered, ravaged face? It looked like—what was his line?—like his face caught on fire and they put it out with a pitchfork. I settled for:

"A very menacing face. Pockmarked skin, drawn tight over the bones—like parchment that had shrunk. He had huge hands."

I could see that face, the thin lips, the curious hair—mouse colored, or no color, really. As if it were artificial, doll's hair . . . too thin, too wiry, too sparse to be a wig, the bony skull showing through. Small, flat ears, pulled back, irregular—as if they'd been added on from different bins, or reconstructed.

"So, his basic technique, as a policeman, was to intimidate people?" she asked. For some reason I was not displeased by her expression of disapproval.

"It's not uncommon," I said. "Though Grootka was better at it than most."

"Is it so effective?" Agge asked.

"Amazingly so. Grootka told me when he was on the street, in uniform, they put him out on Hastings. That was the heart of the old ghetto. They called it Paradise Valley. It was a tough place. He said he grabbed the first guy he came to and whacked him over the head with his stick. 'I'm Grootka,' he tells the guy. 'Tell everybody. Grootka's in town.' He meant, you know, that he was in charge. He says it worked."

"So that's where you get this image," she said.

"You mean of Grootka 'keeping the law'? No, no. Well, maybe in part. But the image really seems a later development. But don't get me wrong. The people liked him."

"You mean the black people? Because you are talking about black people, aren't you, when you talk about Paradise Valley?"

And the tan, I thought. She was more the tan. The café au lait. Hard to equate that with black, somehow. "Sure. The black people, the African-Americans. He was respected. And liked. But Paradise Valley was just the beginning. He worked the city, the whole city. What we call the Street." Don't tell her about the Kid. "The Street people liked him, generally, even the bad guys. He was tough, but he wasn't a brute. He didn't bullshit you."

"He beat up that one guy," she said.

"Who? Oh, the guy, when he first went on the Street?" I laughed. "That *was* bullshit. He never did anything like that, I'm pretty sure. He probably caught some guy shaking down a paper-boy, gave him a rattle, and let him go with a warning and the notice."

"Catch a nigger by the toe? If he hollers let him go?"

I suppressed a sigh. It wasn't like that, but how could you explain? "I wouldn't say that. Grootka wasn't one of those."

"One of what?"

"He wasn't a racist." Maybe I should tell her about the Kid. No. Well, you had to try. "Grootka was hard on everybody, white or black. Polish-American, African-American . . . 'Americanus kentuckianus' he called the hillbillies, with an emphasis on the 'anus.' But when I say he gave him a rattle, I don't mean . . ."

Well, what do I mean? Of *course* he gave him a rattle, and probably a knuckle or two. "It's just . . . to *me,* to another cop, he would say he decked the guy and gave out the notice—'Grootka's in town.' He's maybe overdramatizing it, that's all. It's like that famous bank-robbery line. You know, 'Die on a dark day.'"

Agge hadn't heard that one. I was surprised. Surely someone would have told her. It was the main Grootka story. Crap mostly, but there had to be something to it. I had to tell her.

"Grootka goes into a bank to cash his paycheck, something like that. It's crowded. Then he notices a guy in front of him has a very large leather briefcase, a satchel, and it's exactly like the one a guy in the next line has, and another guy in another line. This is too much coincidence for Grootka. He looks around, sees another suspicious character standing over by the counter where they have the extra forms, deposit slips, that kind of thing. This guy, he's eyeballing the whole scene closely and he also has the same kind of satchel, plus Grootka is almost certain he's armed. He checks out the rest of the room. It looks like four guys, that's the whole gang. So he draws his own piece—he always carried this cannon, a huge .45 revolver—and jams it in the back of the guy in front of him.

"'Blink and you'll die on a dark day,' he says. The guy on the right sees this and hauls around with his satchel. Grootka clubs him with the barrel of the gun. Grabs the guy in front of him around the neck, for a shield, waves the cannon out at the end of his arm at the guy at the deposit-slip counter, freezes him and the guy in the other line. Beautiful piece of work, really. He was famous for it. But I think the 'dark day' line was made up by a reporter, Doc Gaskill, who used to hang out at Lou Walker's Bar."

No point in telling her that Grootka had shot the guy at the counter, blew him away in front of thirty or forty lunchtime patrons. Fortunately, the dead man had been found with a gun in his hand. But good Lord, shooting an armed man in that kind of a crowd. I'd screwed up the story anyway. Was it the guy in front of him he told not to blink? Or did he yell it? Or whisper it? Something like that. All bullshit anyway. Grootka never made up a line like that in his life. Gaskill more likely. But it could have been Grootka. He could surprise you.

"He could surprise you," I said. She seemed impressed. I watched her carefully jot down the legendary line.

"What did he do during the riots?" she asked.

I thought she'd forgotten that line of questioning. "That was thirty years ago," I said. "I don't remember."

"Oh, you must remember something."

I pondered. "Nothing comes to mind. It couldn't have been anything significant. I guess he just ran around like everybody else, trying to hang onto what was left of the city. I don't recall him ever talking about the riots."

"What did you do?"

"I stayed home." Pretty much. I went fishing.

"You weren't interested?"

"It wasn't historical, yet." Shouldn't have tried that. Too flip. "Well . . . I mean . . . I wasn't interested in the situation that much. I lived outside of Detroit. About ten miles, or so. Still do, more or less. But it was very rural in those days. I didn't make much connection with the city. My dad worked for the city—he was the water commissioner—but I didn't really pay that much attention. I was enrolled at Michigan at the time, but it was summer vacation. I was probably thinking about school."

This was annoying. Why was I babbling away like this? And what did she really want? I couldn't believe all this interest in Grootka. He was a guy who, in his lifetime, most people wanted to avoid. Now that he was long and safely dead, no one could really be interested in digging him up.

"So . . . is that it?" I said.

"It? About Grootka?" she said. "Why, no. Not at all."

I subdued a sigh and tried to look easy. "Ask me anything," I said, "I'm easy."

She looked frustrated. "Well, what was he like?"

"Grootka was a hard man. Tough. Mean. Not very pleasant, most of the time. He was almost never a fun guy to be around. Difficult, annoying. He's never going to buy the drinks. He was bright, he was direct—so in that sense he was kind of an antidote to the timeservers, the smarmy, lying, back-stabbing, whining, conniving . . . well, the usual kind of stuff one runs into in public work. Organizational work. I'm not being a critic. I'm a bureaucrat, too, like my dad; our life, our civil life, depends on organization. Everybody claims to hate bureaucracies, but without them we couldn't function. There's good ones and bad ones. When you have a lot of people working together, as in any large corporate activity, you get a lot of friction, and therefore it is necessary for there to be a lot of oil if the organization is going to function. I understand this, but

I'm not sure Grootka did. Grootka was not an organization man. There was no oil in the man. He was more like gravel."

She nodded. Some people, not just women, are not as attractive at first as they become later, once you've had a chance to look at them. Agge was immediately pretty, and the more you saw of her the prettier she got. In fact, you began to see that she was beautiful.

I wanted to think of a good story about Grootka, for Ms. Agge Allyson. I presumed that her search for a historical character—say Grootka, for the sake of argument—was based on the notion that the individual can function as a kind of lens through which we can view the period in question. The idea, as I understood it, is that a fellow human being enlists the interest of readers . . . after all, we are more interested in other people than we are in abstract ideas. But to be really effective in the telling of history, it seemed to me, the chosen person ought to somehow represent, or embody, some significant historical event or, perhaps, an idea or principle. Now, how did Grootka fit into this concept? Grootka was about as unusual, as unrepresentative as I could easily imagine any cop to be. How did writing about him say anything about the Detroit police force?

When I offered this question to Ms. History, she nodded almost enthusiastically throughout my lengthy explication and then said, with a flip of her hand, "Exactly! But, of course, it doesn't matter."

"It doesn't matter? Then what the heck is the point? If it doesn't matter, then why bring it up? Why bother with Grootka?"

Her face suddenly lit up, glowing a pleasantly pinkish brown. "It doesn't matter that he isn't *especially* representative. Who is? On the other hand, just about anybody is, in some sense. The point is, Grootka's interesting, and he is, after all, a cop. Whether you think so or no, all cops are more like other cops than they are like . . . well, schoolteachers. The reader is interested in his amusing adventures, and in the meantime, I can tell the history of the force."

"But," I protested, "when you hold up before your reader the spectacle (or is it spectacles?) of Grootka, won't he or she be tempted to believe that this is a typical policeman?"

"To an extent, yes," she conceded. "That's an inescapable consequence of writing about an individual as a member of a group. But if I do my job right the reader should see that Grootka is not every cop. Anyway, what is this Grootka? Some kind of monster? Everyone holds within herself an essentially human character, and as different as individuals might be, they aren't usually *so* different that they don't exemplify in some way the basic human experience."

"The basic human experience," I said. "What would that be?"

"Oh, you know . . . like nowadays anyone watching TV or reading the paper sees the word 'Detroit,' and they think: Dr. Jack Kevorkian. Well, we know that most cops don't have anything to do with that, but still . . . it happens on one's watch. Possibly, it has something to do with one's experience. So Kevorkian is relevant to any Detroit cop today, and vice versa. But that doesn't mean any cop is *deeply* relevant."

I could only gaze at her.

"You're pursing your lips," she said. "What is it?"

"The Germans have a word, *selbstmord*," I said. "It means suicide, but somehow I've always felt that it said a little more. It seems to say 'self murder.' As if one went out looking for one's self and, finding it, then murdered it. A more complex and dramatic notion, perhaps, than passively inhaling a gas or taking a jar of soporific pills."

"There you are," Agge said, obviously pleased.

"I'm not thinking about Dr. Kevorkian, not *deeply*," I said. "I'm thinking about Grootka. But when you mentioned Kevorkian it reminded me of Grootka using that word. I don't know where Grootka picked up any German, but he meant it in the sense I was just mentioning. He said there was someone going around being him and he had to get rid of him."

Agge looked at me as if she didn't believe me. "Somebody was going around pretending to be Grootka, so he had to track this guy down and . . . *kill* him?"

"No, no, not *pretending*," I said. "Somebody was *being* him. I made the same mistake when he told me about it. It wasn't a case of someone impersonating him or resembling him, it was another *him*. So, of course, he had to kill this other Grootka."

"Of course," Agge said, with an uneasy laugh. "Why?"

"It seems obvious. If another you is walking around, who knows what he or she might do? And whatever this other self did, you would be, in some sense, responsible. You would have to kill this other you in defense of your primary self, so to speak. Eventually, I imagine, the other self might come looking for *you*. No, no." I shook my head. "Two selves would never do. Can't be tolerated. The question is: How did Grootka come to think this?"

"What happened?"

"I'm not sure. It was several years ago, at a time when I was no longer working with Grootka. I don't think anyone was—he didn't like partners, found them difficult to work with, and the feeling was mutual. It was not long before he retired . . . which was a whole 'nother set of problems, believe me."

"Do you think he was cracking up?"

"It sounds like it, doesn't it? But thinking back, I don't know that I felt that way at the time. It seems to me that he was pretty functional, he seemed okay."

She wanted to know, naturally, how this peculiar problem was resolved, but I couldn't satisfy her. As far as I could recall, it wasn't resolved. I didn't see much of Grootka at about this time and when I did more or less resume our previous relationship, the question had disappeared. Presumably he had worked it out. History Lady wasn't satisfied with this. It seemed such an unusual situation, calling for extraordinary measures. Surely Grootka must have worked it out. You just don't suggest one bright morning, she pointed out, that an alternate self is loose on the planet and has to be eliminated and then, some unknown but evidently not lengthy period later, pretend that the situation had never occurred.

"Oh, I don't know," I said. "I think that is what happens a lot of the time. Problems pop up then fade away. They seem remarkable on Monday, familiar on Tuesday, boring on Wednesday, and hard to remember on Thursday. Anyway, I wouldn't know how to find out what happened to this one."

"Really? I thought you were a detective."

I sighed openly. "I could look into it," I said.

"Great. When could we meet again?"

I thought about that. It seemed like a pleasant enough prospect. At present I was not urgently locked into any investigation. In fact, I'd decided to take a few weeks, even months, and just work at the precinct, clearing up back cases, helping out. In short, instead of rushing about focusing on major investigations, as I'd been doing until recently, I had now envisioned a lengthy period of simply pulling duty. There was no reason not to incorporate this little historical project into my unpressing agenda. And, of course, the prospect of seeing this young lady was not oppressive.

I figured I'd have to locate the files on Grootka, such as they were. That might take some time. But, what the heck . . . "Why not tomorrow?" I suggested.

"Terrific. And while you're at it, maybe you can find out what Grootka did on the Hoffa case."

"Hoffa? The Great Mystery. As you say, who didn't work on that one? Sure, why not?"

3

Come Out

"I had to like open the bruise up and let some of the bruise blood
come out to show them."
—Daniel Hamm, from Steve Reich's "Come Out," 1966

It puzzled me, all this interest in Grootka. The man
had been dead for . . . well, how many years, now? For the first time
I realized it had been a good while. Four years, anyway. He had never
interested anybody so much when he was alive, at least, not since
he had retired. Well, that was not true: a killer is always of interest.
People want to know what he's like, if he's different from the rest
of us because he has killed a man. As an occupational group, cops
have a high rate of killers among us. Still, even among cops, the
killer is unusual. I used to hear about so-called killer cops more, it
seems. There was a guy, Steve Something, who was supposed to be
a killer cop. He'd killed fourteen men, all legit. That's what I heard.
But later, when I tried to verify this, nobody seemed to remember
the guy. They'd "heard of" him, but they "never took it seriously."
And finally, I just couldn't track down this myth.

But I remember well, when I was in uniform, an older cop
pointing out Grootka with definite awe in his voice. "See him?" the
sergeant said. "That's Grootka. He's a killer." And it was a little scary.
It meant: One of your colleagues is a killer, he has killed another
human being. And: You may be called upon to kill, like this man.
Scary. Later, I found out that it was even scarier than I'd suspected.

I hadn't worked with Grootka long before he confided to me
that he was, in fact, a multiple killer. Well, I knew he had killed at
least one bank robber (some said two, but I never checked it out for
some reason), but one early morning, after sitting over a drink in a
blind pig, on our way back to the shop, he obliquely referred to having
killed another man, a mafioso. The conversation at the blind pig was
one of those supercynical cop macabre routines. The guy who ran
the pig, Jimmy Singleton, told about seeing a movie where murder
victims are substituted for wax images in a museum—an early 3-D
thing, I think. That launched Grootka on a long ramble about bodies being encased in freshly poured concrete, dissected, ground into
burger, dumped into sausage-making vats, immersed in acid baths . . .
it went on and on. But later, as we were driving home, he observed,
"Of course, the usual way is to bag 'em up and dump 'em in the trunk
of an abandoned car. That's the way the Mob does it." Then he snorted
a crude approximation of a laugh and said, "It works. If the bastards
only knew that was how I got rid of Raspa." He wheezed with laughter.

Raspa was an old-time thug, Grootka told me—before my
time. His death had never been reported. "I don't even know his
real name," Grootka said. "He was a real primitive, one of the guys
from the old country, from Lucania—that's down in the south of
Italy, somewhere. Hill country. I guess they're like hillbillies down
there. Raspa could hardly speak any English. These guys, they came
over here and they were like wild animals, they would do anything.
Yanh, they were dago hillbillies, like these Paducah types we got.
Peasants. You got a village up there, maybe five or six hundred
people, half of them never been to the next village. They were hard
men, full of superstition, real killers. Most of 'em was bandits back
there, but kind of like folk heroes, like Robin Hood or some fuckin'
thing, 'cause they're against the landowners and the gentry. They
believe in witches and elves, the evil eye, that kind of shit. You could
never get in their heads."

I enquired how it had happened. Grootka shrugged. "It was him or me. I hadda blast him." He waved a hand cavalierly. It wasn't so much a confession as a kind of drunken boast. "These guys are—whatchacallit—disposable. They don't have no real family or nothing, no attachments, see. Nobody gives a rat's ass what happens to them, beyond a certain—you know—'Did he get the job done?' If he didn't, if *he* got popped instead, then it's 'Fuck 'im.' I threw his ass inna car trunk that got crushed and sold to Zug Island for smelting. I got the idea from them, from Umberto's old man, in fact. It's a good way to get rid of bad rubbish. Anyways, it saved the taxpayers a lot of grief and money . . . prob'ly saved a few taxpayer lives down the road, too."

Grootka's own words, more or less. Who Umberto or his old man were, I had no idea, then.

I don't know if I believed him at the time. I think I must have been a little loaded myself. Anyway, I forgot it until the Galerd Franz case. This was a weird, complex case involving a rapist-murderer who reappeared after a long absence. I won't go into it except to note that Grootka had confided to me that he thought he'd killed Franz once already, twenty years earlier. Obviously, he was wrong, but I think Grootka genuinely relished the opportunity to kill Franz "again."

Another significant aspect of this case was that Franz had accused Grootka of the rape-murder of a young girl, Mary Helen Gallagher. Several people have asked my opinion of this charge by Franz. I think a lot of them believed that Grootka was capable of the crime. To be sure, he was a violent man, no doubt a troubled man, and who knows what were the sexual complications of that mind. But I do not believe that he killed Mary Helen Gallagher. If Galerd Franz hadn't suggested it, no one would ever have thought it of Grootka, and Franz was a psychopath.

It makes a difference who you kill, I'm sure. It even makes a difference who you *say* you killed. I never gave it a thought, at the time, though I occasionally reflected on it, later, after Grootka died.

(He died in the act of saving my life, by the way, which is something that I won't pass on to Ms. Allyson.) But here is the chief significance of this rambling discourse: Grootka set a trap for Galerd Franz, and incidentally inveigled me into the investigation, by the technique of using an abandoned car as a crypt. So you can see, when I reflected on his earlier confession it had the ring of authenticity.

Grootka lived alone in an apartment on Van Dyke, not far from the Detroit River. He claimed he spent most of his time trying to avoid his landlady, the widow of a rabbi, whom he believed was trying to entrap him into marriage. But the thought of anyone, much less a nice Jewish widow, wanting to marry Grootka required imagination. More than imagination: a willing suspension of disbelief. Grootka had been raised in a Catholic orphanage, St. Olaf's, I think, and whether he was a good Catholic or not, he was definitely a Catholic: he was still having nightmares about nuns, by his own account, as late as a week or two before he died. (In fact, I think he had a superstitious fear of nuns, or it may be of ghosts—this man who was otherwise as fearless as a badger.)

And now, in two days, two different people had asked me seriously about Grootka—not just "Hey, remember how that asshole Grootka used to stick a cigarette in his nose and blow smoke out of his ears—how did he do that?" but real, genuine questions. Ms. Agge Allyson seemed sincere, once you got past the notion of someone actually funding a history of the police department. But why would a Mr. Luckle from Accounting be interested? I didn't even know there was an Accounting office in the Detroit Police Department. Well, that's not quite true. I knew there was an Accounting section, but I thought that was part of the Racket and Conspiracy division. I decided to call my old buddy Andy Deane at R&C.

"Lucky?" Andy said. I could just about see Andy's freckled face wrinkled in confusion. He resembled a middle-aged Huck Finn. "The only Lucky I know is some kind of gink over at Internal Investigations."

"He said 'Luckle,' but maybe it's the same gink. Is this Lucky a major gink? A dinky gink? A rinky-dink gink?"

"That'd be your elemental finky gink," Andy said. "They're mostly finks in Eye-Yi."

"Hm. Well this Lucky gink was asking me about Grootka."

"Grootka? What about Grootka?"

"That's what I said," I said. "He said he was from Accounting, or something like that, and that he was inquiring about funds that Grootka may have expended for informational services . . . something like that."

"Something like that, hunh?" Andy was being wonderfully informational today. "We're talking about music lessons, right?"

Music lessons were what one might waggishly call payments for information—squealer stipends, fink funds. I told Andy that Mr. Lucky seemed keenly interested in Grootka's music tuition. But these funds were, to say the least, discretionary. Plus they were awfully petty—chump change. Half the time, the detective paid them out of his own pocket. Still, there was usually a bit of small change around for this purpose. I had no doubt that Grootka would have exploited this resource, no matter how miniscule, to the max. Well, if the department was looking for restitution I could give them his last known address: Section VIII, Lot 2707, Mount Elliott Cemetery.

I said good-bye to Andy and turned my attention to more pressing concerns. Namely, a real live criminal named Humphrey DiEbola, currently residing in Grosse Pointe Shores. It occurred to me, just now, that the first time I'd seen DiEbola, I was with Grootka. We were walking down one of those gloomy, echoing hallways at 1300 Beaubien, the Detroit Police Headquarters, when we approached a small flock of twittering lawyers surrounding a very large and red-faced man who was walking resolutely along, apparently ignoring them. He stopped at our approach, however, and said, with a beaming smile, "Grootka! An honest face, at last!"

That had been good for laughs. At the time, I'd been assigned to Homicide, assistant to Grootka. Nobody else wanted to work with him. But we got along, after a fashion. I spent four years there, with Grootka. It was a record. Guys would come up to me and congratulate me, shaking their heads. But I liked it, pretty much. The man taught me a lot. He taught me things that I don't believe I would have gotten from anyone else. On this occasion, he introduced me to Humphrey DiEbola, who was known far and wide as the Fat Man. Later, when DiEbola ascended to the boss's position, the nickname vanished in the wind. And, in fact, DiEbola himself went on an amazing diet that trimmed him dramatically down to where the nickname would have been inappropriate, anyway.

I was interested that DiEbola seemed genuinely pleased to see Grootka. "I known him a long time," Grootka explained, when we walked away. "Hell, I knew his old man. Another one a them mean-ass Lucanians. He called hisself Gagliano, but I think it was just the name of the village up in the hills that he come from."

I was puzzled: how did a son of "Gagliano" become a DiEbola? Grootka laughed. "He made it up, just like the old man—or maybe that's what the old man told him his *real* name was. It sounds kind of like gentry, see? Like he was the duke of Eboli, in the old country. Eboli is a larger town, down by the coast. These guys come over here and maybe, if they're around their paisanos in New York, they go by names that they were known by in the old country. But then, like old Gags, you set off for Detroit to make a name for yourself, you can call yourself anything you want."

Grootka had known most of the older mobsters. They were all immigrants, he said. "Throwbacks," Grootka called them. "They all look alike, kind of short, dark, round-faced—like Humphrey— they got these wide, thin lips. It ain't that usual Medatrainyun look, that thin eagle face like Carmine. These are some ancient people. Gags told me some of them live in caves. Maybe they're the missing link." They were very tough, he said. Gagliano had been one of the tougher ones, but he and Grootka had gotten along in the peculiar fashion of cops and robbers—a kind of grudging respect.

In many ways, Grootka's experience had been similar to theirs: poverty, a rough upbringing. Gagliano, for instance, had run away from home as soon as possible, getting to New York in his teens. Like many, he had gone back when he had made some money, to play the role of the gentry. But like most of those, he hadn't been able to bring it off.

"It's tough," Grootka observed. "You go back in your flashy suit and Florsheim shoes and you find out they still ain't as good as what the real gentry got, and then they wear out. You buy some land and they cheat you—you pay too much, the land's no good, the well is dry. Pretty soon you knock some peasant babe up. You're just about out of money, 'bout the time the Florsheims wear out on that stony ground. It's time to go back to America, now or never. You're gonna be a peasant if you don't watch out. Gags got out in the nick of time. He brought the kid with him, but not the mother. Maybe she was too ugly or a witch—he believed in love potions, they all do. He hooked up with one a these Sicilian babes in Detroit, she raised the kid like it was her own—Umberto prob'ly thinks she's his real ma. Gags got careless doing a hit and got his own ass wiped when the kid was only about six or something, I don't remember. The kid grew up with Carmine, I think the mothers was sisters, not the real mother, but the step. Umberto was always Carmine's fat cousin. Except he's smarter than Carmine. But the way things were laid out—it's Fate, see, and these mopes believe in Fate like it was the Blessed Virgin—Umberto (he calls himself Humphrey, after Bogart!) ain't never going to be boss, unless he's very patient. Which he is."

Grootka was prescient. At the time, Humphrey was just Carmine's lieutenant. But now he was the boss.

For some time now my chief concern had been with Humphrey and his minions, especially one Joe Service (actually, not a regular hand of DiEbola's, but a favored contractor). Lately, I had managed to bring down Service—he was currently recovering in a Colorado hospital—but Humphrey himself was another matter. He seemed untouchable. What I wanted was an entrée into the big man's field of operations. Every week I spent at least a few hours sifting through old files and trying to make pieces fit, but so far nothing seemed to work.

I was getting weary of this pursuit. Another part of me wanted nothing more than to just be a harness bull, as the old movies have it. Just work the precinct. By contrast with the complex strategies that would be needed to bring down a Humphrey DiEbola, the day-to-day chase-and-file grind of the precinct looked like a vacation. But it's never a good idea to think that you can take things easy.

I must have been thinking out loud: Jimmy Marshall knocked on the doorjamb of my office. Jimmy used to be my assistant; now he's my boss. We get along fine. It's a good thing to train the man who becomes your boss. He tends to do things the way you would do them. Now Jimmy had the headaches and I had the pleasant task of commiserating with him and encouraging him. At the moment Jimmy had the unenviable task of informing me that I was in violation of basic police department regulations. To wit, I was not living within the Detroit city limits, as required by chapter 3, section 48, of the police manual.

This was not news. But it was an embarassment. For many years it had become commonplace for officers to reside outside the city. The issue had become an open scandal in the last few years, since the extraordinary transformation of Detroit had become so pronounced. Between the 1980 census and that of 1990, there had been a population decline in Wayne County (which comprises just about all of the city), of about 220,000 people. Almost all of these were whites. There had been a corresponding decline in the number of police officers, most of whom were also white.

Presumably, to forestall this defection of white officers, not much was said when a white officer moved to Warren or Royal Oak, or, in my case, back to my original home in Saint Clair Flats, which is in Macomb County. But it was expected that the officer would maintain at least an accommodation address—i.e, an "official" address in the city. After a while, though, quite a few of the officers neglected even this, including, I confess, me. Nothing was said, but it had been in the back of my mind, and I knew that one day it would become an issue.

I agreed with the basic principle here: a police officer should reside in the community where he or she has power and responsibility; to do otherwise is to court disaster. The citizenry are always skeptical (to say the least) about the responsiveness and empathy of the police power. A healthy community cannot afford a police force that is not resident in the community where it hopes to function. I knew this and understood it, but I wasn't easy with the popular notion that this problem was a consequence of simple racism: i.e, that the whites (including the police) had left Detroit out of racial hatred. There is no denying that race was a huge factor; it's just that I thought there were other, not unrelated, economic and psychological aspects. It's not worth splitting hairs about, however: it was race.

My excuse—or really, not an excuse, but merely a reason—was that I was only temporarily absent and, anyway, it was merely a matter of convenience. I expected to return to the city, oh, just about any time now.

I'd had an apartment in the city, years before. It had been fun, for a while. But then other guys had begun to exploit the situation, asking me to list them as roommates and so on. And then they had taken to using the place as a trysting site. I finally got fed up with it and, since my mother didn't seem to mind. . . . Well, let's be clear about this: at one time I thought my mother was happy to have me move back home.

In those days, not so long after the death of my father, she was still in a conventional-widow mode. She wore black dresses and pinned a hat with a veil to her gray hair when she went to teas, where she conspired with her Eastern Star cronies about marrying their daughters and granddaughters to me. When I recollect this, it's shocking. I wonder if it shocks her.

She had never been very impressed with my police career, to say the least. It had quite stunned her, I gather. But then she began to develop new and compelling interests. Bird-watching was the key. She became obsessed with birds, which led to a more serious concern with the environment, and travel. Soon, she was hardly ever at home. And she began to get younger as I grew older, curiously enough, transforming herself from a conventionally maternal woman, a widow in corsets, into a slender, somewhat unisex athlete who traipsed about in Gokey brogans when she wasn't dashing about in spandex. She bought a mountain bike, and rode it! Correspondingly, she lost any interest, it seemed, in my marital status or career aspirations. She didn't have the time.

For my part, I had become conscious of the racial implications of Detroit's transformation but, as I say, not totally convinced of a racist character. On the surface, I felt, it had an overwhelmingly racist quality, but I'd always been a little suspicious of the conventional view of racism. I had a gut feeling that many seemingly racist behaviors might be more accurately attributed to a variety of other, more complex, factors. For instance, leaving aside the racial composition of Wayne County, there was the fact was that there had been a considerable decline in the earning power and income of all Detroit residents, generally. When people are poor things get dangerous. It wasn't safe, no matter who you were. In short, it had become an increasingly less attractive place, and as a consequence, the nearby suburbs, particularly just north of the city, in Oakland and Macomb Counties, seemed more attractive. But who could afford to move there? Only white people, particularly since (and here is really where racism came into play) black people were largely discouraged to do so, especially by the realtors, who probably told their consciences that they were simply acting in a businesslike manner. I'm being a little facetious, but not completely. Realtors widely believe that white people don't like black people— they don't look beyond conventional notions—and so they exacerbate real racism (i.e., deeply held notions of some white people about the inferiority or undesirableness of blacks) by adopting an economic racism to protect their business interests.

No doubt the problem was much more complex than this, but I won't dilate on it. For now, my problem was to accommodate to the new reality. My boss was under pressure to bring his department into compliance with the regulations. Specifically, that meant enforcing the residency requirement for white officers. Jimmy was not accusatory. But he was the lieutenant. I was the sergeant. It was time for me to move to town or resign.

"So, I'll move to town," I said. "I knew it was coming. I'm sorry I didn't do it on my own."

"Good. Thanks, Mul. But." He hesitated, then plunged on. "It has to be soon. No delays. They're talking ninety days."

"Ninety days. You got it. There's lots of vacancies in town. Rents are low. Shouldn't be a problem. What else you got?" He was carrying a sheaf of papers.

What he had, he said, was a "grounder," which is what one might call a nonjob. Some kid was getting a weird transmission on his computer and he was worried about it. He thought it might be criminal in some way. But it didn't seem criminal, on the face of it.

The transmission was a message, from some kind of cover name or alias, it looked like. Somebody named Hexam. Gaffer

Hexam. The transmission featured a crudely animated cartoon, or "graphic," that depicted a woman being killed. She was being killed in a series of buffoonish ways, as if it were a Road Runner cartoon, except that the cartoon wasn't anything like as slick as the Road Runner. A sort of generic stick-figure woman with exaggerated pyramidal breasts and a cloud of white or blond hair, in a triangular skirt, stalks jerkily along a city street, a business district of tall buildings, arms swinging. A huge chunk of concrete, part of a building, falls on her. Her hands and feet stick out from under the concrete slab. In another sequence, the woman is walking on a bridge over what appears to be the Detroit River, judging by the skyline in the distance; in fact, it seems to be the Belle Isle Bridge. She stops to talk to a much larger figure, a man in a dark outfit of some kind— a cloak, or maybe just a long overcoat. Suddenly, the man's arms fly up—there's no other way to describe this—and then the woman tips over the railing of the bridge and disappears. In the third and final sequence, the woman is smashed by a speeding limousine that flattens her. After that, a question mark rises on the screen, followed by the words, "Where? When?"

The kid had recorded this on a little square disk. He seemed like a nice enough boy, about sixteen, a student, tall and gawky but nice looking. "It seemed kind of weird," he told me. "You see weird stuff on the Net sometimes, but this seemed so direct."

"Is there any way of checking back, through the channels or something?" I asked. I wasn't familiar with the system, as you can tell. The kid, whose name was Kenty, didn't think it could be traced. Or maybe it could be, but it would be very difficult and time-consuming and if it wasn't of any interest to the cops then he sure wasn't going to waste time on it. But he thought it might be interesting because it had what seemed to be a specific person's name attached and it bothered him because it had been sent directly to his E-mail.

The "graphic," as the boy called it, was directed to "Sgt. Fang Mulhiesen [sic], 9th Precinct." Directed in the sense that the opening panels of the "graphic" carry a title or heading as above. And the closing panels also carry a heading: "by Gaffer Hexam." It was a mystery to me. But I said I'd look into it. Just the utterance of that fateful cliché seemed to sink the boy's heart, and mine too. He muttered something about "Let me know" and "I'll see you" and left. I sighed and set the disk aside.

"Why would a 'disk' be square?" I asked Jimmy. He shrugged. "A disk is a round thing," I said. A blank look. "If it was meant for me, why send it to him?"

"It got to you, didn't it?"

"Yeah, it got to me, but why not send it direct?"

"How would you do that?" Jimmy asked. "What's your E-mail address?"

I thought about that. What was there to say? "Oh well, what else have you got?"

We had a young man who had come all the way from Mexico, looking for his brother, who was last known to be employed at Krispee Chips, a potato-chip factory in this precinct. This young man did not speak English and we had no Spanish speakers in the precinct. He had been to Missing Persons, downtown, but they had sent him out to us. Communication was difficult, but somehow, with the help of a couple of other officers, we pieced together a little information. We were interested in his story because Krispee Chips is an important feature of Mob presence in Detroit. Humphrey DiEbola is the C.E.O. It is believed that innumerable aliens are cycled in and out of the country through Krispee Chips, as putative employees. These are almost always Italians. We'd never heard of Mexicans at Krispee Chips.

The young man showed us a letter from his brother, Pablo "Pepe" Ortega. It was postmarked Detroit, in January. Pepe Ortega brags to his family about how he has become the manager of Krispee Chips. He is making so much money, soon he will be a millionaire.

The brother tells us that Pepe went to Europe about four years ago. The family, which apparently is middle class, living in Mexico City, heard little from him, but he had written that he was learning to be a chef, in Paris. Then he was in Italy. Then they got this letter. They wouldn't have become worried, but then they got another letter, ostensibly from a concerned friend of Pepe's. The brother did not have the letter, alas. His mother had thrown it away. She thought it was obviously from some girl Pepe had gotten pregnant. It was mailed from Grosse Pointe, Michigan, but no address, no name. Just a message that Pepe's family should contact Mr. DiEbola about the whereabouts of their son. It was important, the letter said.

"Was this letter in English?" I asked.

Mr. Ortega, a very handsome, well-dressed man of thirty, indicated that it had been. When he'd learned of it, his mother— who could read and speak English *"un poco"*—had already destroyed it. She didn't take it seriously, but he wrote to Krispee Chips and received a letter from them. He showed me. It was from a Chris Oresti, designated as office manager. Ms. Oresti wrote that Mr. Ortega had resigned his position of production adviser at Krispee Chips in January, not long after his letter to his family. They had no idea where he had gone, but he was thought to have left Detroit.

This really was too good an opportunity to pass up. With Mr. Ortega and a taciturn detective named Field, I drove to Krispee Chips, which is located down an extraordinarily long block on an otherwise residential street that runs off the river.

Chris Oresti was new to me. She was an attractive and intelligent-looking woman in her late thirties, perhaps early forties. I appreciate people like her. They're bright, competent, and pleasant. Very understanding and quick to anticipate difficulties and head them off. She grasped our purpose quickly.

"Mr. Ortega was a valued employee," she told me. "Mr. DiEbola thought very highly of him and was distressed when he learned that Mr. Ortega had quit and left, without any warning." She said that Ortega had simply called one morning, instead of appearing for work, and said he was leaving town. He didn't say where he was going, but mentioned that he would contact them later about his pay.

"But he didn't contact you," I said.

"No," Ms. Oresti said. She went on to tell us that Ortega may have exaggerated his role at Krispee Chips. He was nominally carried as a production adviser, but that was more of a ceremonial title that Mr. DiEbola had created for him. He was apparently developing a new line of taco chips, without so many additives. He came and went as he pleased; in fact, you could hardly call his activities at the factory regular employment. Mostly, he worked at DiEbola's house. She thought that, in fact, he had been Mr. DiEbola's personal chef, but she wasn't sure. She wasn't privy to that kind of knowledge of Mr. DiEbola's private life.

Alas, Mr. DiEbola wasn't in. She wasn't even sure if he was in the country. She would certainly take our message asking him to call. She knew it was important.

That was disappointing. But it wasn't as if there wasn't plenty to do. Shootings, robberies, rapes . . . business was brisk. When Field and I got back to the precinct Detective Ayeh asked my advice about a case that was already three months old. If you didn't get something going within a week or two, a case tended to disappear, buried under the eternal blizzard of new offenses, new outrages. But this case interested me, as it had all of us at the time.

A woman had gone into a supermarket, around nine P.M., and pulled a gun, attempting a robbery. Three customers had responded by pulling their own guns, and all of them shot at the would-be robber, at least one of them killing her. Pretty amazing, even for Detroit. It made the national news, for the usual fifteen minutes, or seconds. And it was later noted by a few more serious editorialists. Inevitably, the incident was seen as symptomatic of a gun-obsessed society.

For the investigators it was more interesting that one of the other pistol-packing customers happened to be a woman who knew the dead woman or, more germanely, knew the robber's husband. Knew him all too well, it turned out. This was a coup for one of the precinct detectives, young Ayeh, he of the keen eye and hawk nose and better known as Ahab. But, alas, the business came to nothing, since the bullet that killed the woman turned out to have come from the gun of one of the other customers, a man who had no relationship of any kind with the victim. Indeed, it was difficult to prove that the woman who knew the husband had even fired her piece.

Like everything else, all the information about this case was on a computer file. I'm not tremendously handy at this, but even a cursory scan through turned up at least one interesting fact: the supermarket was way the hell and gone over on Eight Mile Road, a couple of precincts away from where the victim lived. Ayeh said that he had noticed that and he had ascertained that Mrs. McDonough, the victim, had gone to the store separately from Miss James (the once suspected killer.) Both their cars had been parked in the store parking lot. The husband, Ted McDonough, had been home asleep (he worked the night shift at FedEx, at the airport). Ayeh had also ascertained that Mrs. McDonough was pushing a grocery cart that contained breakfast cereal, a half gallon of milk, toilet paper, shampoo, a plastic container of chocolate-chip cookies from the store bakery, and a half gallon of chocolate swirl low-fat frozen yogurt. She had not paid for these items when the shooting broke out, although the cashier had rung them up, which was how Ayeh knew exactly what was in the cart—it was on the scanner printout receipt.

I hadn't known any of these details. They seemed very intriguing. I agreed with Ayeh that if Mrs. McDonough wanted to rob a grocery store she wasn't likely to do it in her own neighborhood, where she was well known. But would she actually buy things she needed? Frozen yogurt? If your purpose was robbery, why bother with these items?

And sure, if Miss James wanted to kill her lover's wife she might have followed her to the store, or she might even have been tipped off that Mrs. McDonough was going to attempt such a thing, perhaps by the husband. Though it seemed a bit too convenient that Mrs. McDonough's gun was unloaded—she actually fired no shots herself. But was this the whole story? Could it possibly be the whole story?

"Where did Mrs. McDonough's gun come from?" I asked Ayeh.

It seems she had bought it herself, a month earlier. A legitimate purchase, over the counter, from a legitimate dealer. It was registered, although she was not licensed to carry it on her person. It could be transported in the trunk of a car, from the police station where it was registered to her home, and to and from her home to an approved firing range or gun club. Mrs. McDonough didn't belong to any gun club.

The fact that Miss James had not, in fact, killed her rival had stymied the investigation. But I wondered if it couldn't be jump-started again. For one thing, it certainly looked like Mrs. McDonough—"What was her first name?" I asked Ayeh. "Mildred," he answered—had actually shopped for groceries and was planning to pay for them: she had more than enough money in her purse. I asked Ayeh to find out, if he could, whether that grocery list corresponded to needs or preferences in the household: i.e., did they usually buy Honey Bunches of Oats and Swan's Neck toilet paper? Were they out of or low on those items? Did someone in the house like chocolate-chip cookies and/or low fat chocolate swirl frozen yogurt? In short, were these usual, regular purchases?

The other thing was, could there be any normal or reasonable excuse or cause for Miss Ardella James to be in that neighborhood at 9:08 P.M.? For this Ayeh had a reply. Yes, Ardella James had been at a record store on Eight Mile Road, which had obtained an old blues recording for her. She was a fan of Etta James, who she liked to tell people was a cousin, although there was no evidence that they were related. Ardella was a blues collector, in fact. The record shop had previously obtained unusual or hard-to-find records for her. She didn't like CDs. She liked vinyl. "She says it has a better sound," Ayeh told me. "The surface noise is a problem, especially on older records, she says, but the recording is fuller or something. It didn't make sense to me. She picked up the record— paid twenty-five dollars for it!—some time between eight-twenty and eight-forty. The store closed at nine. Then she showed up at the Food Fair at nine. She hadn't done any shopping there. She apparently had just come into the store."

And no one else, none of the other people present, could be linked to either Ardella or Mildred. The man who actually shot her, whose bullet had killed Mildred, was Albert P. Fessel, age sixty-six, a retired baker. He lived in the neighborhood, was married, in good repute, and had a permit to carry the .38 caliber Smith & Wesson revolver. He used to own a bakery on Chene Street, about a mile away, but had given it up when he was robbed for about the twentieth time.

I remembered the bakery. I remembered the man, I thought. He made wonderful raised donuts, incredibly delicious and appall-ingly fattening. I suppose I had eaten several hundred of them in my lifetime. Could this be the same guy? Ayeh assured me that Al Fessel was indeed a lightly colored African-American of about five feet and eight inches in height, weighing about two hundred and thirty or forty pounds, with a neatly trimmed mustache and sparse, gray hair cut very close to his round skull. He wore heavy black-rimmed glasses. No known or even suspected relationship with the deceased.

Al Fessel claimed that he thought the woman was going to kill him. She had a gun in her hand and she shot at him at least twice, he was certain, at the time. *At the time.* Later, he supposed that he must have been mistaken, since the checkout clerk said that

Mrs. McDonough had only waved the gun and hadn't fired it. But somebody had fired, and Al Fessel had thought it was her. "Must of been someone else, then," he'd told Ayeh. "And he knew," Ayeh said, "'cause he'd been shot at plenty."

All this was interesting, certainly, but I thought something was amiss. I wondered if there wasn't a fundamental misstep here. How did we know, for instance, that Mildred McDonough had been intending a robbery? I kept returning to the fact that she'd had more than enough money in her purse to pay for her groceries. The more I thought about it, the less Mildred looked like a would-be robber. I discussed it with Ayeh and he agreed to go back and talk to the clerk. Though where it would get us, I didn't know.

In the afternoon Mr. Luckle called back. (His name *was* Luckle—it was often misspelled and mispronounced, he said. I could commiserate, having been called Millhowzen, Mulhouser, Millhozer, Mullice, and even Malice.) He said he had important business with me and he hoped that I could come down to headquarters, to Internal Investigations, "So that we can clear this matter up," he said. "Would four o'clock be convenient?"

It was neatly performed, but I was familiar with this dance routine, having used it myself many times. Obviously, something was *vermischt,* to use an old NATO term (which I think must have meant, once, "screwed up, messed up, perhaps missing"). Four o'clock wasn't at all convenient but I motored on downtown compliantly.

Mr. Luckle was one of those truly white men, apparently quite hairless, who seemed devoid of blood. You couldn't really imagine him bruised. Where would the bruise blood come from? But to give this ghostly pale man credit, he seemed pleasant enough and he also wasn't noticeably on the prod, as most cops fear when dealing with Internal Investigations. He seemed as puzzled as anyone about the funds that Grootka had presumably misappropriated. They amounted to $4,017.39—enough to be concerned about but not enough to fuel a scandal, considering that the figure encompassed more than thirty years of detective work. Still, it couldn't be ignored. Mr. Luckle wasn't the kind of guy who ignored any misdeed.

I was willing to help, though hardly eager to devote my time to a painstaking search for legitimate payouts by Grootka, especially since the man was safely dead and anyway his reputation had never exactly been honorable. But Luckle changed my mind.

"Your name is on several of the chits," he said.

These "chits" were mere slips of paper on which Grootka had scribbled a sum—anywhere from five dollars to fifty dollars, never any more—and a name, plus a signature (usually his own, but sometimes "Mul," or "Mullein," or something not really recognizable, but which Luckle seemed to believe was an approximation of my name). I had not signed any of these chits. I was willing to swear it. The names were those of informants, or so it appeared: Shakespeare, Red Hen, the Sparrow, Homer, Pudokyo (I remembered him: a sex pervert whose penis got longer every time he lied), Motor Mouth, Caruso (and Mario Lanza), Dickbreath, 33 1/3 (a.k.a. ElPee, a notorious ear bender), the Turdle, Books. Many of them were familiar to me, although I reckoned that most of them were dead. I couldn't recall seeing any of them lately. Books was very dear, in more ways than one: a good old friend both of Grootka's and later, mine, and also the recipient of several hundred dollars. Luckle believed that there was more missing, since the chits accounted for only a portion of what the department had actually appropriated for this purpose. But at least this much was nominally accounted for.

I didn't see what the big deal was. Mr. Luckle readily explained.

"These chits are in no way adequate accounting for departmental expenditures. Since their originator is no longer available for clarification and/or restitution, his associate—you, Sergeant Mulheisen—will be held accountable for any funds you are unable to justify."

That was pretty clear. Unless I could explain a bunch of barely legible scraps of paper, the department was going to make me pay up. I gave Mr. Luckle my most vulpine grimace, but it didn't seem to faze him. Armed punks have cowered in corners before that grimace. Luckle didn't blink and, to be sure, no blood rose to his cheeks. It was a lot of malarkey, of course, and the Policemen's Benevolent Association wouldn't stand for it, but it looked like a hassle. I said I'd give it my best shot.

Since I was at headquarters I went by Records with an idea that I'd look into Grootka's cases, make a list of his informants, and justify it that way. It didn't work. For one thing, most of Grootka's cases were precomputer, and while some of that stuff has been logged onto computer tape, or whatever they do, a lot of it hasn't and never will be. It's just too expensive and nowadays the government is so strapped for operating funds that we can't be spending it on things that don't show an immediate payoff. These files were, in fact, more neglected now than they would have been had computers never been invented. It's a long story and a boring one, about the unanticipated drawbacks of a major technological transition, so you won't hear it here. The upshot was that if I found it so important to ransack Grootka's files I'd have to do it myself, and be prepared to spend a few dusty days in dark caverns.

But then, of course, there was Ms. Agge Allyson. *She* might be interested in spelunking Grootka's dark past. Hell, it was her vocation, so to speak. When we met tomorrow I'd suggest it.

Records had actually packed up many of these records and were storing them in an old warehouse down by the river. I recognized the address. It wasn't very far from where Grootka had once found a corpse and called me in to help investigate. He'd identified the corpse as Books Meldrim, one of his "music students," as it were. It seemed ludicrously appropriate that the body of Grootka's work, so to speak, was now immured in an adjacent warehouse.

4

Dining with
the Dead

After Grootka's
death I'd searched his apartment thoroughly. It was a nice apartment, a ground-floor back in an old town house, a style of building that had been constructed in Detroit in the twenties and thirties to house upscale management types in the auto industry. They were typically three stories (any higher and the code required an elevator) and built within walking distance of major trolley lines. They were usually solid brick with a fairly grand foyer that featured marble walls, terrazzo tile, and an ornate central staircase that led to a gallery on the next floor, which connected more humbly by a narrower staircase to the third floor. So the third floor often featured more actual floor space than the two lower stories, because there was no great yawning open stairwell.

Grootka's building was a couple of blocks from the Detroit River, out Jefferson Avenue east of the Belle Isle Bridge. His main-floor apartment was spacious, with a large living room, a couple of bedrooms, a large kitchen and bath, even a good-sized pantry. In the original layout, his part of the building would have been the kitchen and living quarters of the servants, the front rooms being reserved for the gentry. That was where the rabbi had lived and his widow still resided. Grootka kept his quarters very well, although I suspect that Mrs. Newman, the rabbi's widow, actually cleaned the place for him.

The bedroom that he slept in was dark, the only window opening onto the central airshaft. Grootka used to tell me that he liked its darkness, that he had difficulty sleeping with any kind of light. "Anything comes for me in the night, it better come with a flashlight, and ghosts don't carry flashlights."

The room was furnished military style: a simple iron bed frame with a thin stuffed mattress lying on a lattice of flat metal strips fastened by springs to the frame. I had slept on a bed just like this in the air force; we called it a rack. In fact, Grootka's rack could have stood up to inspection in any barracks I'd ever lived in. The two blankets were rough gray wool, evidently from a military surplus store. He made the bed in a military way, too, with the blankets tucked under the mattress, hospital corners, and one of the blankets stretched tautly over the pillow as a dust cover, rather than under it in the white-collar inspection style. To my knowledge, Grootka had never been in the military, so this style may have reflected some orphanage-inculcated habitude. Perhaps the desire for utter darkness stemmed from this experience as well.

There was a single dresser, made of pine and painted gray. The top drawer contained socks neatly rolled and tucked in pairs, both silk dress socks in gray, black, and navy blue with red clocks on them, and dark wool socks also rolled and tucked. Other drawers contained neatly folded white boxer shorts, T-shirts, dress shirts, a couple of old well-worn wool V-neck sweaters. In the closet were hung three double-breasted wool worsted suits, in brown, gray, and blue, along with two silk ties in solid colors and several pairs of casual slacks. His usual tie, as I'd told Agge, which he wore just about every day, was red and it was never untied, just loosened and slipped on and off; normally, it was hung on a spindle of the chair by the bed—

I remember having seen it there, but he'd been wearing it when he died and it had been packed up with other items from the morgue. There were three pairs of dress shoes, in brown, tan, and black, very good shoes, evidently made to his last. (He had been buried in his police uniform, but as far as I knew, the funeral director had not required shoes.)

In a hall closet near the entry, I'd found a couple pairs of rubbers, including six-buckle arctic galoshes of a type I hadn't seen in years. Under the bed was a pair of carefully lined up leather slippers, very expensive and well cared for. Another pair, rather cheaper ones of boiled wool with rubber soles, very likely the ones he used when he came from the bath, were in the bathroom, along with an old, somewhat threadbare blue terry cloth bathrobe hanging on a brass hook on the door.

It was an interesting apartment. Even one who lives very simply, as Grootka appeared to, leaves a surprising amount of things. Some nice paintings, or prints, were hung in the living room and in the other rooms. So Grootka had been interested in abstract art. Possibly more interesting to my colleagues were the dozen or so guns, stashed all over the place—behind books on a shelf, under sofa cushions, in the liquor cabinet, in an otherwise empty box of Sanders' chocolates on the coffee table. One of them, a .32 caliber revolver, had been of use to me in the scene with the killer, and another, a small silver-plated revolver, had discharged three fatal shots from Grootka's hand into the killer.

Almost as interesting, however, was the music room. It was a rear bedroom. It was bare except for an upright piano (battered, but in good tune), a stool, a music stand, and two gleaming saxophones on separate stands—a huge baritone and a straight soprano. A large sash window looked out onto a rear porch that was little more than a walkway with stairs going up and down and beyond that a small courtyard and a gate. (This was the way Grootka used to "sneak in," to avoid his supposedly matrimaniacal landlady.) The window was heavily curtained and barricaded with a mesh grid. There were pictures on the walls, pushpinned reproductions of what looked to me like a nineteenth-century American seascape (gray and placid, with sails in the distance) and an Eakins scene of rowers on the river: perhaps they gave the musician a scene to look at, or into, while practicing scales.

And there was quite a lot of sheet music in this room, including some very complicated-looking scores, ultramodern stuff, some of it by composers with European-sounding names. There were several folders of handwritten music featuring a blizzard of notes and some odd-looking notation that could have been computer generated. Did Grootka play this, on the piano, on the saxes? He did, according to the neighbors, some of whom grimaced when they recalled the fact, not because he didn't play well, they said, but because the music itself was "awful." ("Why couldn't he play 'Danny Boy'?" one of them said. "He could play as good as that guy on *Lawrence Welk*.")

I wasn't familiar with this music, but then I'm not a player. The handwritten stuff had numbers rather than words where one might expect a title, and the stuff on the accordion-folded computer paper may not have been music at all, but it was titled "Nigger Heaven: A Suite for Quartet and Six Others, by T. Addison."

There was an excellent stereo or high-fidelity system in this room and many long-playing records and a surprising number of compact discs, mostly classical recordings, but many jazz recordings from a wide range of music—Louis Armstrong to Anthony Braxton. I was frankly astonished. I kind of knew that Grootka liked jazz, but before I saw this if you'd asked me I'd have said he was probably a Tommy Dorsey fan. There were no Dorsey boys here.

The most attractive neighbors shared the back porch: a handsome woman of middle age with a strikingly beautiful daughter of about sixteen or seventeen. They were genuinely grieved at the death of their dear neighbor, Mr. Grootka, whom they seemed to remember as a kindly, helpful, and (I gathered from some unspoken gestures or sentiments) protective older man. They were not the ones who disliked Grootka's musical performances. A youthful gay lawyer upstairs and a somewhat older bachelor managerial type on the top floor, both of whom had bedroom windows that opened onto the airshaft, were not so appreciative.

Much more significant than neighbors, now that I recollected it, were Grootka's notebooks. I don't know why, but I'd completely spaced them out. Three boxes of mostly pocket-size dime-store notebooks, filled with pencil scribblings, usually containing miscellaneous items like business cards or ticket stubs, each secured with a rubber band. That was why I'd spaced them out, no doubt: just a peek into those miserable scribbles was enough to make your guts turn to cold, gelid coils. There were also some larger notebooks, but I'd ignored them at the time.

It appeared that Grootka, who was not an overly methodical man, had nonetheless evolved a familiar method: he kept notes on cases in separate notebooks. I hadn't examined them at all closely, but I'd gotten the impression that the method was a familiar one: basically, a main notebook would contain the day-to-day notes. Then there would be a number of satellite notebooks, each one dedicated to a single case and containing information about that case alone. I had found all these notebooks jumbled in a couple of cardboard boxes stored in the rather spacious pantry of Grootka's apartment. But what had I done with them?

I'd seen the system before and I'd even tried it myself, for a while. But then I'd gotten in the habit of restricting all my notes to the actual files in the precinct or the bureau. I kept a daily notebook, of course, just to jot down stuff as it occurred. My daily logs were filed in my office file cabinet. As soon as I got back to the precinct I consulted the appropriate aide-mémoire now to see what had happened to all of Grootka's property. To my surprise, I discovered that I was in possession of most of it.

Getting old, I thought. I had totally forgotten that I'd been named conservator of Grootka's estate by the court, in the absence of any known relatives or even other interested parties. It isn't usual for the investigating detective to "inherit" a subject's petty goods, but it isn't unheard of. A home or an automobile, now . . . the state is sure to take an interest in the estate. But it doesn't want to be bothered with books and records and kitchen utensils. Paging through my logs I was reminded that the musical instruments had been donated to St. Olaf's orphanage. It seemed to me that his clothes had gone to Goodwill or the Salvation Army. Other than that—and, I almost didn't remember, a Seiko wristwatch, probably worth five hundred dollars, that I'd given to his friend Books—Grootka had accumulated very little of value. He'd had a fairly new Buick, which the state had claimed and one of the guys had been tipped to buy at auction. And he'd left a savings account, though I doubt that it had amounted to more than a few thousand. But Grootka's notebooks and music were stored in my attic, I was pretty sure.

Would there be anything in there about *selbstmord?* I was willing to bet that there wouldn't be. Somehow, it just didn't seem the kind of thing that Grootka would notate. It would be like keeping a dream journal—just a little too flaky for a no-bullshit bastard like Grootka. (Well, that's what he used to say: "Hey, I'm just a no-bullshit bastard, but. . . .")

Thinking about all this, I remembered that Agge, the History Honey, had asked where was Grootka when Hoffa disappeared. Possibly there was something in his notebooks. Another reason to look.

I couldn't remember Grootka ever saying anything about Hoffa. Which was odd, come to think of it. I remembered the furore. Everybody was checking their traps, trying to get a lead. Not a dick in Detroit, but wanted to know what had happened to the bastard, hoping to get lucky and make a name.

I stuck my head out into the hallway and bellowed, "Maki!" A tall, bony, red-nosed detective with rubbery red lips stuck his head out of the squad-room door. Maki was a nice guy. Been on the force forever.

"What do you know about Hoffa?" I asked.

"They found him!" he declared, with a red rubber grin.

I stared at him. His eyes were beady, blue, and a little watery. He was not known to be a joker. "Where?" I asked, suspiciously.

"Jeffrey Dahmer's autopsy!" he guffawed, and his head vanished.

I sighed and returned to my desk. Apparently the world had gone completely loopy.

A few seconds later, rather sheepishly, Maki appeared at my door. "Mul, I'm sorry," he said, abjectly, "it was too good an opportunity to pass up. I don't know what got into me." He laughed a little, thinking about it. He was embarrassed now.

"I know, I know," I placated him. "But seriously. . . . What do you know about Hoffa? Did you work on the case at all?"

"Hoffa? Seriously? Sure. Sure, I worked on it. Didn't you? I just did the usual."

"No," I said. "I wasn't a detective yet. What usual?"

"Oh, I don't know. . . . I checked out some alibis, tried to locate some possible witnesses, snitches . . . that kind of stuff. I didn't try very hard."

"Why not?"

"Well, it was Hoffa," Maki said, almost apologetically. "He was not exactly a policeman's pal, you know. Anyway, everybody knew the Mob whacked him. It was bound to happen. You fool around with those guys, eventually they dump on you, especially if you aren't one of them. Right?"

I shrugged; it happened. "Did you know him?"

"Hoffa? I met him once. I was on the West Side, then. I went to check out a tussle over at the local, Two ninety-nine, Hoffa's local. He beat some laborer up. The guy was protesting because the laborers' union—A.F. of L., you know—was on strike at Zug Island and the Teamsters didn't honor the picket line. So a bunch of them went over to the local and stood around, yelling, calling Hoffa a labor traitor, and finally he came out with some of his heavies. There wasn't much to it. The guy got his ass kicked. Or, I should say, his nuts. Hoffa kicked the guy in the nuts. Really stomped him. Pretty nasty stuff. Nothing came of it, though."

"No?"

"The guy never pressed charges. It was kind of iffy, anyway. But the thing I remember is Hoffa chewed our asses. You know, the old rant about 'Where were you when I needed you,' and 'Who do you think pays your salary.' The man was abusive. And a crook. You never saw him, hunh?"

No, I'd never seen Jimmy Hoffa, live. He was all over the press and the television, of course. Hoffa was not a hero of mine, although I certainly didn't share Maki's dismissive attitude. I had been brought up to respect unions. In my home, men like Eugene V. Debs and Walter Reuther were revered. Others, like George Meany and Hoffa, were viewed with mixed feelings. They were allowed some respect for being at least chosen, whether honestly or not, to lead enormous bodies of union workers. There was no denying in Hoffa's case that an overwhelming majority of his constituents supported and even loved him. Doubtless, there were some, perhaps many, disaffected and even anti-Jimmy Teamsters; but it seemed that the great majority were more or less enthusiastic supporters. You can't ignore that.

Too, Hoffa was a genuine character, an original. There was no one in public life quite like him. He was tough, not in the least abashed by polite society, and quite willing to speak from the hip. In Detroit a guy can dine out for a long time on candid comments like Hoffa's about the Mob: "You're a damned fool not to be informed what makes a city run when you're tryin' to do business in the city." Even as a cop, I had to admit that it didn't make sense to pretend that the Mob didn't exist, like most public figures did.

I wondered if Grootka mightn't have been at least a grudging, if private, admirer of Hoffa's, but I couldn't recall even a single mention of him. That seemed odd, considering how Hoffa had been in the public eye more or less constantly for decades, to say nothing of the tremendous hullabaloo about his disappearance.

Oddly, I had misspoken myself, to Maki: I *had* been a detective at the time of Hoffa's vanishing, but to the best of my recollection I hadn't had one single thing to do with the case. And I was certain that Grootka had not mentioned it, not even on the occasion when we were discussing ways of getting rid of bodies, as in abandoned cars.

The Hoffa case was sure to be on the computer. I called up the clerk in Records; she did a quick scan for me and reported, almost immediately, not a single reference to Grootka in the records. So Grootka had never worked on the case. Too bad. I'd have bet that it would have been worth an amusing anecdote or two for Agge's history.

Then the clerk from Records called back. She'd been interested in my query and had taken it on herself to make a cursory scan of the F.B.I. liaison file—it was, after all, essentially an F.B.I. case. Here she came up with one reference to Grootka. A memo from a Special Agent Senkpile to D.P.D.-Homicide: "Please keep your man Grootka out of this. Highest priority." Which meant, the clerk thought, orders from the director himself.

"Hoover?" I said. But no, Hoover had died three years earlier. Webster? Gray? Who could remember these nonentities?

Well, this was fascinating. I called the F.B.I. They had no Agent Senkpile anymore. And, naturally, they had no comment about this former agent's comments re Grootka. But they'd get back to me.

I called a guy I knew in the U.S. marshal's office, P. G. Chelliss, better known as Pedge. An old-timer, he remembered "Stinkpile." "A true FBI man, Mul. Stinky was Dutch Reformed. He got his hair buzz-cut even before he joined the bureau. Shined his shoes every day, stood tall, looked you right in the damn eye. This man could *soldier*. Absolutely useless as an investigator, of course. Couldn't find his ass with both hands."

"Why would he warn Grootka off the Hoffa case?"

Pedge, remembering Grootka, snapped: "Who wouldn't?" But on further reflection he confessed that he had no idea. It was ridiculous for Senkpile to even be *on* the Hoffa case, much less in a position of apparent authority. He promised to check around.

I have a small window in my office. It looks out onto Chalmers Avenue. It was a swell dark and rainy March day, temperature about fifty degrees with periodic blasts of wind that could tumble a pig. The trees were bare and wet, the street glistening, reflecting the headlights of cars already, at four in the afternoon. A great day to get out of the office and run down to Lake Erie. As bleak as Detroit looked on a day like this, the southern Ontario plains were bound to be even gloomier. I do enjoy a gloomy prospect.

I was not disappointed. The wind and rain off the little jetty in front of Books Meldrim's cottage was absolutely doleful. You could hear lost ships out there in the murk, moaning for guidance, lamenting their trespasses, pleading for mercy.

Books was looking okay, not noticeably older. He was in his seventies for sure, possibly his eighties or nineties. I couldn't tell. He was a small brown man with grizzled hair and mustache. He reminded me of an old jazzman, but I couldn't recall who, exactly. In fact, he was a player himself, a well-regarded nonprofessional pianist in the Teddy Wilson style.

My intention was to ask him about the list I carried of Grootka informants. Maybe some of them were still around. But I got distracted by the jazz suggestion and asked him about Grootka's surprising predilections.

"I knew about the soprano sax," Books said. "Will you have some tea? I also have whisky, but I haven't been drinking it of late, so I forget to offer it."

I took the tea. For some reason I'd gotten fed up with whisky myself. A day like this called for tea, and Books's strong Darjeeling answered well.

"Grootka was always a surprising one," Books observed when we had settled near the fireplace. It was a very snug cottage. "I believe he learned music at the orphanage. He told me he played a C-melody sax in the band. In our younger days he was very fond of the kind of small group swing that one could hear in the joints down on Hastings Street. You know, there was always a considerable jazz movement in Detroit. Many great players got their start here. Why, I remember Don Redman's band, McKinney's Cotton Pickers, and Benny Carter played with them, too. What a wonderful player *he* was—still is, in fact. Oh, it was a swinging town!"

I was quite aware of this. My own preference was for the small bands of the thirties and forties. I had inherited it, obliquely, from my parents. Not because they were jazz fans—they had never shown any particular interest in jazz—but because they were of that era and I longed to be of it myself, to share that life with them. It gave me a fine and unusual pleasure to listen to Books reminisce about the period.

"In the forties, down on Hastings, I used to hear guys like Lucky Thompson and Wardell Gray. That's when I first met Grootka. He was hanging out—'course, he was a cop, but he was a fan, you could tell. Bop was coming in. I believe Milt Jackson was around then, too, before he went with the Modern Jazz Quartet."

"How did Grootka get onto this avant-garde stuff?" I asked. "It seems out of character, somehow."

Books shrugged. "You never know with Grootka. And you know, I think the idea that the swing players hated the boppers and the boppers hated Ornette and that gang . . . well, a lot of that was just the media, you know? I mean, some of those old guys, they didn't like the new stuff, said the boppers couldn't play in tune and where was the melody, all that stuff . . . but I believe that most of the real players weren't really like that. The critics and the reviewers, they liked the controversy. I guess it sold magazines and records. But you know how the real players are: they like everything. Hell, you couldn't get Basie to admit that Lawrence Welk was bad—'Man's got a hell of an organization.' Ha, ha." He paused suddenly, remembering something, then related a tale about the fine old cornetist Bobby Hackett, who evidently was even less capable than Basie of finding anything critical to say: "Cat asked him, 'What about Hitler?' And Bobby thinks for a minute, then says, 'Well, he was the best in his field.' Ha, ha, ha!"

We both had a good laugh on that one. "Well, Grootka certainly got into free-form jazz," I said. "He had a baritone sax, too."

Books's face lit up. "Really? I bet that was Tyrone Addison's influence."

"Oh yes, there was some music with Addison's name on it, on Grootka's music stand." I'd heard of Addison, the obscure genius. But I hadn't heard much. I thought of him as a quintessential Detroit star—greatly admired locally, but unknown to the outside world. There were precedents for that kind of obscurity, but it's an old story in provincial circles. His music, which I couldn't remember ever hearing, was said to be wild and difficult. But I hadn't heard anything about Addison in years. I had a vague notion that he was dead—dope, probably.

"Did Grootka know Addison?" I asked.

"Oh yes. I remember he talked about him incessantly for a while. I think he was taking lessons from him! That'd be that baritone. Tyrone was a bari player. Gone now, I guess. I've kind of lost touch."

Astonishing. But then, Grootka was unusual. Imagine, taking lessons at his age. Then it struck me: "When was this?"

Books frowned. "Back in the seventies, about seventy-five, seventy-six, in there." And then, to nail it down: "It was when he was working on the Hoffa case."

"Oh yes," I said, casually. "Did he ever talk about the Hoffa case?"

"Not much. I got the impression he thought it was all open and shut."

"In what way?" I asked.

Books made a face of careless certainty, a comical moue: "Oh, you know . . . Hoffa got all screwed up with them Mob boys. There wasn't much to it, but I guess Hoffa was stubborn and wouldn't let it drop, whatever the beef was. So he had to go." He shrugged. That was all there was to it. Open and shut.

I pursued it a little further, but Books didn't know any more. We fell to considering the list of names I'd brought and that was good for a laugh or two. Books confided that a couple of the names on the list, Shakespeare and Homer, were alternate tags for himself.

I was happy to accept Books's invitation to dinner, which turned out to be black-eyed peas with ham hocks and cornbread. It was delicious, particularly with the poke sallet greens. I was curious where Books would get these things locally; it seemed unlikely that supermarkets in this region of southern Ontario would feature the makings for soul food. He said he drove up to Detroit once a week to shop, or sometimes a friend would come down. Something in his tone made me ask how he enjoyed living down here on the lake.

"I like it fine," he said. "I have my books, my records. I generally enjoy solitary living. But, you know, once in a while a fellow longs to see another dark face."

He smiled thoughtfully and sipped at his wine. We had finished the dishes and withdrawn to the fireside again. He drew on the H. Upmann "Petit Corona" I had provided. "When a man lives alone," he said, "he is tempted to philosophize. I am not immune. I have come to believe that race is one of the biggest servings of bullshit that man has ever tried to digest. But look at it this way: say you're sick. You got a tumor and you need help, right now. There are two doctors available to you and both are named Brown. But one of them is white and one is colored. Which one will you go to? As long as you don't know that they're different races, there's nothing to choose. But if you do know which is which . . . well, if you're me, it would be hard not to at least see the colored doctor first, don't you think? It would be easier, more comfortable. And I'll bet you would see the white Dr. Brown first. That's 'cause there is nothing but skin color to distinguish these two doctors from one another, so race becomes at least a minor factor. But say that one of them is a well-known surgeon and the other one practices holistic medicine—you know, herbs and naturopathy, that kind of thing. Well, if you're me, you wouldn't give a fart in a whirlwind what color that surgeon was: you'd go see him. Another man, like my old friend Henry Chatham, he's a naturopathy man: he'd go to a witch doctor or a conjure woman before he'd let a man of any color cut on him. You see? But." He looked a bit wistful. "Sometimes I miss Nigger Heaven. Maybe I should have retired there."

I was momentarily nonplussed.

Books chuckled. "I'm sorry, I don't mean to embarrass you. I should have said Turtle Lake. It's a colored resort up in the Thumb. Maybe you heard of it?"

I had, though it seemed ages ago, and I'd even heard its nickname. And now I made the connection with the piece of music that I'd seen attributed to Tyrone Addison, in Grootka's apartment.

"Did Tyrone Addison have a place up there?" I asked.

"Tyrone? Naw. Why, Tyrone wasn't no more than a boy when I used to go up to, ah, Turtle Lake. I had me quite a nice place over by the golf course, actually closer to the casino. Oh yeah." He shook his head. "I had me some *times*! But, you know, come to think of it, I used to see Tyrone up there. His uncle had a place there. Lonzo. Now what was Lonzo's name? He was a bail bondsman, great big 'ol black fellow. Yes," he said with triumph, proud of his memory, "it was Lonzo Butterfield! My, my, what a fellow. Talk about conjure men, or women, ol' Lonzo was one. He could walk that walk and talk that talk. Mmmmhmmm. Yeah, and there was something going on up there once, too. I remember Grootka coming to me about it."

"Really! What?"

"Grootka was after Lonzo for something," Books said. He shook his head with regret. "I'm doggoned if I can remember what it was! But you know these bail bondsmen, they're a wicked bunch. No telling what it was."

"When was this?"

Books stared at the fire for a long moment, seemingly focusing into its depths. Finally, he nodded and said, "If I had to put a date to it, I'd say July or August of . . . oh, let me think . . ." Suddenly, his face brightened. "I just had bought a brand-new seventy-five Continental, except that it wasn't exactly brand-new. So it must have been 1975. August of seventy-five." He beamed.

I was impressed. But alas, no amount of encouragement could dredge up from the past the details of Grootka's interest in Lonzo Butterfield. All he could remember was that Grootka had asked him to drive up to Turtle Lake and see if Lonzo was there.

"Was Lonzo there?" I asked.

"No. But somebody was. I guess it must have been Tyrone. Yeah, come to think of it, Tyrone was there, with that white wife of his."

"Tyrone was married to a white woman?"

"Nice lady, too," Books said. "Man, she had tits like melons. And she didn't mind showing them, either. She wore a little skimpy bikini down to the beach. Oh yeah. I wonder if Tyrone put her up to it, or did she do it to piss him off? You know, I believe he put her up to it. I don't believe she wanted to show herself like that. But some of these fellows . . . they want the world to see what kind of woman they got."

"What did Grootka say about all this?"

"Nothing. He was only interested in Lonzo."

"You don't say. I wonder if he knew Addison then, or was it later? You know, the lessons and so forth?"

"Well, he might have known Tyrone beforehand," Books said. "But I wasn't aware of it."

From there the conversation drifted to music and I asked Books if he had any of Addison's stuff on record.

"Well, you know, I don't. I'm not even sure there is anything. But, damn, there oughta be! The cat was a stone genius. I'm not taking Grootka's word for it, though he knew a thing or two about the music. Tyrone was supposed to be pretty hot stuff back in the seventies—hell of a player. He played with Ornette and Charlie Haden, Marcus Belgrave—all them cats. I remember Yusef—you know Yusef? Lateef? Yeah. The man is heavy. Yusef told me once Tyrone could *burn* on the bari, like he reinvented the horn, man. And he could write. Very heavy stuff, but basic. It made you think. But . . . I don't know what happened to him."

"Drugs, you think?"

"Well, when you're talking about these fellows, it does come to mind. But I don't recall that Tyrone ever was into drugs. Course, that don't mean a damn thing."

I had to agree. Junkies were notorious for concealing their habit. "What kind of stuff did he write?" I asked. "You saw him play?"

"Oh, hell yes. He worked quite a bit around town. He'd be playing hard bop, mostly, with Joe Henderson and Marcus. I saw him in a really hot group with Woody Shaw and Louis Hayes." He shook his head, marveling. He was looking through his record and compact disc collection. "Ah, here's something. You might like this."

It was a CD entitled *A Parvus Fanfare,* by one M'Zee Kinanda. The cover featured a remarkable photograph of a small country church with a few barefooted black children perched on the steps, smiling. Church was not meeting, evidently.

There were fifty-nine minutes of blues-tinged music on the disc, mostly featuring soprano sax and some remarkable drumming. I can't say that the music really grabbed me, although it was interesting. It swung, but only sporadically. Most of the time it was very serious music. Myself, I'll take Ellington any day.

Books insisted I take the disc along. He wasn't interested in it, he said. And he gave me a tape, also by Kinanda. "A little something to listen to on the drive home," Books said.

Before I left I remembered to ask Books if he'd ever heard Grootka talk about suicide, or about another self on the loose.

"Haw! That's a good one," Books said, grinning. "He actually told you that? Well." He shrugged, his face becoming thoughtful. "Grootka could surprise you. If he did have some notions about that, a good person to see would be that conjure man Lonzo Butterfield."

"I thought you said he was a bail bondsman."

"Yeah. Conjure man, too. From New Orleans, you know. Look him up. He'd be interesting to talk to."

One thing about unpleasant weather: it's no fun to drive in. But I took it easy on the way back to Detroit and mulled over the things I'd been hearing. The Hoffa disappearance really was remarkable, more remarkable than I'd ever considered. The thing that stood out the most for me was the way everybody blithely concluded that

James Riddle Hoffa, deposed union leader and well-known crony of infamous mobsters, had been murdered and disposed of by those same old pals of his. I didn't find this so easy to accept. If Hoffa was so buddy-buddy with the Mob, why would they knock him? The Mob doesn't hit people for fun. There has to be a reason, especially when the target is a very visible guy who has a long-standing reputation as a friend of the Mob.

I had long contended that the Mob, considered as a corporate entity, was not one of the better-run organizations. It has a reputation for ruthlessness and constancy, not to say implacability—characteristics of successful corporations (Ford Motor Company comes to mind). The fact was, the nature of much of their business meant that a high degree of personal trust and loyalty, of reliability, was essential. The Mob had often fallen back upon actual blood relationships to ensure this crucial loyalty, even when it meant accepting perhaps a lower standard of performance. In the modern hard-driving and technical world, that factor was often a serious drawback. Still, I figured no mobster could be so stupid, so indifferent to general syndicate approval, as to hit Jimmy Hoffa out of anger or annoyance or even bad judgment. Except maybe Carmine, I thought. But even Carmine wasn't that dumb, and besides he always had Humphrey DiEbola, the Fat Man, to counsel and restrain him. No, I figured there had to be some as yet unknown reason . . . *if, indeed, the Mob had done the number.*

What the hell, Hoffa was a pretty rough and reckless guy. He'd stepped on a lot of toes, shot off his mouth an awful lot, had surely ruined a few lives on his road to fame and fortune. There ought to be no shortage of candidates without Mob associations who would want him dead and be willing to do the job themselves. I would sure like to see the F.B.I. file. I wondered if Pedge could help.

And, of course, I was most interested in looking through Grootka's old notebooks, to see what his findings, if any, had been.

I stopped at the precinct, although it was nearly midnight. To my surprise, Maki was still there. He was an old hand; it wasn't like him to linger after his shift. But he said he'd been waiting for a guy to come in and see him, and then he'd gotten sidetracked by some old files.

"You know," I said, "I've been thinking a lot about Hoffa. He must have made a few enemies, wouldn't you say?"

Maki snorted derisively. "A few? You'da thought the guy was drafting an army of assassins."

"That's what I was thinking. Take that guy, for instance, the one he stomped at the local . . . the laborer."

Maki shook his head. "Well, that's one he didn't have to worry about. That was Sam Peeks."

The name was familiar to me but I couldn't place it. Maki filled me in.

"About a week after his run-in with Hoffa, Sam took his act to his own local. He got maybe a hundred guys to picket their own leaders for not supporting them, not negotiating in good faith. So the president over there, what's his name . . . McKenzie—he's dead now—invites Sam up to the office to discuss his grievances . . . *alone.*" Maki frowned, remembering. "I heard there was over thirty shots fired inside that office. Somehow, all but five of them found their way into Sam Peeks."

The M'Zee Kinanda tape was pretty good, an improvement over the CD. He had a better bass player, I think, and the horns weren't so determinedly atonal and abrasive. Even haunting, at times.

5

Evening
Blues

It really is a damn shame to set yourself up for something when a little thought would have armed you against almost
certain disappointment. It's common as hell, for instance, for a grown
man to get the blues because "his team" has failed. I'm talking about
professional sports. How is it, I ask myself from time to time, that a
guy can invest so much emotionally in a group of hired men who
purport to represent the community, although everyone knows
they aren't *from* Detroit? You would have to be more naive than
any Detroit child to believe that the average professional player really
cares about Detroit. The pro is from somewhere else, has no significant amount of his history invested in Detroit, and is probably hoping
to get traded to New York or Los Angeles, where he can get the media
attention he "deserves" and make some real money.

And yet, there are these entities called the Detroit *Tigers,*
Lions, Pistons, and *Red Wings* that readily earn the devotion of
Detroiters (mostly boys and men) for their entire lives. Guys here
still talk about Bobby Layne and Gordie Howe, although few are
around who were adults when they saw them play. Even profound
obscurities like Johnny Lipon and Eddie Brinkman are still mentioned daily. And when the Tigers are doing well, why, the whole

city seems to perk up. But when they're awful, as they often are, the city has got the blues.

Why is this? How can it be? Is it just that most of us have such an unassuageable hunger for community that even a squad of avowed mercenary athletes, all dressed up in the same costume and proclaiming that they are the Detroit team, suffices to bind us into a semblance of unity? Is it because we followed the fortunes of the team on radio and television and in the papers from our youth on, so that even when the names of the individual heroes change the corporate image remains and that image is cloaked in our childhood dreams and heartbreaks and longings, to the extent that at the age of forty, or fifty, or even ninety, we pick up a newspaper and automatically look to see how the Tigers, or the Red Wings, are doing?

How can this be? I don't know. But every cop in Detroit knows that when one of the teams loses a game that they were expected to win, an "important" game—well, look out! More assaults, more robberies, more everything.

The current wrench was the shocking turn in the fortunes of the Red Wings, the Detroit hockey club. Here was a club enjoying one of the greatest seasons in the history of professional ice hockey, yet they were losing the playoffs to a miserable overaged team, the Saint Louis Blues. I was surprised by how sick this made me. I was even having dreams about the Red Wings! And I knew that it wasn't doing the spirit of Detroit in general any good.

You don't have to live in Detroit, either, to feel this pain. You only have to have lived there as a child—or nearby, as I had, and again did, in Saint Clair Flats. It's a rural place, still: the house is an old farmhouse and there's a barn and a few other outbuildings, and the ten acres or so still border the Saint Clair River. I came across old Red Wings' memorabilia in the attic that night, while I was looking for Grootka's stuff.

Ma had met Grootka once. She had invited him to dinner while talking to him on the phone; to my surprise, he'd accepted. I think she wanted to know who my friends were. The occasion was not particularly memorable, except that afterward my mother had observed that Grootka was "formidable." When I asked what she meant, she related an incident that had occurred as they were sitting in the backyard, sipping cocktails, while I ran to the store for some herb or spice (probably a put-up job, now that I think of it: Ma probably wanted to grill Grootka about my love life). At one point, she said, a meadowlark had perched on a fencepost nearby and begun its vociferous song. Grootka swiveled his head and looked at the bird, which faltered in midphrase and fell silent.

"I don't believe your friend is a bad man," Ma had said, "but he *silenced* a songbird with a glance!" Other than that, she'd gone on, "He seemed a perfect gentleman."

By the time I got home from Books's the house was dark and Ma was gone again, and when I trekked up to the attic I couldn't find Grootka's stuff. There was quite a bit of old stuff up there, neatly stored and not too dusty. I had to wonder when Ma ever got a chance to dust. But there was no sign of the cardboard boxes in which I'd packed away Grootka's notebooks and music.

I fell asleep listening to M'Zee Kinanda and, I must say, I was beginning to like it. In fact, I began to see what all the fuss was about. While I wasn't looking, jazz had moved on. Oh, I don't mean the hyped jazz, the youthful superstars that seem to pop up on television shows. But the music had changed. It had become more daring harmonically and rhythmically, and from what I could hear, the men and women who played it were tremendous technical players. This was nothing new, of course, but there was a suggestion of virtuosity, which made me a little uneasy. Virtuoso music is thrilling at times, as when an Art Tatum appears, although it has a tendency to become boring, too. The nice thing about this music is that an element of antic goofiness is present, as well. I'm thinking of the Sun Ra shtick: the man from the future, from Saturn, as he called himself—although it was pretty well known that he was originally Herman Sunny Blount from Birmingham, Alabama.

One of the things I especially liked about the music was that, while unabashedly modern, advanced if you will, it didn't turn its back on earlier jazz. It clearly was based on an admiration for what had gone before, in a way that bop hadn't seemed to manage. That is, the boppers seemed contemptuous of their predecessors, although as Books had suggested, perhaps that was more hype than reality. Anyway, this music did not make me feel that I didn't want to listen to Ellington anymore; indeed, its echoes of Parker and Monk and Powell, as well as Ellington and Basie, made me want to get out some of my old records.

But what endeared the music to me was its ingenuousness. It didn't try to be liked. And it didn't take itself too seriously. It was full of self-referential humor, I felt. From childhood I had been very wary of my own tendency to play to others' liking for me. It was not an attractive trait. I had to learn, in a way, not to be loved—no easy task when you're the only child of overaged parents. This music was intelligent and splendidly performed, but it got that way without trying to be loved, which is my point.

My first thought in the morning was: Where can I buy more of M'Zee? I thought of a jazz shop on Mack. I thought of this while I wondered what had happened to Grootka's notebooks. My mother, as I now realized (this was thought number four, while drinking the last of the microwaved coffee) was in Siberia. Yes, actually in Siberia, in cruel April, to observe the arrival of some rare cranes to the great marshes. I hoped she had remembered her boots; no doubt she had. She wouldn't be back for at least a week, perhaps longer.

Siberia, of course, was the birthplace of one of the Red Wings' new stars, Vladimir Konstantinov, alias "the Gladiator." I'd dreamed about him last night, along with the rest of the Russian Line, skating furiously through a kind of Sun Ra Ice Show Extravaganza.

All of these things were swirling in my mind when I saw in the *Metro Times* (the *Free Press* and the *News* were on strike, still) that M'Zee Kinanda was performing in concert tonight, at the Detroit Institute of Arts. Ordinarily, this would simply be viewed as a serendipitous occasion: an opportunity to go see the man himself and hear his interesting music up close. But I also had tickets to the seventh game of the Red Wings–Blues playoff, at the Joe Louis Arena. Even for a cop, these tickets were hard to come by.

The million-dollar question: Since the Wings were in some kind of weird spiral of self-destruction (probably a consequence of relying so heavily on a brilliant front line of ex-Soviet stars—Fedorov, Konstantinov, Fetisov, Larionov, and Kozlov [talk about alien mercenaries!], who were subject to spasms of Slav fatalism, apparently), ought a fan to desert them in this perilous hour and go to the M'Zee Kinanda concert? Or was it not true that since one's presence at the other games had not helped, that one's absence at this game might be a decisive factor that would make victory possible?

I decided to abandon my Red Wings tickets. It was a bold move, one that only a true fan could understand and appreciate. I invited Agge Allyson to accompany me to the M'Zee Kinanda concert and she accepted. This made the sacrifice of the Red Wings tickets easier to bear, as did the eager purchase of the tickets by Maki, for little more than I'd paid for them.

But I emphasize that this was no minor gesture. Much against my will I had found this team occupying my thoughts. Particularly the Russian Line. I had a notion that the Line was constituted of at least two distinct and well-known Russian types: the aristocratic, intellectual, poetic, or even mystical type, as exemplified by the brilliant and dashing Sergei Federov, Slava Kozlov, and Igor Larionov, and the pragmatic, indomitable, tough, salt-of-the-earth-peasant, tank-commander types embodied in Konstantinov and, especially, the thuggish-looking Vyacheslav Fetisov.

Of course, I hasten to say, these are mere simplifications: I'm sure none of these men were in fact mere exemplars of such a reductive dichotomy. That is, in real life they are certainly more complex, complete personalities. But these categories are sometimes useful. There *was* something dreamy and creative, romantic even, about Fedorov: he fairly swooped about the ice, creating plays, flashing brilliantly across the blue line in his scarlet road jersey like a cardinal (*Cardinalis cardinalis,* according to my mother), a regular Ariel on skates. But then, at times, he would go into eclipse and seemingly brood, despairing, paralyzed, as if in molt.

And no one could deny that the brutal faces and the hard, mean body-checking style of Konstantinov and Fetisov had something of the earthy peasant about it. Chekhov and Tolstoy would have recognized it, I'm sure; and especially would have Gogol. They were hard men, actually former officers of the Red Army, strong workers, untiring, the kind of men who led tank regiments into Kraków. And naturally afflicted with a semimystical fatalism. This seemed to be the current problem. It was as if an overwhelmingly superior Red Army had stalled in the suburbs of Berlin because they knew, deep down, that they were inferior. (Just for a day, of course: the following day they awake with a familiar hangover and without hesitation roll on, crushing all opposition.)

I had dreamed that their brilliant, interweaving ice dance was suddenly thrown into chaotic confusion, not unlike the music of M'Zee Kinanda, which was playing furiously. I feared that they had fallen pray to a despairing belief that they could not win, and so the beloved Red Wings were doomed. I knew this was bullshit, but in my "Russian mood" I couldn't shake it. As rational a person as I like to think I am, I fell back on the petty magic of seemingly ignoring them—in the hope that they would then prosper.

It was all nonsense, to be sure, but I think it's fairly common nonsense among American men, perhaps among Western
men generally. (I'm thinking of what I've heard about European
soccer fans here.) I took the precaution of programming the VCR
to tape the game, just in case.

In the afternoon Agge Allyson and I had gone to the warehouse on Atwater (an apt name) and been confronted with the
boxed files. With the help of an amiable clerk we were dismayed to
learn that the files were organized on a principle of case histories,
which meant that you had to start with a file name and number
and then begin to ransack the boxes. It was no use asking, "Where
are the Grootka files?" It didn't work that way. It was dusty and dirty
and daunting.

Nor was there, for instance, a master file entitled "Riot—
1967." You had to know what you were looking for before you could
look. I had some experience with this, of course, but without the
assistance of the clerks at Records, it's the old haystack again. Agge
took a few notes, but after only an hour or so of cursory poking about,
she declared that she needed to rethink her approach. She fell
eagerly on my suggestion that we'd better get out of there if we
were going to go home, shower, dress, and so on, before the M'Zee
Kinanda concert.

The M'Zee Kinanda performance, as often happens, was
nothing like I had expected. I suppose I was influenced by the Sun
Ra image, although the only comparison was in the music rather
than the appearance. Kinanda and his musicians did not wear ludi-
crous costumes, robes and bizarre headresses from the B-movie
space-opera property room, as I'd seen in photos of Sun Ra. (Some
of those getups were wildly wacky, suggesting that his mom had
whipped them up out of towels and sheets; the headgear often had
a suspiciously ex-pantry aspect: you wouldn't have been shocked
to detect a handle obscured by the glued-on antennas.) It was this

theatrical tawdriness and spoofery that had hampered serious appreciation of Sun Ra's music, in fact, and I'll be damned if it wasn't
hard to shake.

M'Zee Kinanda and his ensemble were only vaguely suggestive of Africana. There were some stylized masks and fancy drums
on the stage, as decorative props, but the players were dressed in a
variety of more or less ordinary casual clothing—jeans and sweaters, a tweed jacket, a kind of Nehru jacket, running shoes, for
heaven's sake. The woman who played the synthesizer wore something that might be construed as a dashiki, though most would just
call it a colorful dress. And most of the men wore a hat or cap of
some kind, usually a round one with colorful patterns or brocade,
rather like a yarmulke, although the French horn and tuba player
wore a Detroit Tigers baseball cap.

All the musicians were evidently African-Americans, to use
the currently favored term. The titles of the musical pieces were
ostensibly African in origin, though even that wasn't clear. I wasn't
sure what to think when Kinanda, in his rich, attractive voice, said,
"And now we'd like to perform a piece that I wrote a few years ago,
entitled 'Kilwa Kisiwani.' It's in three parts, reflecting the Indian,
Bantu, and Portuguese influence on this medieval trading center
of East Africa. The first part opens with a soprano sax interlude,
followed by Mayanna's solo on the Yamaha DX-7 . . ."

I don't know . . . it didn't sound particularly *African* to me. It
sounded like wild and beautiful Free Jazz. The percussion was terrific, but it was mainly a bop drum kit, as far as I could tell, and the
drummer sounded a lot like Roy Brooks, an old Detroit player and
drum teacher, who was pretty familiar to me. It wasn't Roy, it was
a younger man, but it sounded like him.

The tunes, or whatever you call these musical pieces, were
wonderful. They weren't tunes, in the sense of "My Funny Valentine," but they weren't ragas or fugues or concertos, either. They

were fairly brief, somewhat evocative tone pieces, or mood pieces, with definite melodies, some of them even a little bluesy. There seemed to be a basic simple structure, a theme or a melodic phrase, and a general but fluctuating rhythm, with a lot of improvisation. But I think I'd have to listen to a lot more of it before I'd like to describe it further. And I plan to hear a lot more of it.

The audience definitely loved it. The audience seemed more familiar with the music than I was, certainly. It was a mostly African-American audience, young but not very, and evidently a bit upscale, judging from the dress and the cars in the Art Institute parking lot. There seemed to be at least a minority academic element in the audience: beards and conservative suits, horn-rimmed glasses.

I was happy to take up Agge's suggestion that we go to the reception after the concert. It seems that she knew one of the musicians, or a friend of one of the musicians, and she thought we could at least meet Kinanda and shake his hand. I was all for it, although these scenes often seem a bit uncomfortable or awkward to me—but then I'm not averse to social awkwardness: you can often learn something from such situations. It isn't always clear just what is supposed to be happening. Are the musicians really interested in talking to their fans and admirers? Or is it an obligatory thing? Or maybe they're just happily greeting their old pals and other musicians who have come to pay a little compliment, a courtesy. Anyway, as a cop, I'm naturally curious, not to say nosy. I want to know what's going on, what different kinds of people are like. I don't mind seeming awkward.

Kinanda was a pleasant man about my own age, tall and good-looking, with a graying beard that made him look distinguished, an effect aided by horn-rimmed glasses that he hadn't worn onstage. He had, as I mentioned, an especially fine voice. Agge's friend introduced us.

"So glad you could come," Kinanda said. "Did you enjoy the program?" He seemed genuinely interested in our reaction. "You're familiar with the music?"

"I'm just getting into it," I told him. "A friend introduced me to it and I like it. I like it a lot." I started to say that my listening background was in hard bop, but he interrupted, asking the name of my Virgil—that was his phrase. I started to say "Books Meldrim," but that didn't seem quite appropriate, and for the life of me I couldn't remember Books's real name. I ended up stammering out, "Buh—, uh, a guy named Meldrim."

Kinanda frowned. "Is he a musician?"

"Sort of semiprofessional," I said. "He plays a little jazz piano . . . Teddy Wilson style, maybe a little 'Fatha' Hines."

"Books Meldrim? Why, I know Books. Is he still . . . around?" This last was phrased as one might say "still alive."

"Sure. I don't know if he plays in public anymore, but he's still kicking, still in good health. I saw him last night, as a matter of fact."

Kinanda seemed interested. A young woman came into the room, a gallery of the Art Institute actually, a kind of reception area. They were serving wine. The young woman wrapped herself around Kinanda, perhaps seeking warmth, as she was inadequately attired (if you take clothing as essentially a form of shelter, rather than decoration; she certainly didn't need clothing for decoration). "Baby, you were bewitching," she declared. It seemed an appropriate appreciation. The music had been bewitching. Kinanda tolerated the frankly erotic embrace with a graceful reluctance. Not obviously insane, he didn't, apparently, want to cool the young lady's ardor or affection, but he was also not comfortable with her demonstrativeness. He may have been conscious of Agge's sniff of disapproval.

I should say something here about Agge. She was looking rather stunning herself. I never knew you could wear a T-shirt with an evening gown. She certainly perked up when Kinanda managed to fend off his sultry assailant long enough to ask, "Is Books still hanging out with Grootka?" I know it caught my attention.

"You knew Grootka?" I asked.

"Knew?" Kinanda said. "Do I detect a past tense? Yes? I'm sorry to hear it."

"It's been a while," I said. "Four years, anyway."

Kinanda pursed his lips. "Line of duty, I suppose?"

"Well, yes," I said. "Although he was supposed to be retired."

"Hard to imagine Grootka retired." But he didn't ask for details and I didn't volunteer them. "You are a policeman too, I suppose." I admitted I was. "Mulheisen," he voiced my name, almost to himself, as if committing the name to memory.

"How do you know Books and Grootka?" I asked. But Kinanda had turned away, happy to talk to the young woman and several other people who were eagerly demonstrating to one another how familiar, even intimate, they were with the celebrity of the moment. "My man!" they exclaimed and, "Brother!"

My old friend Jimmy Singleton suddenly materialized. Jimmy will occasionally run a blind pig, for a few weeks at a time, until its natural half-life expires. "Mul, what you doin' here? You dig this shit? I didn't know. It's cool, eh?"

"What happened at the Joe?" I asked, referring to the Joe Louis Arena, the home of the Red Wings.

"Blew 'em out," Jimmy said. "Six-two. Yzerman scored two goals, the Russians got all the others."

Blessed relief. My sacrifice had paid off. I was shocked at how good it felt.

"Do you know these guys?" I asked, meaning Kinanda.

"Known 'em for years," Jimmy said.

"Kinanda says he knew Grootka."

Singleton nodded. "Yeah, he would."

"Well, Grootka knew everybody," I said. "But is Kinanda, or was he, a local guy?" I was puzzled: Grootka's unusually wide acquaintance could hardly extend to, say, New York, or Chicago, which is where I presumed Kinanda was based.

"He used to play around here, in a previous life," Jimmy joked, "but he made his name in L.A. He usually has a couple of the home cats in his band."

"Ah, that explains it. I guess he likes the Detroit sound." Although, I thought, what is the Detroit sound?

"You mean that hard edge?" Singleton said.

"Yeah." I thought I knew what he meant. It was a legacy, I thought, of a couple generations of Detroit players, dating back to the twenties with the McKinney's Cotton Pickers, through boppers like Wardell Gray, and up to and including Roland Hanna, the Jones boys, Barry Harris, Paul Chambers, Ron Carter, Kenny Burrell, Louis Hayes, Pepper Adams, Donald Byrd, Marcus Belgrave, and Geri Allen. It was a straightforward, technically brilliant style that was devoid of sentimentality, but not unemotional.

Reflecting on the music I had just heard, I found a definite affinity. This music was not mainstream, certainly not bop, but there was that same wry, unsentimental edge that said "Detroit" to me. The only thing I missed was a lack of a strong tenor or baritone sax presence. The only sax in the lineup tonight had been a soprano, played virtuosically by a young black woman named Karen Tate. She was a terrific player who doubled on clarinet and bass clarinet, but she didn't blow with that characteristic Detroit edge. I mentioned it to Singleton.

"The man didn't blow," he pointed out.

"You mean Kinanda? I thought he was a piano player." The tape Books had given me had listed Kinanda as a keyboard player and composer, but there had been some mention of "saxes." I'd heard some powerful saxes on it, but I'd gotten the impression, as I had tonight, that Kinanda was a pianist.

"He also plays sax," Singleton said. "Damn good, too. Tenor and bari. I guess the music didn't call for a big horn."

The featured composition had, in fact, been an extended series of reflections on a theme, presumably about African life, except that the composer didn't bother to tell us anything about the theme, just the somewhat evocative titles of the relatively short pieces that made up the suite: "Kilwa Kisiwani," "Victoria Nyanza," and so on. It wasn't unusual: music lovers are used to titles that are vaguely evocative without being very descriptive of the music itself, as in Schubert's "Trout" quintet.

When I saw an opportunity I approached Kinanda again and asked him straight out what the composition was all about.

"It's about jazz," he said, promptly. "Music and instruments. Keyboards, drums. Music is always about that. But we give it other names sometimes, maybe because we think it should be *about* something . . . something out there." He waved his hand vaguely in the direction of the city. "Tchaikovsky got together an orchestra and wrote a piece about Napoleon and the invasion of Moscow, but it's really just orchestral music, no matter how many cannons are fired."

"But what do names like 'Kilwa Kisiwani' and 'Victoria Whatever-it-was' mean, then?" I persisted.

"Oh, yes." Kinanda looked thoughtful. He didn't seem in the least put out by my impertinence. "You know what? I think at the time I had some idea . . . maybe some memory or image of visiting Tanzania. I had been there on a State Department–sponsored trip a few months before. So I had that thought. But"—he shrugged, as if in apology—"I can't say that the pieces, despite their names, are *about* Tanzania. I was taken to see Lake Victoria, so I remembered the African name, which is really a holdover from colonialism—Victoria Nyanza/Lake Victoria."

"So you're saying," I pushed on, "that music can never be about something other than itself?"

"Well, it's just music, you see. It's purely abstract. Of course, once you add words . . . a *song* can be about something other than itself, than music. A hymn, for instance, is about God. And Bach's Mass in B Minor is about God, or about religion, at least. But I don't think that a Bach fugue is about God, although I guess some would say that God is in the details. But for me, it's about something else—rhythm, harmony, tonality. I have written music that was about places and people, events. But 'Kilwa Kisiwani' probably evokes an ancient African capital only for me."

Agge had listened to this with great interest. "What did you write about people?" she asked. "An opera?"

Kinanda screwed up his handsome face. "No, not really. It used some lyrics, some narrative . . . it's never been recorded, or even performed. It was an early work. But"—he brightened—"you know, I may do something with it yet."

"Does it have a name?" Agge said.

"Well . . . ah, I think I'll have to rename it—*if* I rewrite it." He turned to me. "Are you a player?"

"A jazz player?" I shook my head. No one had ever asked me such a thing. "No, of course not."

"Of course not? Does that mean you don't play at all?"

"Well, I took piano lessons, as a boy. But no, I never thought of myself as a player." Now that I thought of it, I wondered why I had never attempted to play anything other than my lessons. Why not a jazz tune? "I don't know why I never tried it," I said. "It never occurred to me."

"There are two kinds of people," Kinanda said, his voice taking on a certain pontificatory inflation, "players and auditors."

"I would be an auditor," I affirmed. "I love music. But there are people, you know, who don't seem in the least interested in music. A third type. I wonder what they would be called."

"Idiots," Kinanda said, decisively.

"What was Grootka?" Agge said.

As one, Kinanda and I said, "Player."

I think at the moment I was taking Kinanda's dichotomy to be one of those great generalities that people often invoke, and that what he meant by player was an activist, a doer, as opposed to someone like myself, who was more an observer. Although I hasten to say that I don't subscribe to these gross dichotomies: I've never been content, for instance, to merely observe; and there is no doubt that Grootka was a crocodile of a watcher.

"There are certain kinds of players, however," Kinanda said, "who probably should have stayed auditors."

6

Fine and
Dandy

"**I** believe that Lao-tse says somewhere that you should govern an empire as you would cook a little fish," said Books Meldrim. He was cooking a little fish. Several of them, in fact. Bluegills. We were on the deck of his house on the Lake Erie shore. I nodded and smiled and sipped some more of the excellent champagne he had provided, a Moët & Chandon, not too brut.

"I'm not familiar with Lao-tse," I said. "He was a Chinese philosopher, I guess, but what period?"

"You heard of Lao-tse! Very early, pre-Christian. He wrote the *Tao-te ching*. Lately, folks call him Lao-tzu."

"Oh, *that* Lao-tse." I was embarrassed.

"He may be just a myth," Books said, as if to comfort me, "though usually there's something to a myth. Anyway, the *Tao* certainly exists. It's a basic text, good for rummaging through. And I have to admit"—he smiled as he turned the fish on the portable grill—"that's what I do, rummage. I never really studied it. I get these pithy quotes that sound like good rules for living. Nothing wrong with that, of course. Even Charlie Parker quoted from Ellington. It's knowing that it's a quote, not something you invented your own self, that's important. A feller gets to believing what he stole is what *he* made is when he gets into trouble."

I felt like saying "Amen," but thought that might sound phony. I contented myself with my cigar and watched the sun continue to fall into the great lake of the Eries, scene of fierce battles among the Hurons and Chippewas, the Potawatomis and the English, and the Americans and the Canadians. It looked peaceful enough now, with a scattering of clouds to the west, black and blue and red and gold. A few large seagoing ships were barely moving out there. Gulls were stroking their steadfast way home. It was pleasant, indeed, and the fish were as well governed as an empire, according to Books: "Not overdone."

I had come down at Books's invitation. He'd said he wanted to show me something and he also wanted my reaction to the M'zee Kinanda concert. I was happy to comply, especially if it meant a fish feast on the deck. And especially since Books condescended to play the piano. His house was small, but very cunningly and beautifully designed and accomplished. It featured, for instance, heavy glass doors that essentially opened the living room onto the deck, which in turn gave onto the jetty itself. On a warm night like this, with little breeze, a pianist could comfortably sit in the living room, as on a stage, and perform to a gathering of dozens, sitting on the deck chairs or the seats built into the railings—it made the lake itself an extension of the house. But I was the only fortunate auditor this evening.

"When I had this house built I was a little worried about these windows," Books confessed, talking while he rummaged through sheets of music, in the manner of all musicians. " 'Cause I know how the wind can howl off that lake in the winter and I didn't want my piano ruined. But the carpenter got these good insulated doors and he put them in so they seal tight."

He arranged some sheets on the music stand and peered at them. "I got this piano out of the old Graystone Ballroom, many, many years ago and I spent a lot of money getting it restored. It's a great piano, a Bechstein. It was just thrown into a basement corner, a waste. This was before the Graystone's reincarnation as a rock palace in the sixties, so I figured the piano must have been left over from the heyday of the big bands. I like to think that it may have been played by Fletcher Henderson, or the Duke, maybe 'Fatha' Hines, or even *God Himself*—Art Tatum. Ahh, here it is."

I was sprawled on the rail seat, smoking and enjoying the first really warm evening of the year. The piano under Books's fingers suddenly blossomed into sound that filled the air. It was almost miraculous, like watching a bud unfurl into an apple blossom, rich in not only color and texture but aroma. The tune was simple, a plaintive blues, but Books had a remarkably soft touch, seeming to prod the keys gently, barely moving his fingers. It raised the hair on the back of my neck. For a moment I had the peculiar impression that the piano was alive, filled to the bursting with music, and when Books pressed gently it released these sounds into the air.

I told him at the end, when his long, thoughtful exploration of an idea had evaporated on the evening air, that I was amazed by his ability. I could tell he was pleased, but he was also genuinely rueful.

"I wanted to be a player," he said with a sigh, "but I just didn't have what it takes."

"Oh, you're wrong," I insisted.

"No, no . . . I know what it takes. For one thing"—he held up one slender hand—"the Lord didn't give me the hands. Too small. A feller can learn to play within these limitations, in jazz anyway, but it's a limitation. I'm sure I could have made a living in the clubs, maybe even cut a few records, but I could never be first-rate with this span."

"You're too hard on yourself," I said.

"Maybe. I envy the people who aren't. Like Grootka. He never worried about being first- or second-rate. I talked to him about it. 'That kind of thinking is bullshit,' he'd say. And he was right. It is bullshit. It's giving in to vanity and ambition, social pressure, other people's opinions. I know it, but I can't help it. I never pursued the piano, except for my own uses. I can't help admiring those who push ahead with their own agenda—they get things done. Even if you're somebody like Grootka, who couldn't play a horn for shit. But he didn't care—if he was even aware. He enjoyed it, so he went at it, full speed and damn the rocks."

"Though, sometimes, the consequences are terrible and someone else has to clean up the mess," I observed. Books nodded agreement.

"I got something for you," Books said and disappeared into the interior of the house, returning shortly with a neatly wrapped parcel, about the size of a book. "Open it when you get home," he said. "And here's a little tape to listen to. It's Kinanda, from a jazz festival that a friend of mine taped off a broadcast in San Francisco. I think you'll like it. He calls it 'A Fine and Dandy Lion,' after the old tune, which a lot of jazz musicians have used as a basis for other tunes. The chord progression is conducive to blowing, I guess, but as you'll see, Kinanda doesn't stick to the chords . . . he blows them away."

I really had no idea what he was talking about. He tried to explain what a chord progression was, but it was either too simple or too complex for me. I guess there are people, perhaps most of us, who are introduced to music at home and at school, take a few lessons, learn something about harmony and so on, without ever really penetrating its secrets. Basically we just *like* music. That is, it's important to us, more or less, but it's not important the way it is for those people who become musicians. We don't *breathe* music. I nodded and said "Unh-hunh," and promptly forgot what a chord progression was.

I listened to the tape while driving home and it was great. It sounded kind of familiar. It was a blues, all right, and I'd heard it recently . . . and then it hit me: it was the blues that Books had played when I was sitting on his deck. I hadn't recognized it because it was a much more complicated exploration of the basic theme, plus it heavily featured a baritone sax.

This was what was in the package. A notebook, or composition book, as I've already described. I put it here because this was actually book #2, although it was the first one to come to my attention. Like book #1, it was written in blue ink, in a nice hand, and I've edited it for ease of reading, retaining a few of Grootka's usages for effect.

Grootka's Story

I walked quite a ways, not really dressed for it, in my street shoes and a suit. The day had warmed up a little by now, but it was pretty breezy and anyway, I never was a guy for shorts and sport shirt, and I didn't bring none with me. So maybe I looked a little funny to the farm lady when I knocked on the door.

[*I could imagine. Say you're an Amish farm wife, probably cooking pies or something in your kitchen, wearing an apron over your floral housedress, with the characteristic babushka, or scarf, on your head, and suddenly you hear this pounding on the front door. It's out in the country. Usually, people drive up into the barnyard, or whatever, and honk their horns or get out and halloo and you go out to greet them. You don't expect someone to come walking up to the front porch and pound on the door, certainly not a big, mean-looking Detroit police detective. No wonder she wouldn't come out. Grootka says she peered through the muslin curtains (I assume they were muslin—isn't that the see-through stuff that your mother hung on frames to dry?) and talked to him through the door. I don't know the life of these people—I get the impression that they're very chary of strangers, especially the womenfolk.—M.*]

Jon A. Jackson

She won't let me use the f——g [*The dashes are G.'s curiously delicate usage. Sparing my sensitive eyes, I suppose, but you will notice later that when he's excited he forgets the dashes.—M.*] phone, to call Books, and by now it's pushing noon. I don't want to walk all the way back to the f——ing resort, but it looks like I got to. She did let me get a drink of water from the well, which they got a little hand pump out by the side yard and you can sit down on a bench under a big maple or oak tree, I don't know which it was. I was sitting there when I seen a big car pull up at the gate to the resort.

This gate is just beyond the farmer's driveway and it's the way a lot of the resort people go in and out to avoid the prick on the front gate. But the farmer insists that they gotta keep the gate closed, to keep his cows out of there. It's a barbed-wire deal, a kind of loose fence that goes across the road and the pole fits into a hoop at the base of the regular fence and another hoop slips over the top of the pole—you got to pull the gate kind of tight to do it—and it works fine, except that once in a while some jerk don't bother to reclose it after he drives through, so then the cows wander in and the kids have to go round them up.

Anyways, the guy who gets out to open the gate is a white guy, wearing a golf shirt and fancy slacks, big black shades. I knew him right away and I wondered if he made me, but he didn't seem to even see me. A course, I was sitting under the tree, in the shade, and I suppose he didn't expect to see nobody there anyway. It was Cooze, a boy from Buffalo that Carmine liked to use from time to time when he had a problem, a real asshole and a guy who I always thought oughta give thanks every morning if he wakes up 'cause nobody blew his f——ing head off yet. Cusumano is his real name—Valentino, God help us, which is why he goes by Cooze. So I know that Carmine must be in the car, and maybe the Fat Man too, since I can tell from the way Cooze is acting—not being a smart-ass, just taking care of the gate like a normal guy would do—

that he's not on his own. But naturally, the windows of the Caddy are tinted so the peasants can't ogle His Holy Eminence when he's out riding around. Cooze hops back in the car and off they go, not bothering to rehook the gate, naturally.

Now where could these high and mighty Crime Lords be going? There must be something damn important in Nigger Heaven to bring them all the way up here. I thought it over and it seemed to me that it had to be Lonzo. He was the only one of these guys who was connected at all. I mean, there was probably twenty tinhorn drug peddlers and thieves down there, but none of them was likely to attract the exalted attention of the big bosses, actually bring them driving up to a Negro resort. Not even Lonzo, really, so he must be onto something f——ing huge, and since they were shrewd enough to use the back gate either somebody was showing them the way or they knew the place.

So I had to get my ass back down to Lonzo's, which was about a mile away on a bad road. I seen a old Schwinn bike leaning against a barnyard fence. It was one of them fat-tired kinds, with a lot of chrome and handlebar tassels—some kid's dream. I figured one a the Hamish kids had earned this bike the hard way, bucking hay and shoveling cow shit. I ran to the house and pounded on the door, but of course the old lady ain't coming out for me. So I yelled that I was a cop and I had to borrow the bike, but here was a fifty-dollar deposit, which I would bring the f——ing thing back, don't worry. And I stuffed a fifty in the doorjamb and I jumped on the bike and went pumping away.

This was not the road to hell. They didn't have no intentions, good or otherwise, of paving it and even with fat tires it wasn't so easy to get going in the sand, especially since them old Schwinns didn't have no fancy gears. It was just stand up and crank that mule. But it was better than walking by God and I got down to Lonzo's in about ten minutes and sure enough, there's Carmine's

Caddy sitting in the driveway. I hauled the bike into some bushes down the road and decided to hunker in myself, to wait and see what might be going down. What the hell was I gonna do anyway, bust in wavin' the Old Cat [*Grootka's nickname for his revolver, an enormous old .45 caliber Smith & Wesson.—M.*] and arrest everybody? For what? And anyways, I'm outta my precink.

I don't know if you ever sat in the bushes in the summer, Mul. It's innarestin'. I don't know if I ever did, but it seemed to bring back something. These were pretty thick bushes out back of the house with just a weedy field beyond and then some woods, honeysuckle bushes, I guess, and a few little poplar or willow saplings, but I don't know bushes much. There was a lot to see, though, if you're just taking a squat in the bushes on a summer day with nothing to do but observe nature—ants taking a regular road they got, but very busy, hauling pieces of trash like a bit of seed or a part of a dead beetle. A spider is hanging in a web. A robin flies in once in a while. It was pleasant and cool, the leaves rattling in the wind. I was comfortable, leaning back against a sapling, the sun kind of flickering green and gold, and there was that musty old cool dirt smell. So I kind of drowsed, sitting there waiting, about a hundred feet up behind the house. There were only a couple houses on this ridge, so far, none of them close and there wasn't nobody about.

But I woke up when Vera comes out. Vera is Tyrone's wife. She was the broad I seen earlier, which I thought it was a whore of Lonzo's, not that Lonzo actually runs whores, he's not a pimp by trade, but he's into just about anything and so I figured this blonde with the big boobs must be one of his whores. But she looked familiar, like I said, and now it hit me—this is Vera Addison. I met her before a couple of times. She seemed like a nice enough babe. I didn't pay her any mind after I got through scoping that frame, like any guy would. She's one of these gals that loves to show it—low-cut dresses, miniskirts, real high heels, and, of course, hair blonder

than what's-her-name, the Swedish bombshell. You run into babes
like this in jazz circles, groupies. They're into black stuff, it turns
'em on, I guess. Usually they're low-life babes, attracted by the myth
of the big black cock, I guess. But not always. I had a vague notion
that maybe Vera was different, I guess because Tyrone was different.
Tyrone wasn't a nigger.

I should take a minute to get this straight. There's niggers
and there's niggers. Some of them are white and some are black.
You heard me talk about this, Mul. To me a nigger is any f——ing
lowlife regardless of race, color, or creed. A loser, a shiftless, no-
account kind of guy. They make a mess ever' where they go, they
take more than they could ever give if it even occurred to them to
give. You know what I'm getting at. There's an awful lot of niggers
in this world. They're a f——ing drain. But the average person,
white or black, ain't a nigger. The average person has got more
sense than to shit in his own nest. Okay. Enough of that.

Vera comes out in the back. She's wearing a lot of clothes for
Vera, a blouse and jeans, a big straw hat and wraparound shades.
But she's carrying a blanket and a straw bag and she walks back by
the bushes where I'm hanging out. There's a little ditch or something behind the bushes and she jumps across. Back there is a nice
little private space, shielded from view from the road by the bushes
and the willows, and there aren't any close neighbors anyways. She
spreads out her blanket and starts taking stuff outta the bag—a
book, some lotion, a towel, a little radio. She turns on the radio and
it's tuned to some jazz station. It ain't much of a day for sunbathing,
being kind of cool and the sun going in and out of the clouds, but
by God she starts taking off her clothes and, believe me, it's a real
production number. You'd think she was in a skin flick. She's
moving kind of easy, swaying her hips to the music, slowly rotating
like she's on a stage, each button of the shirt and the jeans is a
number in itself. It turns out she's got a bikini on under the jeans

and shirt but that don't stay on for long and it seems like she's already got a pretty complete tan. I mean this babe is an eyeful. The breeze is raising a lot of goosebumps and her nipples are tighter than an Eskimo's asshole, but she sure is enjoying herself. And I'd be happy to spend an afternoon filling my eyes, but I know that a pretty girl can maybe find a place where no one is looking if she's alone on a desert island. I figure I got maybe a minute before someone starts looking. Someone from the house for sure, and maybe from somewhere else, a airplane or a balloon. Somebody will spot this gorgeous babe lying out here, getting a little sun, especially now that she has taken off the bikini. Mul, this broad has tits like what's-her-name, the Swedish actress I mentioned before. You wouldn't think tits that big could stick straight out like that, sort of like the nose cones on a 747. And I might as well tell you right now—Vera is not a natural blonde. Anita Ekberg. That's who I was thinking of. [*Grootka actually spells it "Needa Heckburger."*—M.]

But as much as I enjoy the view, it also means that someone is likely to spot yours truly, lurking in the f——ing bushes like a goddamn Peeping Tom. So I figure I better make the most of it. I creep over to the nearest point to Vera and I whisper, "Hey! Vera!"

Jesus, you should of seen her! If she'd been wearing underpants she'd of spoiled 'em for sure. [*Grootka has scribbled a little note here, in the margin: "I don't mean that she actually peed, or nothin', this is just a figger a speech."*—M.] She flops on her belly and snatches a towel, but finally, when she's covered up, more or less, she says as angry as a bunch of ants whose hill you been pissing on, "Who is that?" Or words not exactly like that, but the same idea.

I kind of stick my head out a little bit and grin. "It's me, Grootka. How ya doin'?" For some reason this don't calm her down. I finally hadda pull the Old Cat on her. That chilled her.

"Whatta you want?" she says, her eyes as round as silver dollars. But give the woman credit, she is whispering outta the corner of her yap and not letting on that she's talking to me.

"Who's inna f——ing house?" I ask.

She looks puzzled for a minute, then it clicks and she says, "You're Grootka! Oh my God! Oh God, oh God!"

I had to shake the Old Cat at her to get her attention. "Who's in there? What the hell's goin' on?"

At first she claims there's nobody there, just her and Tyrone, but after a second or two she says "some friends."

"What friends? Tyrone is friends with Carmine? You're kidding."

Just about this time I get this feeling that she's not as spooked as she seems. I mean, sure she's spooked, but now there's something cool in her face. And I notice she ain't exactly clutching the towel like it was the only thing between her and the preacher man. One big fat tit is peeping out, her ass is definitely feeling the breeze, and she keeps stealing a look at the house. And finally it dawns on me—the chick *is* putting on a show. But for who? Not me, she didn't know I was here. Must be for the house.

I take a quick look at the house, what I can see of it from this deep in the bushes, and I'll be damned if I don't see a shadow or something, like somebody sneaking around the corner. It's a real quick glance, believe me. Who ever it was has disappeared. But he looks kind of short and stocky.

"Grootka, you idiot," she whispers outta the corner of her mouth, "get the hell out of here! You're screwing up everything." But all the same, she starts doing some exercises. Touching her toes, twists. Man, forget the f——ing towel, it's a show! And I just sit back to enjoy it.

But too damn quick the back door opens and Tyrone sticks his head out and yells, "Hey, Vera! Come on! The guys are leaving!"

Vera real quick yanks on her bikini and her jeans and blouse, ignoring me now. Without looking up she says, again, real low, "Get the hell out of here. Somebody's gonna get hurt."

I tell her, "Won't be me, babe. Nobody knows I'm here. Except you." I emphasize that last point and she nods to show she gets it.

She sashays on back to the house and I hear people talking out front in that familiar way, saying good-bye, that kind of thing. By now I've worked my way back toward the front of the bushes but the best I can make out is the Fat Man and Cooze, bringing up the rear as they go down the drive and get in the Caddy. From the little I could hear, which wasn't nothing, it must of been Carmine and at least a driver—probably Carlo what's-his-name, plus the two I mentioned. And Lonzo and Tyrone. Where Lonzo's boys went, I dunno. Probably to the casino. I see Lonzo's Caddy is not there.

After all the usual *so long*s and *see ya*s, Carmine's Caddy drives off and Lonzo and Tyrone walk back to the house. Well, I sit back, chewing all this over. I don't know what the hell it means. And I'm just about ready to get the hell out of there, like Vera said—which I gotta admit has got me puzzled now—when I see that fucking Cooze slippin' back down the hill. On foot!

Let me tell ya, it's one thing when you see Grootka out flappin' the soles, but at least I got a history of walkin' the beat, anyways. You see a sharp Dago like Cooze tiptoein' through the pasture on his Florsheims and you're lookin' at somethin' that's no good. The chick was right. Somebody was gonna get hurt.

Cooze gets within about twenty feet a the back door and he has to jump for a tree trunk 'cause Tyrone sticks his head out the door and he whistles. Naturally, being Tyrone, he don't just give your standard wolf whistle. This is about a G-major/B-flat/D whistle, sort of a blues. Followed by "Yo! Janney," or something like that. That's what it sounded like. Janney. But it could be Jamie, or Jimmy.

He does this a couple times, looking all around the back-yard. Fucking Cooze is trying to squeeze his skinny frame into the trunk of a elm. But I notice he's got his arm hanging straight down and at the end of it is a fairly large piece, like maybe a Python [*a Colt revolver, usually .357 caliber—M.*].

Pretty quick a short, stocky white guy sticks his head out of the bushes on the other side of the house. He's kind of tentative. "They all gone?" he kind of whispers.

Tyrone comes all the way out on the back steps and he gestures with that big hand of his. "Sure," he says, "come on back in."

And at that, out jumps old Cooze and waves the cannon. "Okay, Pops," he says, "let's go for a ride."

But Pops don't want to go ridin' with Cooze, it seems. He was only a step or two outta the bushes and now he turns and bolts, like a rabbit, diving for the briar patch. And Cooze, he don't hesitate. He hoists the cannon and takes one shot. *Boom!*

Actually, the trees and bushes must have muffled the shot pretty good. It was more a flat, cracking sound, like breaking a big limb. It looked to me like the bullet must of hit Pops in the back of the head. Anyway, there wasn't much doubt he was dead, cause he just pitched forward into the grass.

And then, of course, I took out Cooze.

Now, Mul, I can just hear you saying, "You what?"

Yeah, I took him out. I had to. It was reflex, almost. I had the Old Cat out and I just gunned the fucker down. Yeah. You can't stand by and watch a clown like Cooze blowin' folks'es heads off and not do something. I hit him in the middle of the upper back. A very good place. I figure it blew his cold fuckin' heart right out of him. And afterwards, in case anybody axed, I said, loud enough to hear, "Halt, or I'll fire."

You wanta read more? I got more. A lot more. What you need, Mul, is a good read. Kick back and smoke one a them Havanas yer always talking about. Put a nice berg in yer black Jack and marvel at the story he'll give you.

7

Grave Groove

It wasn't too hard, when I put my mind to it, to figure out what Grootka's cryptic little message at the end of book #2 meant. It was the combination of *Havana* and *berg.* I used to get my cigars from a man named Marvin Berg who ran a store over on Fort Street, downtown. He was a big, fat man who was a little creepy in ways, but basically a gentle soul. Alas, he had long since passed on and the store was no longer in business. But I remembered that his last amour—if that's what she really was (it was hard to imagine Marvin Berg actually engaging in amorous activities)—was a strange little creature named Becky, who had a fast mouth. She didn't seem to care what she said, or to whom, but Marvin was clearly delighted by that. I enjoyed her lip, as well, for all it's apparent sourness. I wondered if she was still around and if she knew anything about this notebook of Grootka's.

The problem was, I didn't even know Becky's last name. And now that Marvin was long gone, how would I find her? Well, being a wise old detective I looked up Berg in the phone book, thinking that I might get a lead, anyway, though I hardly knew what it could be. But there was a Marvin Berg, in Pleasant Ridge. This is an odd little suburb, out by the zoo, no more than a hundred acres, or so it seems. I called the number. A woman answered who I thought might be Becky. When I asked if she was, she snapped back, "Who the hell is this?" When I identified myself, there was a snort of disbelief and then a truly Beckyesque comment: "I'd have thought you'd disappeared up your own asshole by now."

That was our Becky, all right. It was never difficult talking to Becky; the trouble was getting to a conversation about something, rather than mere badinage. But she sounded great. It had been at least five years since I'd talked to her. My last image was of a woman of about thirty, dark hair in bangs, very white skin, and wearing exceedingly red lipstick. It would be interesting to see what she was like post-Marvin. "Drop by, or drop dead," she replied to my suggestion, which appeared to mean that she had no objections, anyway, although she claimed to have no knowledge of any material that Grootka might have left with Marvin.

I took the Chrysler Freeway to the Walter Reuther Freeway and swerved off at Woodward—thinking, as I did, that Detroit would never name a freeway after its *most* famous labor leader— no, no, there would be no James R. Hoffa Freeway. Marvin's house was quite large, suitable for a family of seven, rather than a diminutive widow. It was an old house, but in excellent condition, set back from the road among some mature maples.

"I like it," I said, and I did. Becky was standing in the yard, dressed in an old University of Michigan sweatshirt and jeans that had dark wet dirt on the knees. "I'm looking for a new place to live, but this looks too big for one person. Maybe I should move in."

"Do I have a choice," she sneered, "or am I Poland welcoming Hitler?"

She looked pretty nice, actually, pale as ever but her eyes were bright and she hadn't neglected her lipstick. Kind of a dashing little figure in rubber boots, amusing and gamine. She said she'd been cleaning up the flower beds. "I get a lot of guys asking to move in," she said. "For some reason they're all old farts, like you. Are you really looking for a place?"

I was a little taken aback by that last, but of course, I was looking for a place. Unfortunately, it wouldn't help my situation to move to Pleasant Ridge: I'd still be "out of town." I explained that and she shrugged, then moved toward the front door. "Too bad. I could use a cop around the house, and we might have had some fun." No smile. For some reason I shivered in the spring sun.

"So what's all this crap about Grootka?" she asked when we were seated in the huge living room, with its solid oak wainscotting and cold fireplace. I had refused a drink, but she was sipping a Stroh's from the bottle. "He's still dead, ain't he?" She displayed a comic alarm.

"Oh sure. Not even Grootka can beat the Man with the Axe," I assured her.

"Man with the Scythe, you mean," she said. "The Man with the Axe is the jack of hearts, I think."

"Or a saxophone player," I said.

"Anyway, it'd be the Devil who took Grootka," she said.

"Do you think so? Hey, listen, did you give any thought to what I asked you about?"

"You mean some notebooks of Grootka's? Well, they might be in a box of stuff that Marvin left for me to return. Toward the end he was kind of getting ready. You didn't come around. . . . Okay, okay!" She held up a hand to stop my protests. "You didn't know 'cause I didn't tell you. He had about five heart attacks in his last couple of years, you know, and after he got over the first two, I quit calling people and rushing around like it was the end of time. And then, naturally, he has the big one. Well, what can you do? C'mon, we'll go downstairs and look."

There was a tremendous basement, all very clean and orderly, complete with a workout room with its de rigueur treadmill and weights, all nicely dusted and polished. Evidently not anything that Marvin had ever used, but judging from Becky's lithe form they were still in use. The boxes were stacked in a little enclosure in a corner, up off the concrete floor, and she uncomplainingly took down one after another and set them out, opening them and casting quickly through the contents.

"Ah, here's something you'd like," she said. She handed me a large wooden casket or box, obviously a cigar humidor. "You can throw this crap in the dump if you don't want it," she said. "In fact, I think Marvin said something about getting you to haul it away." It was full of genuine Havana cigars, from the wrapping rooms of H. Upmann. Fifty or more Coronas. I was astounded. I started to protest but a glance from her hushed me.

"I'm not smoking them," she said, "and I sure as hell ain't handing them over to Customs. Besides, for all I know, they came in before the embargo. They any good?"

I felt a couple of them, rolling them in my fingers and thumb. They were in excellent condition. "They're wonderful," I said.

"Good. I got about twenty more boxes, never opened. You can haul those off to the dump for me, too."

Fifteen minutes later we came upon a box that contained, among a lot of old cigar catalogs, a familiar-looking notebook. I snatched it up. It was full of Grootka's writing.

Grootka's Third Notebook

[N*ote:*
Grootka had written a note congratulating me on finding this notebook, and it was attached inside the cover with a paper clip.—M.]

Actually, Mul, I just put all that shit in there about the guy being shot in the head to make me look good. Cooze never got a shot off. The way it went was when I saw Cooze lift his gun I took him out. I had to do it. I didn't know who the guy was. For all I knew, it was Hoffa. But it wasn't. It was some pal of Tyrone's, a Dutchman named Jacobsen. This damn guy, Janney, I never liked the sonuvabitch, but Vera, she kinda liked him. He was always hanging around. I seen him in the clubs, once I thought about it. He's one a them jazz buffs. Sorta like you, come to think of it. Except that he's got some money and he don't mind spending it on a guy like Tyrone, which is better than he could probably find to spend it otherwise. [*That's what he said.—M*]

The thing is, when I popped Cooze I seen Jacobsen jump in the bushes like it was him gettin' shot, and maybe he thought it was! Only when the smoke cleared he noticed he wasn't shot after all, so he come crawlin' out and seen it was Cooze who was dead. Which sets him to rockin' on his knees and sayin' *Oh God, Oh God,* which seems to be a regular thing for folks to say when the shit starts flyin', did you ever notice?

So now I got a dead asshole on my hands. No sign of Carmine and Fats, by the way. They musta been around somewhere, but they sure as hell ain't stickin' around to trade lead with the Old Cat. I don't know, actually, if they knew it was me, but they knew when Cooze didn't come back from the shootin' that he wasn't comin' back. So they must of split. So now I got a bunch of f——ing loons, black and white, staring at me and sayin' "What we gonna do now?" like I'm their big brother, or something.

I got them to find some tarp, it was that black plastic stuff, VizQueen or whatever they call it, that the contractors use, and wrap ol' Cooze in that. Then we went in the house and everybody had a good, stiff drink.

Now, who all was there? You'll wanta know. It was me, Vera, Tyrone, Jacobsen, Lonzo, and Mr. Jimmy Hoffa, no less. Pretty soon along comes a couple of Lonzo's boys, which I think their names are Krizmo and Baits [*Evidently, Charismo Fredericks and Johnee Bates, both of Detroit. Both deceased as of this writing.—M.*]

Mr. Jimmy Hoffa was in the bedroom, but he came out when I came in. It seems that Vera's little strip show was meant to entertain the Mobsters while Jimmy hid under the bed. How's that for crazy bullshit? And Jacobsen wasn't even supposed to be there, but he'd showed up maybe ten minutes before the Mob, 'cause he'd been looking all over town for Vera and Tyrone, 'cause they'd stood him up for dinner at the Red Fox, which was where they'd run into Hoffa. But I'll get to all that. The important thing was, somehow he got thinking that they might have gone up to Nigger Heaven (which I'm not gonna even try to apologize for or explain, any-more—that's what everybody called it, even to me).

Okay, so here's the scene. They're all goin' nuts, blaming each other, suspicious of each other—you know, Who let the Mob in on this?—and Hoffa is . . . well, he's kinda cool. Hoffa is think-ing. The immediate rush is over, but his little *punim* is scrunched up in a frown and the Great One is thinking. He's thinking he's gotta get the hell outta there. Which I don't blame him, but where's he gonna go?

But, first things first. I gotta get rid of this body. I see it's up to me, mainly 'cause these guys can't wipe their ass with both hands, but also 'cause he's *my* corpse. I mean, I popped him, so I gotta get rid of him. Well, it's no big deal, but I'm not in any hurry and I figure I oughta get some help. So I get on Lonzo's case.

Lonzo is taking a lotta shit at the moment 'cause everybody figures he's the prick who tipped Carmine that Hoffa is here. Who else would do it, unless it was some neighbor or something, or maybe Vera or Tyrone let it slip when they were out shopping or talking to someone on the phone, or something? But Lonzo is a good suspect, 'cause he's in with the Mob, so even though Tyrone is his dead sister's boy (a point he keeps making) everybody figures he sold Hoffa to the Mob, if only to keep them off his own ass when they find out that Hoffa is his guest.

Jacobsen, to give him credit, don't agree. "I think we owe Lonzo," he says. "It was Lonzo who kept telling Carmine he was sure Jimmy wasn't here. Why would he say that if he brought the killers here?"

"Aw man, that was bullshit," Tyrone says. And of course, Vera agrees, very loud.

"He had to say that," she claims, "'cause he couldn't let on that he was the fink." She's pointing at Lonzo and screaming.

Lonzo is glaring around with those yellow eyes. He looks like he was about to kill him a couple of whiteys and maybe Tyrone, too. Fortunately, I'm there to keep the peace, with the Old Cat.

I can see that all of this is making Hoffa real nervous, but what the hell, there ain't no way of settling it real quick and there are more important things to do. "So, Lonzo," I say, "what's the deal? Did you tip Carmine?"

Lonzo reels off a coupla yards a language that woulda had Sister Mary Herman kneeling on his chest crammin' a bar of Fels Naptha down his throat, but all it means is "Nope." So I explain to him, in case he don't get it: "These folks all think you set them up. You got to admit, that's the way it looks. Now you and me know Carmine can't be interested in nobody but Mr. Hoffa, here, and I don't even know why he's hot about that, but these folks are in the way and they could get zipped, so you can see why they're hot." (They were listening and had quit yelling, so I just kept on yapping—sorta thinking out loud for their benefit.)

"Carmine ain't gonna bring a heavy shooter like Cooze out here just to get some fresh air. He meant to take out Hoffa. Probably he, or somebody, was watching that little shoot-around out there. They seen, or think they seen, Cooze take down a short, white, middle-aged guy and unless they know something we don't expect, they prob'ly think it was Hoffa. I don't know if they seen

Janney crawl back outta the bushes, but they sure must of seen me take down Cooze."

They didn't seem to get the point right away, but I'm sure you do, Mul. Like I said, Cooze didn't come back on his own. My guess was that Carmine didn't know that Hoffa wasn't hit. But it was only a guess. And anyway, they hadda know that Cooze was down, whether they knew it was me took him down or not. My second guess, and this was more than a guess, was that they would be back as soon as they picked up some more soldiers. And when they did, you can bet they wasn't going to do nothing less than clean house.

So, should we blow this pop stand? Would you of stayed? Where was there to go?

This is where my man Lonzo comes through. He says, "What if we was able to convince Carmine that Hoffa was dead?"

"Good idea," I say. "Let's shoot the fucker our own selfs and throw his ass in the Red Fox parking lot."

Krizmo and Baits start laughing their asses off, but Hoffa, of course, don't like this kind of talk, even in fun. He gives us a pretty good imitation of Edward G. Robinson, telling us all to shut up and start thinking again.

But really, I explain, Lonzo's got a idea there. We got to get the word out on the street that Hoffa was croaked, but that there wasn't gonna be no corpse to show for it. If the Mob bought it, the chances were real good that they wouldn't be back. Then after a couple a days, Hoffa could tiptoe back home and by then everybody's had a chance to cool down and see that it's better this way and Hoffa could tell the F.B.I. some bullshit thing about he was fishing, anything. And the Mob could see that Jimmy's a standup guy and nobody's gonna get hurt and we can get back to business as usual. That seemed like the best bet to me.

I had an idea of some people I could sing this lullaby to, kind of leak it, who I figured would buy it, but my man Lonzo shakes his head. He was sure that it'd never sell, not to Carmine and specially not to the Fat Man (who I allus figured was smarter than Carmine anyways) if the story could be pegged to me. It would look more like butter if *he* put it out, and he knew just the chumps to lay it on. It turned out a couple of them were the same chumps I was thinking about, but Lonzo's idea that it was better if he told the story seemed right. As for Cooze, it was the trunk of an ayban for him.

So now, Mul, you're asking all kind of questions, I can prac'ly hear it: What's with Hoffa? What does he think? Why am I trusting a stinking rat like Lonzo? What the hell is going on?

Okay, okay. Don't get your p.j.s in a tangle. I talked to Hoffa, but first I had to get the show on the road. I walked out with Lonzo while the boys were loading Cooze into the trunk of the Caddy and took him aside. "Screw all that shit inside," I told him, "you get the word to the Fat Man that Grootka is here. And you tell him that Hoffa is dead. We ain't got time for no street rumor. Those boys'll be back within a couple hours, soon's it's dark. I know you sold Hoffa to the man and I oughta blast your sorry ass right here, but this way you got a chance to live. You hear me?"

I swear the sonuvabitch looked me right in the eye—which is never fun with Lonzo—and said, "I never tol' nobody nothing about Hoffa. When would I have a chance, even if I wanted to git my own nephew croaked?"

I let him talk. He obviously hadda justify himself to somebody, so why not me? He said somebody up at Nigger Heaven had called him and told him that something funny was going on at his place and Grootka was hanging around, so he come up to see. But it never occurred to him that Hoffa was up here and sure as hell not that Hoffa was at his place! The only reason he come flying up to check it out was because I was there.

Well, it sounded good, anyways. I just shrugged and let on that I believed it. The trouble was, if he didn't sell Hoffa, who did? He didn't have no comeback for that.

Lonzo took off for town with Krizmo and Baits, to spread the good news on the right corners and let the Fat Man know what was playing at the Bijou, and they took the late Cusumano with them. I never heard no more about Cooze and neither did you, so you know they must of did a good job on that. Then I sat down for a chat with Jimmy.

Mr. H. wasn't too happy. He'd been on the lam for three days already and he hadn't talked to his wife, or let her know he was okay. That was bugging the shit outta him. The guy really was worried about his old lady—it was pathetic. I didn't know what to tell him. What could I tell him? If he got word to her that he was all right, one way or another it would get out and that could be fatal. It was hard, but there it was. Well, he knew that, I didn't have to tell him.

But the thing was, he claimed it was all a big misunderstanding. If only he could talk to Carmine and maybe Tony Jack [*Anthony Giacalone, an organized-crime figure in Detroit with known associations in the Teamsters union.—M.*], maybe a couple others, it could all be straightened out.

"You want to hire a hall?" I asked him. "Maybe you should go on *Johnny Carson.*"

But no, it was just that Tony Jack had sent a couple of punks to talk to him at the Red Fox, instead of coming hisself, like he was s'posed to. And then they were late, and when they tried to explain he blew up. He knew the guys, a couple of minor leaguers named Beano and Zit. [*Long since deceased.—M.*] The three of them had gone for a little walk away from the parking lot—there's woods around there, where they're putting in some developments, and they walked over that way, he says. Hoffa says the Zit pulled a gun.

"Was he gonna shoot you?" I asked.

"I don't know," Hoffa says. "I think so. I was yelling at the bastard and he says, 'Hey, asshole, I'm telling you,' and he yanks out the piece and he's waving it around. Maybe he wasn't meaning to use it, but I panicked. I swung my briefcase and whacked the gun hand. He dropped the gun and I took off."

That was when he ran into Tyrone and Vera. They were just pulling into the parking lot to meet Jacobsen. Hoffa jumps in their van and asks them to help him, which they did. They ended up bringing him up here.

"Why were you carrying a briefcase?" I asked.

"I had some important papers I wanted to show to Tony Jack, but of course Tony didn't show up. Look, you're the hotshot dick, Grootka," Hoffa says, "you get me out of this. I'm sick of this stinking joint. It stinks, I don't have no clean clothes, there's nothing to do—it was better in Lewisburg [*the federal penitentiary where Hoffa was incarcerated, March 7, 1967, to December 23, 1971—M.*] Between him"— he points at Tyrone—"playing that goddamn sax all day or playing these crazy records, and her"—Vera, natch—"walking around here half-naked, I'm going nuts. You talk to somebody, straighten it out."

"Well, what's to straighten out, that's what I want to know. What's the deal with Carmine?"

"It's nothing!" Hoffa insists. "He thinks I'm gonna blow on him and Tony Jack to the grand jury in Pontiac. Hell, I never blew on nobody yet, why would I now? I don't know nothing!"

"What does the grand jury want?" I asked.

"It's something about a loan Tony got from the pension fund, a long time ago. What do I know about it? What am I, a friggin' loan officer? I told the grand jury, I don't know nothing."

Well, I kept pushing, but Hoffa wouldn't give. He had some kind of deal with Tony Jack and Carmine, I could see, but he wouldn't give me any details, nothing. "Me and Tony and Carmine and Fatso, we're like brothers," he said. "We been through a lot together. We do a little business, why not? But our deal, we go back a long ways, to we were kids on the street. I can't believe that they

would put out a hit on me. It was just those friggin' hothead punks
Carmine sent."

"And your hot head," I said.

"Yeah, and my hot head. Jo says I got to watch my temper."
Jo is Hoffa's old lady, Mul.

All I can think, Mul, is that maybe it was all a misunderstanding. It seems like Hoffa really was confused. But pissed, too.
Mainly 'cause Tony Jack had sent two punks to talk to him. Things
got out of hand and now the Mob was looking to just get rid of
Hoffa before they got stuck with the dirty end of the stick. Can you
beat that? These guys, they're like high school girls, or opera stars. I
know it don't sound like much, but you and me have seen deals that
got nasty on less. Naturally, I didn't let on to Hoffa.

"Gee, it don't sound like much," I says. "I mean, Carmine
ain't gonna spring for a hit on a public figure like you, and you
being a old buddy, just 'cause you might let something drop to the
grand jury. What the hell, the guy knows you. Right?"

"Right," says Hoffa. And when I shrug and look all mystified,
he shakes his head and says, "Oh, I dunno. I been trying to figure it
out. I been thinking . . . why are these guys so down on me getting
back into the union?"

And this maybe is it, Mul. Hoffa tells me that he'd come to
think that maybe Carmine and the others didn't want him to get
back into the Teamsters. The deal was, when Hoffa got outta the
can, when Nixon give him a pardon, he didn't realize that there was
this special condition, that he couldn't participate in the union
until 1980.

"When they let me out they told me there was no special
conditions," Hoffa told me. "I hadda sign a paper, Conditions of
Parole, and all it said was that I hadda live in Detroit and report in
like anybody else. I told 'em I could live with that and I signed it.
But a day later I find out, when I'm already home, that there's a

special condition. That ain't constitutional, and the stinkin' Feds
know it. You can't have the government screwing around in union
business. Now that we got Ford in and this new attorney general,
Levi, it'll get thrown out. You'll see. But it looks like Tony Jack and
Carmine and them have been listening to Tony Pro. [*Anthony
Provenzano, a New Jersey Teamsters official who was connected to
organized crime.—M.*] He hates me since I wouldn't get him a
pension from the fund."

I didn't know nothing about any of this, but I could see that
Hoffa was still boiling about it. What it comes down to, was that
the hoods was pretty happy with Fitzsimmons being the Teamsters
president now, even if Jimmy had been their fair-haired boy in his
day. But as far as they were concerned, Jimmy's day was over. At
least, that's what he was afraid of. And he'd reacted when they sent
the kids to talk to him, 'stead of coming their selfs. And then he got
to thinking that maybe they didn't want him back so bad that they
were gonna make sure he didn't come back.

I dunno, Mul. I can't say I was totally convinced. It's a big
deal, putting out a hit on a guy like Hoffa. The guy who did it
would have to be either nuts or really confident of who he was.
Maybe both. But the thing is, this is what I had. This is Jimmy's
story. And it kind of fed into my main pitch, before, that if we
could just get the Mob to cool it for a few days and get Hoffa back
home, show that he wasn't gonna blow the whistle on them, then
maybe everything would be cool.

But you know how it is Mul . . . when all's you want is
something simple and all's it takes is for everybody to just be cool,
that's when you can't get 'em to sit still.

Which reminds me. By now, if you're reading this, you
must of had Carmine and the Fat Man down for a little talk, or
maybe you went out to see them, maybe at the potato-chip

factory. I should of said something before, but maybe it ain't too late, I hope not.

WATCH OUT FOR THESE FUCKERS, MUL!

I mean it, don't get too cocky around them. This is a bad situation. It could mean prison for the whole bunch of them. But I ain't telling you nothing, I guess. The trouble is, Mul, and I hope you don't take it the wrong way, but you never was much of a street cop. I mean, your deal is to study the evidence and ponder the case and talk to the witnesses and all that shit. *And that's good. I mean it.* But when it comes to going and knocking on the Big Bad Wolf's door, for the love of Mike, take some muscle with you and carry a big stick. If I ain't around, and I prob'ly won't be by the time you're reading this, get one a them guys like Stanos, or Dennis, from the Big 4. Don't fall back on Jimmy Marshall, he's a good kid, smart and all that, but he's too much like you, you asshole. Take some muscle. And watch your ass!

8

Hockey
Hell

I went to the hockey game and I came away so depressed that I can't talk about it. What *is* this? I'm watching these splendid men in brilliant red wheeling about the ice as if they own it, as if the other team wasn't there . . . but they don't win. A spectacular pass play culminates in Fedorov ripping a terrific, unstoppable shot to the high far corner of the net, but it *is* stoppable and so is the rebound. The Red Wings outshoot the creaky old Blues almost two to one, but they lose. It's not right. These guys are clearly superior; how can they lose? And beyond that, when they do lose, why do I care so much?

I forced myself to push it out of my mind. I had plenty else to think about. For one thing, the guy from Accounting was back on my butt. Where is my accounting of discretionary funds? And Ahab wanted to talk about his supermarket shooting. I could barely remember the case. I had to put him off; I promised to see him later. And then the kid, Kenty, was back. He'd gotten another transmission on his computer.

It was another little cartoon. Like the first, it wasn't a moving picture, just a series of panels. In this one, addressed as before to "Sgt. Fang Mulhiesen" (I don't know why people can't get the spelling right, it isn't that hard), we are back on the bridge, as in the first disk, except that now the lone character is a man instead of a woman. This man is little more than a stick figure with an overcoat and a hat and he encounters a couple of much larger men, one of whom has an axe and chops his head off, after which he's thrown off the bridge. It's a fairly simplistic drawing, but perhaps a little more sophisticated than it seems. Whoever is drawing the cartoon does know something about movement.

As the cartoon goes on the scene shifts to a kind of residen-tial neighborhood. Now we see the blond woman again. She runs down a street of detached houses, pursued by three big, dark fig-ures, presumably men in overcoats and hats and carrying large square guns in their hands. Finally, she runs into a house and slams the door, and in the last panel the pursuers are attacking the house with axes and the woman's head sticks out the upstairs window with a balloon attached that says, "Help!"

We watched the thing on the computer in Jimmy Marshall's office. Afterward, I took the kid back to my cubicle and we talked. He said, "I guess she figured her first message didn't get through to you, or you didn't take it seriously."

"Her?" I said. "What makes you think this is sent by a woman?"

The kid shrugged. "I don't know, it just seemed to me that since a woman was yelling help, she must be the one who made the thing." He shrugged again. "No big deal, I guess."

I sat back in my office chair and thought about it. It was true that I hadn't taken the first transmission seriously. It wasn't a legitimate complaint. Presumably, someone was just playing around with a computer and, having come across my name, perhaps in the newspapers, had sent the cartoon to someone on the Net who might be likely to take the thing to the precinct. It was a gag. Of course, the police have to take gags more seriously than would, say, an insurance officer, or a schoolteacher. But we don't always, obviously.

I looked at the kid. He was a smooth-faced, innocent-looking, ordinary black kid in baggy pants and shirt, except that he wasn't wearing Air Jordan sneakers that cost about one hundred and fifty bucks a pop. Instead he had on some kind of boot with a CCM label. That being a manufacturer of hockey equipment, I wondered if he was a Red Wings fan. I thought he probably wasn't, being an African-American, boots or no boots—maybe he just thought they looked cool; but then I wondered if that was a racist notion. I knew black men who were hockey fans. But not many boys. I asked him, "What do you think of the Red Wings?"

"The Red Wings suck," he said, bitterly. So he was a fan. I felt a little warmer toward him.

"Why do you say 'her,'" I asked. "The last transmission was signed 'Gaffer Hexam.' Do you know who that is?" When the boy shook his head, I told him, "It's a literary character, from a novel by Charles Dickens."

"Oh yeah," he said, with a look of interest, "like in *Tale of Two Cities*."

"That's right," I said. "I wouldn't have got it myself, except that I just happened to reread this novel recently. Gaffer Hexam is a river scavenger, a guy who picks up floating stuff in the river that runs through London."

"The Thames," Kenty said, pronouncing the "th" as in "thumb."

"I think they say 'Temz.' But yeah, that's how he makes his living. At the beginning of this book he recovers a body, which everybody thinks is the body of a young man who is the heir to a fortune. But it turns out that the body is that of a man who only resembles the heir, who has been the victim of a robbery and murder plot that nearly succeeded. But the funny thing is, the author—Dickens—doesn't seem all that interested in that side of the story, after a while. He's got too many other stories to tell us about, so the central murder mystery is kind of pushed aside. Life goes on is the message, I guess."

Kenty looked interested, but I didn't want to test his patience; he was a true child of the computer age, with the attention span that implied. Still, people always seem to be interested in a story, so I went on. "You'd think for a novelist that a murder would be the main focus, wouldn't you? But Dickens just pushes it aside, pretty quickly, so he can tell us all about a bunch of other people. I guess Dickens got more interested in Lizzie Hexam's story."

"Who's Lizzie?" Kenty interrupted.

"Sorry. That's Gaffer's daughter. She also works the river with him in his skiff." Kenty nodded. "Anyway, the idea is that Gaffer starts the story rolling, but then he sort of fades into the background—he dies, and you kind of get the impression that Dickens kills him off, just to get rid of him. But Lizzie's story does become important. It kind of drives the last several chapters, and lots of other characters are caught up in it. But what does all that have to do with this . . . ? What is this thing? I mean, what do you call it?"

Kenty looked confused. "What is it? It's just a thing somebody sent to my E-mail address, but it wasn't for me, it was for you."

"This is E-mail? Hmmm. So now I've gotten my first E-mail. Second, really. Well, what does it mean? Maybe what our person here is saying, is that somebody has been killed, thrown in the river, and she knows about it and the killers are now after her. But," I concluded lamely, "so what? It's only a cartoon. Do you get a lot of this stuff? Things just popping into your E-mail?"

"Nope. Mostly I get people on the Net, people I talk to, mostly about games, that kind of stuff. Sometimes you get folks playing jokes, or they leave stupid messages, but this seemed different."

"What do you think it means?" I asked.

Kenty shrugged. "I ain't no detective," he said. "You are . . .

or you s'posed to be. To me it sounds like somebody is scared and they need help."

I tried not to sigh. "This kind of thing happens all the time, Kenty. Not exactly this, not misdirected E-mail, but this basic situation. People get worried because they think someone is trying to hurt them. Sometimes it's true. We have to take it seriously, to a degree, but that degree is based on the message. Here we have a somewhat mixed message. It seems to be a serious threat, but it's in the form of a crude cartoon that isn't even sent directly to the police but to a . . ."

"A kid," he said, with a serious nod.

"Well, yeah, a kid."

"So you don't take it too serious," he said. "But what if that's her only way out? What if she has a computer but can't get out, or is afraid, or somebody won't let her? But she can send a message on the Net?"

I had kept the first disk. I located it in my desk, somehow, and got Kenty to pull up the material on a computer screen in Jimmy Marshall's office. As I'd recalled, it was just a series of panels depicting threatening events that would, or perhaps could, befall the blond woman. But there was no explicit message of help. We looked at the second disk, saved it, and copied it onto the first one, so I could keep it.

Kenty was sitting at the desk, his fingers idly riffling across the board, not unlike a pianist. He had called up the cartoon again. "See that?" Kenty said, pointing at the screen. "There's a number on her house."

So there was. And in fact, by backtracking we were able to find a street sign. I had missed all that. Well, it wasn't exactly jumping out of the screen. The kid looked at me, as if to say, And you call yourself a detective?

I got out the address telephone book and looked it up. "Vera Jacobsen," it read. The name rang as pure as a silver bell. It's hard to describe the feeling that a detective can get, sometimes, when he stumbles on something like this. It resonates deep in the marrow.

The address was in Ferndale, not more than six or seven blocks from where I'd been earlier, visiting Becky Berg.

"You live around here?" I asked Kenty. "Come on, I'll give you a ride home."

"Nah, that's all right," he said.

"What are you, afraid? Don't want the homies to see you riding in the cop's car? It's just an old Checker, it isn't like a real cop car."

I don't know why I was pushing it; I guess I had some notion of wanting to see Kenty's house, his setup. It was a neat, well-maintained brick house on Three Mile Drive, off Mack. His grandmother came to the door, a round-faced woman with gray hair cut short, wearing a clean but wash-worn blue pajamalike outfit that made her look like Chairman Mao—she even had his fat cheeks. She was alarmed to see Kenty with a white man, and she quickly pegged me as a cop.

"This boy been in trouble?" she said, quickly. She grabbed him by the shoulder and hauled him inside. Kenty tolerated her handling with a roll of his eyes.

"No, Ma'am," I assured her. I showed my identification. "He was just helping us with some other citizen's cry for help. Trying to warn us, you might say. May I come in?"

She let me in, and I was about to explain that I was just interested in Kenty's layout when I realized that she would never believe that. She would think I was looking for drugs in his room. I said that I was interested in the house. I was looking to move and I'd considered this neighborhood.

"You?" she said, skeptically, looking me up and down.

"Yeah," I said, looking her up and down. "Are there any places for sale around here?"

She shrugged. "Go ahead, look around. It's a nice house. Sure, there's places for sale, up by Forest." She frowned at me, assessing my worth, then said, "This for a single man?" When I nodded she pursed her lips, as if to say, I thought as much. "The church"—she pronounced it *choich*—"is fixing up some houses to sell below Mack, but I don't know . . ." she faltered, but then decided to take a chance and went on, "if you would qualify."

"Well, I've got a steady income," I said.

"I mean, I don't know that the church is wantin' to sell these homes, which they been fixin' up, to um, *single* folks. Single men, anyway. There's lots of single women who have families and need the housing, but . . ."

"What church would that be?"

"That's the Penile African Baptist Church." She gazed at me as blandly as any Chinese emperor, daring me to smile.

"The Penile Church," I said.

"Penile African Baptist, on Joy. You'll find it in the book."

I thanked her and started to leave. Kenty said, "You want me to go with you?"

I didn't understand.

"To see the lady?" he said.

"Oh. No. I couldn't do that," I said. I did want him to go with me, for a couple of reasons, one of which was to find out what this church was, but also because he might be helpful, and then . . . well, I'd enjoyed his company. But it wasn't something I could do. You can't take a kid with you on police business.

Which reminded me, in the car, of Grootka's warning about the dangers of this investigation, as old and stale as it was. I had not, of course, called in the Fat Man—who was now generally known by his real name, Humphrey DiEbola, if for no other reason than that he was no longer fat, but also because he was now *the* Man, his boss Carmine having been put away by assailants unknown, though widely believed to have been Ms. Helen Sedlacek and her lover, Joe Service. That is, the reason I hadn't called Humphrey in was that . . . well, let's face it, the material that Grootka had left me just wouldn't support that kind of action. It was a barely legible manuscript written in old school-exam books, hardly a document that one could rely on for an indictment. I hadn't even told Jimmy about it, and so how was I going to go to him, or to the Big 4, and ask for backup? It just wasn't in the playbook. Still, I had an uneasy feeling that Grootka's warning oughtn't to be ignored. He wasn't easily spooked. This had an edgy feel to it, and the feeling was getting edgier. Too, Grootka was not wrong in saying that I was not really keen on the outside aspects of detective work. I was never one to think of a gun first. It always seemed to me that a detective probably should not be in a situation where the only option was a gun. If he was, he'd probably made a mistake, not done his thinking first, as he should have.

With that in mind, I stopped by the Fifth Precinct, which is also the shooting range, and spent an hour getting rid of a couple pounds of lead. It was good exercise and I was gratified by the approving comments of Sergeant Bell, the range instructor, who noted that my scores were up. He wondered if I'd quit something.

"Quit something? Like what?" I asked.

"Usually the first thing that improves a guy's scores is, he's quit smoking, or even drinking," Bell observed.

Now that I thought of it, I realized that I had not had a drink in several days, which may have been the first time that had happened in some time. But it had not been volitional: I simply hadn't felt like drinking. How odd that I hadn't noticed. Also, I hadn't had a cigar for a day or two. I felt like one now, however, and on the way to Ferndale I lit up an H. Upmann "Petit Corona." It tasted very good and got me all the way to the little white house with the picket fence.

I don't know what I'd expected from Vera Jacobsen. If she was the woman Grootka had talked about, I guess I was thinking of a middle-aged busty blond stripper. She didn't much answer to Grootka's description. This Vera was as ordinary looking as a woman could be. Her graying hair was cut boy-short, which perhaps con-tributed to the impression of handsomeness, rather than feminine beauty. Her face was plain and not very wrinkled, with a smooth brow and firm mouth. The famous bosom had deflated, for another thing. She looked to be about fifty years old, perhaps more, her face rather browned in that way that we associate with yachtswomen and golfers, people who have spent all their lives out of doors. She was about five-seven, lean and lithe, a golfer. She wore jeans and an expensive-looking cashmere pullover, running shoes. An intel-ligent, open, alert face, none of the bosomy, flower-child/earth-mama-cum-sexpot image that Grootka had sketched. But, somehow, I felt that this was the woman in the notebooks. This is what hap-pens to us when we grow up, I thought.

"You must be Mulheisen," she said. "It's taken you a while." The statement was flat and declarative. I nodded. "The kid finally convinced you to look into it, I guess."

"Do you know Kenty?" I asked. She ushered me into a very sparsely furnished living room. There was a folded-up wooden bed, one of those Japanese things, with a colorful pad. There were a couple of straight-backed wooden chairs, strangely attractive for such simple things, and there was a piano, a music stand, a clarinet on a stand, and against the wall a modernistic Scandinavian stereo system of some sort. There were exactly three pictures on the three walls that didn't have a window—small, abstract paintings of sea-scapes, presumably, being simply blue shading to a straight horizon, then a subtly different blue shading to deep sky. The three paint-ings were not the same and yet, somehow, how could they be different?

"I know who he is," Vera Jacobsen said. "I gave him his computer. I don't think he knows that."

"How mysterious," I said, unable to repress a tone of pleasure, I guess, because she smiled complicitly.

"It's nice to be able to do something for somebody, once in a while," she said.

I glanced around the room. I didn't feel in any hurry. "These your work?" I gestured at the paintings. She nodded. "A bit more to this than the cartoons."

"You can't do this on a video screen," she pointed out. "But I had to do something to get your attention. It was time."

"So you're not really in danger?"

"Of course, but I've lived with it for a long time. I try not to let it depress me. Grootka said it would take something serious, preferably with a literary twist, or historical maybe, to get you to pay attention. 'You might have to paint him a picture,' he said."

"No kidding, Grootka said that?"

"In those words. 'With a naked lady,' was his suggestion, but I couldn't quite do that."

"And when was this?"

"By now you should have guessed," she said. "Would you like coffee, or would you like a drink? By the way, you can smoke your cigar, if you want."

"No thanks, I just had one. But the coffee sounds good."

She went into the little kitchen toward the rear and quickly returned with two cups on saucers, brimming with hot coffee. "I just made this a little while ago. It's Ethiopian. Cream? Sugar? Me neither." She set the cups down on a kind of bookshelf that also held a small plant with thick, fuzzy leaves. She brushed the plant with a flickering look of dissatisfaction. "I'm not much of a gardener," she said.

"How's the clarinet?"

"I'm not much a player, either." She waved her hand dismissively. "I like to keep up with the music—well, I have to. In my work."

"Your work?" I asked. "Do you play professionally?"

"Oh no, but I produce. That is, I produce records. CDs. It's just a little outfit, you've probably never heard of it: Hastily Improvised Productions, otherwise known as H.I.P. It's all avant-garde stuff."

She was right; I hadn't heard of them, but I said I was interested. "Who do you record?"

"I doubt if you've heard of any of them," she said. "They're mostly European, but we occasionally get onto some wild tenor player from Montana—there's a guy out there now, somewhere, who used to play in Detroit, but we haven't been able to interest him in a recording session yet. Chuck Florence?"

"Never heard of him," I said. "You ever record M'Zee Kinanda?"

"Oh no, he's too big for us. But . . . who knows, we might be able to get him to 'guest' on somebody else's session."

"Where do you do this?" I looked around.

"Not here," she said. "This is just my Detroit pad. I used to live here years ago, but now I'm mostly in Santa Barbara. Are you familiar with the business? Well, it's not what it sounds like, I guess. Being a record producer doesn't mean you have an office at RCA, it's just a telephone in Santa Barbara, and here, too. A recording tells the caller where I am. I try to put together the artists and we rent a studio, usually in L.A., but also here, or New York, wherever's convenient. But, you didn't come here to talk about . . ."

"No, it's interesting," I said.

"Do you play? No? I guess I knew that. But you are a fan."

"You know a lot about me," I said. "Was this from Grootka?"

"Mainly. He thought very highly of you, perhaps too highly. I don't mean that in a bad way." She had seated herself, or perched, on a high stool against one wall. It was another indication that this was not a room for relaxing, although she didn't seem ill at ease. She held her cup in both hands and sipped carefully from it. I'd already burned my tongue.

"I don't mean that you aren't worthy of his esteem," she amended, "but that his esteem prevented him from being as open with you as he would have liked. He thought you were a bit above him, you see."

"You learned all this from a few hours of . . . ah, of being together up at the lake, at the resort?"

"Oh, no, we kept very close contact over the years," she said, looking at me with surprise. "I kept waiting to have it all come out, but Grootka kept saying, 'No, no, not yet, the time isn't ripe. We'll let Mulheisen decide, when it suits him.' And then, of course, he died . . . well, you were with him. After that, I wasn't sure what to do. But obviously, now, things are coming to a head."

"They are?"

She looked at me kind of funny, but said, "I'm sure you see the problem. How to approach you in such a way that you wouldn't get all alarmed and go official on this. That was Grootka's feeling, as well. He wanted to avoid an *official* response, because he felt that the situation was too . . . too delicate, I guess. Too many inno-cent people stood to get hurt, if the official response didn't prop-erly protect them, which he felt that it wouldn't. He felt that there had to be a way, which you—the great Mulheisen—would be able to figure out, to deal with this so that the little guy didn't get hurt." There was a delicate balance in her tone of skepticism, if not scorn, and genuine concern.

"That's what this is all about? These messages, this crypto-whatchamacallit? To avoid an official investigation, because the Mob might. . . . I mean, *cartoons?*" I shook my head, wondering. "You know, it has just occurred to me, Grootka was some kind of radical, maybe like these militia people. He was in the police, but he didn't trust the police. He really felt . . ." Thinking about his stated desire in the notebooks to just let the case fade away, I was momentarily unable to go on.

"But then later he felt that if it was necessary, that maybe I would handle the situation—"

"Discreetly," Vera finished the sentence for me.

"No, I was wrong," I said, "he wasn't a militia-type radical, he was more like a kid reading comic books, believing in Batman. You know, I was just telling someone the other day about this image I have of Grootka, walking down the street, a gun in each hand, keeping the peace."

"Agge. Yes. It was an appropriate image."

"You know Agge, too?"

"Yes, she's my daughter."

"Agge is your daughter? Are you sure?"

I was a little revved up, but this blurted gaffe eased the tension. "This is my day for revelations," I said. "How about Kenty? What's your relationship there?"

"I'm not his grandma, if that's what you're thinking. I was looking for a way to communicate with you, and I heard about Kenty, through Sena, his grandmother. She used to work for me, sort of. Cleaning house, you know. But she came to be more of a friend. I gave her my old computer, for Kenty, because I was getting a new one. I don't think she knows about Kenty giving you my message, and I don't think he knows that the message came from me. Is there anything else you need to know?"

"Yes, of course there is. Can we sit down? Is this a couch?"

She showed me how to set up the Japanese thing. It seemed comfortable. And when I had another cup of coffee she explained.

"Grootka kept in touch, over the years. I mean, after what happened at Turtle Lake. His theory was that while the Mob might be happy not to make waves as long as the issue was still current, later on someone—he thought it would be the one he always called the Fat Man, Mr. DiEbola—would be concerned that some loose ends had been left, well, loose. And they would send someone to tidy things up, so to speak."

"And did they?" I asked, then stopped myself. "No. No, wait a minute. Let's not get ahead of ourselves. What do you mean 'everything was smoothed over'? You mean at the resort, where you and your husband had taken Hoffa."

"Well, sure. What else?"

"But what was smoothed over? From what I've read in Grootka's memoir, he had shot and killed a Mobster named Cusumano and got a couple of Lonzo Butterfield's boys to dump the body for him. What happened to Hoffa?"

"Oh dear," she said. "I thought you'd read all of the notebooks. How much do you know?"

"Not enough. And frankly, I'm getting a little annoyed. You know, this is blatant criminal—"

"I'm sorry. You'll have to go," she said. "I'll have to think about this. I'll call you later."

She looked grim and determined and began to tug at my arm. I unconsciously rose to my feet before I rebelled, but she began to push me toward the door.

"Hey, hey, wait a minute," I said. "This won't do."

"Sorry, sorry," she said, still pushing, "but you've got to go. I have to think. This isn't going right." She had backed me right up to the front door.

I brushed her hands away. "I think you better come with me," I said. I reached for my cuffs.

That stopped her. She suddenly backed away, her eyes wide with fear. She held up her hands, warding me off. "Now wait a minute," she protested. "Grootka said—"

"Grootka said a lot." I dangled the cuffs before her. "Maybe too much. I'd like to hear more." I advanced toward her.

She backed into the Japanese thing and abruptly sat down on it. "Would you like some more coffee?" she asked, looking up innocently.

"Sure," I said, laughing. "Why not?" I leaned against the wall and crossed my legs, waiting, tossing the cuffs nonchalantly.

When she brought the coffee she handed me mine and carried hers to the window. She looked out on the street as she sipped and talked. "You have to be careful when you listen to Grootka," she said.

"Now you're on the road to wisdom," I said, "as—" I started to say *our mutual friend,* but finished with, "Books Meldrim would say."

"Yes, Books." She looked thoughtful. "He's a nice man, isn't he? He warned me about playing too many games with you. He said you would tire of it. But I guess I just got caught up. And then, these guys showed up."

"What guys?"

"Those," she said, pointing out the window with a finger alongside her cup.

I went over to look. Parked in front of the house was my Checker. There were other cars parked in front of other houses. I didn't see anything. "Where?" I asked.

"In the maroon Continental," she said.

I looked down the street. The glass of the Continental was tinted. I couldn't see anybody.

"They're just sitting inside," she said, calmly. She didn't seem that concerned, but maybe she was always this cool. "They've been coming by for a couple of days now. I saw one of them get out and stretch. He went for a walk around the block, then got back in. He's a young guy, about . . . oh, I don't know. I don't judge people's ages very well anymore. He looked like he was maybe twenty-five, or twenty-eight. Dark hair. Wearing a kind of leisure outfit."

"You didn't recognize him? No? You say you usually live in Santa Barbara. What's that address?" I took it down in my notebook, while I continued to ask, "How long have you been back in Detroit?" I jotted down "week." "And they showed up when?"

"I first noticed them about three days ago."

"But they didn't approach you? And you haven't had any threats, in the mail, phone?" I put the notebook back in my coat pocket. "Well . . . what do you want to do?"

"I thought you would tell me. You're the cop. You're the genius, according to Grootka."

"Let's leave Grootka out of this, okay?" I said. "We're here, he's not. I need to know if you feel threatened, if you want to leave. I don't really have anywhere to take you. I don't know of any place that would necessarily be safer. I can't lock you up as a material witness, or any—"

"What?" she said.

"Unless you are a witness for the Hoffa investigation. And, of course, you are. Would you like me to call the F.B.I.? I'm sure they would be delighted to talk to you. And, of course, they'd protect you. They're famous for it."

She wasn't having anything to do with the FBI, as I had expected.

"Well, I guess if you aren't worried, I'm not," I said.

"I'm not exactly *worried,*" she said. "I'm more scared to death. Those guys are after me."

"Do you think they want to hurt you?"

"I don't know. Why don't they come in? Why doesn't someone contact me, ask me something?"

She turned and looked at me, putting down the cup. She still didn't look particularly upset. I was reminded of her striptease act outside the house at Turtle Lake. She was a cool customer, to be sure.

"Maybe you're mistaken," I said. "Maybe it's not what you think. Maybe they're looking for someone else."

"Don't you have some way of finding out? Can't you call somebody?"

I picked up the phone and called Jimmy at the Ninth. I told him about the guys. He said he'd check and call back. I hung up the phone and looked at Vera. She didn't seem any calmer or more agitated.

"What happened out at the cabin?" I asked her.

"I thought you knew. Didn't Grootka tell you all about it? The notebooks?"

"I don't have all the notebooks. I keep finding them. He's playing a long game, extra innings . . . or maybe, it's 'sudden-death overtime.'"

"I have one," she said. "You want it? He said to give it to you if you asked for it. But I just assumed he would have given you a copy. Maybe this means that it's time."

"Time?" I said.

"Grootka said the time would come, when everything should be given to you. But it had to be done . . . *delicately*."

"I'd say it's overtime."

She went out of the room and returned shortly with a familiar-looking notebook.

"Let's drop the games," I said. I set the empty cup aside and took the book. "Where is Jimmy Hoffa?"

She smiled. "He's in Brazil."

9

Idiots
Avant

Grootka's Notebook #4

So we settled
into a cozy little household. You know, Mul, it was a good time for
me. It was like a family, except that there was no mama and papa
and baby bear. More like brothers and sisters, even if there was
some big age differences. Hah! Brothers, all right—Brother Lonzo,
he be Brer Bear, and then you got Sister Vera, she be Sister Fox.
Just foolin'! I never knew family life, you know, so maybe I'm just
imagining things, but it was kind of nice. The people seemed to
care about each other, even ol' Brer Bear.

For the time being we didn't really have to worry about the
Mob. The food was good and the music was great. And it ain't often
that you get a chance to sit down and talk to a guy like Hoffa, man
to man. I gotta admit, I never thought much of the bastard before,
but he was kind of interesting.

[*Here Grootka has inserted an addition, a piece of paper that
appears to be torn from a spiral notebook of a smaller size, probably one
of those notebooks that many police officers carry to make preliminary
notes during the day, for their reports. The note is handwritten with a
blue ballpoint pen, pressed very hard. This page is taped into the regular
notebook with old, yellowed Scotch tape, or something similar.—M.*]

Talking with Hoffa. Me 'n' H. kinda grew up about the same, except he had a family, only his father died when he was about six or seven. He was a coal miner, in Indiana. Jim's mother took the kids to Detroit after the old man died and they lived on the West Side. He says the kids called him a hillbilly and he used to get in fights, but he had a good time. He quit school, never went to the ninth grade, he says. He used to work at Frank & Cedar's, the downtown department store, as a stock boy! Christ, how long has that been gone? But, get this, he's one a them guys who says the old days was a lot better, that the city has gone downhill. He didn't come right out and say it, naturally, but he blames it on "the niggers." Ha, ha! I love that shit. Here's a fuckin' asshole who starved through the fuckin' Depression, who used to have to beg for a job and then be grateful for the pennies they threw ya—he even starts a union to fight the bastards, and he says "it was better then." The man's nostalgic for his youth. You know me, Mul, I ain't much of a union man. I all's thought the union starts out fine, but then it gets in and it turns out to be like the bosses, just one more layer of horseshit. As for the race crap, I don't know that H. actually believes any of that shit, but it gets said so much, just offhand, that a lotta people stupidly repeat it. He's a stupid man in a lotta ways. [*End of insert.—M.*]

He [*Hoffa.—M.*] hated our music, naturally, and I don't think he much cared for butter beans and ham hocks with cornbread and mustard greens. Brer Lonzo was the cook. He's a hell of a cook, Mul. His barbecued pork butt is outta sight. The babe turned out to be kind of nice to be around, too. But gee whiz, that f——in' Janney, what a f——in' pain in the ass! He'd be the older brother, the smart-ass who knows everything. Also, Tyrone turned kind of sour. I guess he got kinda tired of all these guys grabbing at Vera's buns, speshly since she didn't seem to mind it so much.

It seems like there's always something to make a good time a little f——ed up. But I had a good time. Me and Tyrone got in some good practice, him on soprano and me on the big horn, using his instrument, which I appreciated, it's a hell of a horn. But it's a bitch to pick up an instrument so late in life, 'cause you know you can never get really good on it—I played in the band at St. Olaf's, sure, but that was so long ago. You don't know what a bitch it is to play a E-flat right after a B-flat, in any kind of up tempo. A kid can do it, but old fingers, unh-uh. Tyrone'd get pissed at me, sometimes, 'cause I had trouble with tempo, but mostly he was pretty good about that. We played his concerto, mostly just two parts, except when we could get Books to sit in on piano, playing the bass line mostly, since there ain't really a piano part for the piece. And also, Vera could take a clarinet or a alto-sax part—she wasn't too bad.

It was hot and we couldn't really go out during the day, but after dark we had a good time. I was staying at Books's, just like before, so I could go to the casino every night, which was sort of my listening post, and usually Tyrone would come by for a while, or Vera. But they couldn't leave Hoffa by himself, so somebody always had to be there. Lonzo usually drove out from the city, but he had to be in town, to do his bail-bond business, which meant he also could keep his ears open on the street. It seemed like the Mob was buying the pitch, that Hoffa was dead. Everything was real quiet.

We couldn't leave Hoffa by himself because he was so antsy. He was worried sick about his old lady and was constantly trying to figure out some way to get a message to her that he was all right. But I told him, if he ever wanted to see her again, he had to be cool. In the meantime, we had to figure out what our next move should be, if it turned out like it looked, that Carmine had simmered down. Because Hoffa couldn't stay there forever, that was for sure. By now, a whole week had gone by. The outside world was still buzzing, I guess, but a kind of quiet was settling over the whole shitaree. Still, I know it was driving Hoffa crazy, because it seemed like everybody on the TV and in the papers was assuming that he was dead. That has got to prey on a man's mind, I don't care who he is, 'cause you can't help thinking that if everybody believes you're dead it makes it a little easier for people who want you dead to make you dead.

So after a lotta arguing we come up with a plan, which was if we could get through the weekend, on Monday morning Hoffa could reappear. He disappeared on a Wednesday afternoon. We had a couple more days, is all.

The second big problem was f——ing Jacobsen. It turns out he had a big deal cooking in L.A., to record Tyrone. He got some money together—not that *he* wasn't loaded—to record an album, including the concerto, and he had the musicians all lined up, a studio, but Tyrone had to be there, naturally, in a couple of days.

It's always something, ain't it? Not bad enough we got Carmine on our ass, we got to worry about getting Tyrone to L.A.

This Jacobsen was a weird duck. He was about fifty or so, it's hard to tell, and kind of odd. A businessman, in the printing business. He's got a nice press over on Grand Boulevard. They do fancy stuff, stationery for large corporations, special brochures, class stuff. He's some kind a millionaire, I think, but he's also a jazz buff. You and me are buffs, it don't mean shit, but a rich man's hobbies get promoted. He was crazy about Tyrone. He wants the world to see what a great genius Tyrone is. Also, he wants the world to see that he is Tyrone's patron. He also wants Vera's ass, which it seems to me he must be getting a little of.

The way I had it worked out, if we could get Hoffa out of here on Monday, Tyrone and Vera and Jacobsen could fly off to L.A. and who would give a shit. I would take Hoffa to Pontiac, to a TV station, where he would make a little statement. Of course, we still had to figure out what he was going to say. So Vera suggests we have a rehearsal. She'll be the news babe, me and Tyrone and Lonzo and Jacobsen will be the audience and other reporters. Hoffa wanted to say that he had gone off on his own to "think about his future," especially about his "future with the union."

Sounded great to me, if he didn't get into it too much. The main thing was to give the impression that his absence didn't have nothing to do with the Mob. Just leave them out of it and don't answer no questions from reporters.

But then, next morning I'm sitting at breakfast with Hoffa, the others have all gone off somewheres, and he says he's changed his mind. He said he'd been thinking it over and the way he saw it was he might've been a little quick-tempered, but the real trouble was that the Mob thought they could just about do anything they wanted with the union, especially now that they had Fitz in there. He had always been a realistic guy, he says. He used to figure that he had to do business with the Mob because it just didn't make any sense to pretend that they weren't a major power in the way things operated. He seen that once he was out of the way—when he went to prison—they was just as happy to keep him out of it, because now they could move in, bag and baggage, and Fitz wouldn't say shit if he had a mouthful. In fact, he says, since Fitz has took such a taste for shit, he's gonna like it when Jimmy gets back, 'cause there's gonna be a lot to eat.

"That frigging Nixon was in it up to his frigging neck," Hoffa tells me. "But now we got Ford. Ford is a schmuck, but I don't think he's in the Mob's pocket. Ford will give me an unconditional pardon, like he gave Nixon—he's in the goddamn pardon business, for chrissake! He knows the gov'mint's got no business in union affairs."

Hah! He was still thinking the same way. I knew there wasn't no talking to him about this crap and anyway what do I know. I knew Carmine, though, and the Fat Man. Once they got their fat fingers in this pie, you ain't gonna get nowhere slappin' their fingers. You wanta kick them out, I says, you gotta fuckin' kick!

We move into Lonzo's front room with our coffee and Hoffa looks me right in the eye and he says, "How do you mean 'kick'? Do you mean like I think you mean?"

I gotta admit I was a little flip here, but it's just a coupla guys jawin', right? So I says, "A .45 has got kick."

Hoffa liked this talk, I could tell. He kind of smirks and says, "Who would you kick?"

"I ain't kickin' nobody," I says. "*I* ain't got no kick."

We laughed at that, but Hoffa was serious, I see that now. He says, "No, I mean, just as a sample, who'd you kick? I mean if you was me?"

And I says, "Just as a sample? Well, you could kick Carmine. That'd be a big enough sample for anybody. But, if it was me? I'd kick the Fat Man, DiEbola. He's the real brains there. Carmine wouldn't know what to do without the Fat Man, so it's almost like kicking both of 'em. The eastern Mob would be in here running things before you know it. There'd be a lot of hell to pay and some more people would prob'ly get whacked before it was over, but they sure as hell would be out of your damn union."

I could see that Hoffa liked that idea. He thinks for a while and we go on to some other stuff, but he comes back after a bit and says, "If the Fat Man got kicked, just as a sample, who do you think could do it?"

He was looking at me kind of close and I knew what he was thinking, so I says, "Don't be looking at me, Jim. I got nothing against dropping a fat turd like DiEbola, but if I did it I'd do it for my own self, not for you or nobody else."

"Well, who?" he asks. "Do you know anybody?"

"You're the tough guy," I tell him. "You do it. You've dropped the hammer on a man before."

"Where'd you hear that?" he snaps.

I shrug. Now that I thought about it, I guess I never heard that about Hoffa, hisself, but I says, "Well, that's what they say about the Teamsters. Not so much bustin' a cap on some guy, but I heard you guys were never shy about breakin' heads. I heard you wasn't too worried about scratchin' up your knuckles, yourself." Hoffa smiles, a little half-smile. He liked that tough-guy shit. "Take a hurt and give a hurt, eh?" I go on. "That's the way you bruisers are. You gotta know somebody."

He thinks about that for a minute, then he says, "Do you think if we contacted Carmine, he'd meet?"

I could see what he was thinking, so I says, "You don't wanta ask him out here again. These folks here got enough problems without bringing the Mob down on them. They come out here once, on their own, but I'd say they was desperate, then. If they come back, they'll bring a goddamn army with them. You wanta talk to Carmine, set up a meet? Go ahead"—I point to the tele-phone—"call him. But I'd go for something a little more remote, where there wasn't so many innocent people around. Like maybe the Mo-fuckin'-hobby Desert."

"I know a place upstate," he says, "a hunting cabin. It ain't exactly remote. You can drive to it, but it's out in the woods and this time of the year there ain't no hunters or nothing around. Nearest neighbor is, I don't know, couple miles. It ain't my place, it belongs to somebody else. Maybe that would be a good place to meet."

I tried to talk him out of it. We had a pretty good plan, I thought, with him going to the TV station in Pontiac. No calls ahead, so nobody could set up an ambush, or nothing, just jump in the cars and drive to the TV station and let everybody see that Jimmy Hoffa was alive and kicking and then he'd have to talk to the F.B.I., who would obviously protect him. Why screw around?

Later, when things settled down, he could talk to Carmine, explain the situation, and as far as I was concerned, if he wanted to pop Carmine or the Fat Man then, well, he was welcome to it. But right now . . .

No, no, he was like a kid who gets hold of an idea and he wants to get on with it, right now! The man is hot. He's still pissed because they sent the mugs to deal with him and he still half-ass thought that it was s'posed to be a hit. "You don't know these guys like I do," he says. "They commit theirselves to a plan, an action, and they carry it out. It's their code. They know the Street and the Street respects 'em 'cause they know the Mob always does what they say they'll do. That's why they come out here."

I blew my stack. "Fuck their code! I heard that shit all my life and I never bought it. Sure, some lamebrains think that way, but mainly the Mob is like any other business, except that it has to rely on too many fuckin' blood relatives, 'cause they can't trust nobody, and that's how they're always fuckin' up and why they don't actually run shit. Hell, if you're hard enough to shoot people you can run the whole shitaree, but these assholes, they're mostly too dumb to read plain English, much less a fucking code." I hadda calm down.

"Sure, they're dangerous," I concede the point. "But they're fuckin' businessmen first. If it don't pay, they don't play. So don't think that some fucking code drove Carmine and the Fat Man out here. They're fuckin' scared that the Feds are gonna come down on their ass, that someone seen those two fucks diddling with you in the parking lot, and until they know you're fuckin' takin' the dirt nap, they're gonna be lookin' for you. Those bastards had some information and they decided to take a ride and check it out. If you was here, like they expected, they prob'ly woulda tried to parley. But you wasn't here, as far as they knew. They're suspicious bastards, though, so they sent Cooze back. And you see what happened."

"Get your head outta your ass," Hoffa says. "If I go back and try to pretend like nothing happened it'll just happen all over again. Nothing is settled. I see now, what I gotta do is hash this out with Carmine and Tony Jack and the Fat Man. Then I can make my public appearance, but we'll have all this behind us and everything will be copacetic."

I had an idea. "What's those two kids' names, the ones who came to see you at the restaurant?" I picked up the phone and called Rackets and Conspiracy. "Andy? Hey, I'm looking for some guys, maybe you heard of 'em, Angelo Rinaldi, something like that, and . . . Oh," I says, giving Hoffa the full benefit of my show. "And who was with him? Nicholas Soteri? Mmmm. No, I don't think that's it. Hey, Andy, would I shit you? It ain't them. My guys wouldn't be takin' no nap in the trunk of the same old Plymouth. Yah, yah, same to you." I look at Hoffa. "Seems like Angelo and Nick decided to buddy up in the trunk of an ayban."

"Ayban?" Hoffa was a little dense—maybe it was shock.

"Abandoned auto," I says. "Carmine and the Fat Man are tidying up the mess. They got rid of the fools. Now all you got to do is come out like the sun and say everything is all right."

"And end up in an ayban," he says.

Well, I could see he wasn't gonna listen to sense. What he couldn't see was that if he was hell bent on hashing things out, the only hash was maybe gonna be his ass. But I could see he wasn't goin' to no TV station without he talked to Carmine first. I had a bad feeling, Mul. It seemed like we was so close. I just felt like if he'd gone to the TV station like we planned at first, things could of worked out. But he wouldn't have it that way. So I said, Okay, I'd see if I couldn't set something up.

One thing I knew for sure, I couldn't be dealing with Carmine and Fats myself. I know you think I'm some kind of outlaw, Mul, but I ain't that dumb. Hell, I already had to deal with Cooze and it didn't go too well. But it was something I had to deal with and I did it. A situation come up, Cooze went down. Two and two is four. But this was a whole 'nother ball game. I couldn't be out front on this, no way.

It had to be Lonzo. He didn't like it, natch, but I showed him how it had to be. Hell, he was already in it up to his ears. It was his own fault. Lonzo swore up and down that it wasn't so, that he hadn't brought in the Mob, but he had the contacts, they knew him, he was the logical guy. No matter how it boiled down, the Mob'd blame the spade anyways. If things turned out okay for the Mob, he'd be cool. I explained that his best chance for it to turn out right was to be up front with them, play the simpleminded messenger boy.

The place Hoffa had in mind was up near Cadillac, about three hours' drive. It belonged to a mug named Cess Morgan, who collected for the numbers for Big Sid, until he got sent up for busting some guy's nose who tried to screw him. You remember Big Sid, Mul. Sid is kind of on the outs with the Mob, lately, but I hear he is getting back in business. Well, anyway, this Cess is a hunter, or used to be. Right now he was in Jacktown for a couple of years. But Hoffa used to know him, 'cause Cess drove a truck for a while and was in the union and he used to do some strong-arm stuff for the boys. Hoffa thought of him when I said he must know somebody who would do the job. Cess is on the shelf, but Hoffa knows where he hides the key to his cabin, and it sounds about perfect for the job.

Well, here I am, another book damn near all scribbled up. You know I was looking back over it and it don't read too bad. But I'm kinda sad about the way Tyrone looks here. I don't wanta give the wrong impression, Mul. Tyrone is a really good guy. He was under a lotta pressure and the situation at Lonzo's didn't bring out the best in him. You got to understand that a kid like Tyrone is a

artist. He lives for his art. He ain't like you and me and the rest of
these birds. He'd do just about anything to see his music played and
heard. But he's basically a good, kind kid, don't smoke, don't hardly
drink except a beer now and then, and never did no dope that I
could see, 'though he must of experimented now and then, like a
kid would do.

You could see what kind of kid he was from the way other
people acted around him. Even older folks, like Jacobsen, and hard
sunzabitches like Lonzo, they treated Tyrone with respect and love.
I ain't shitting you, Mul. I wrote "love" there. And of course Vera,
she was crazy about his ass. And it wasn't the sex, I don't think. It
was the genius. In a lot of ways he was a kind of innocent kid, just
sailing along through life with his eyes wide open but not looking at
what you and me would see. He saw something else and it was
pretty beautiful.

Well, enough of this shit. See you in book five. Ask Vera.

10

Jimmy Jam

"**W**hy do you say Hoffa's in Brazil?" I asked Vera. "Do you mean he's still alive in Brazil?"

"I don't think he's alive," Vera said. "That was more or less a joke."

"A joke?"

"A Hoffa joke," she said. "See, Hoffa was born in Brazil. That's Brazil, Indiana. He told me that. We were talking one day and he told me like it was a joke. 'Maybe I should run away to Brazil,' he said. 'You know, like them bank robbers and embezzlers do. Only I already been there. In fact, I'm from Brazil.'"

She laughed, not an out-loud laugh, but kind of fondly. "He told me all about Brazil, what he could remember. The big joke was that the town doctor, this hick town G.P., had got it into his head that Jimmy's mom wasn't pregnant with him, she just had this tumor. You know how doctors are: they make a diagnosis and you can't get 'em to change it, no matter what. And, of course, the Hoffas were very worried about it, about this tumor. You know, Is it malignant? Am I going to die? How long do I have, Doctor? She'd already had a couple of kids, so she wasn't some naive little teenager. But then, on Valentine's Day she goes into labor and little

Jimmy pops out! Nothing to it! I wonder what the doctor said when he saw the kid." She laughed.

"Hoffa told you this? So you must have had some time to talk."

"A lot of time," she said. "Quiet afternoons at Turtle Lake. But Jimmy was funny about it. He said when he was a kid they used to call him 'Tumor.' I liked him, quite a bit."

"So he's not in Brazil," I said.

She looked at me and shook her head, as if despairing, thinking, *Cops.* "Jimmy used to call me Alma. It was a name that Tyrone had made up, when we first ran into him, a kind of alias. And Tyrone was supposed to be Taylor. Well, after a little while at the lake, that was blown, but Jimmy still called me Alma."

"So where's Hoffa?" I asked, the implacable cop.

"I think Jimmy Hoffa is wherever we want him to be," she said.

"What does that mean?"

"I guess you're kind of literary, or you read a lot, anyway," she said. "That's what Grootka told me, which is why I pulled that Dickens stunt, but have you read much of Graham Greene?"

I said I had. I liked Greene.

"Good. Maybe you can tell me what book it is where he's talking about how real live characters, people, who when they die they become like fiction. All right, I didn't say that right." She thought for a minute, then started again, hunching forward on her Japanese couch thing, very intent.

"The person Greene used as an example was Winston Churchill, who was an actual person, right? But after he died he became like a fictional person, like . . . yeah, Don Quixote. That's the example Greene used. Now even I remember that Quixote is famous for not telling the difference between reality and fiction. Real people, if they are remembered at all after they die, become basically fictional, or at least, not a hell of a lot different from fictional characters."

I nodded. "And . . . ?"

"Well, that's the way it is with Jimmy Hoffa," she said. "He was a real live person, sure, but he soon became a fictional person that we all know, 'Jimmy Hoffa.'" She held up her two hands, framing her head, and flexed her forefingers to indicate quotation marks. "TV comedians still tell jokes about Hoffa, twenty years later, but it's really 'Jimmy Hoffa.'"

"So what's your point?" I asked, obstinately dense.

"The point is," she sighed, "the real Jimmy Hoffa and 'Jimmy Hoffa'"—she gestured again—"are one and the same now. Now that the real Jimmy Hoffa doesn't exist. He has no more validity than the fictional one."

"What an interesting notion," I said, dryly. "But I'm not interested in"—I made the gesture—"'Jimmy Hoffa.' You knew the real Jimmy Hoffa. When did you see him last?"

She was surprisingly crisp: "It was on August 8, 1975, about eleven P.M. He got in a car with Janney Jacobsen and Lonzo and drove away."

"What about Grootka? Where was he?"

"He and Tyrone left at the same time, in Grootka's car."

"So they left you behind, at Lonzo Butterfield's house, at the resort?" She nodded. "Did you know where they were going when they left there?"

"Yeah, they were going up north somewhere. Cadillac, I think. I don't know the actual place."

"What do you think happened up there? What have you been told?"

"I don't know what happened. That's the part Grootka would never tell me."

"But what about your husband, Tyrone?"

"I never saw Tyrone again."

I was stunned. I didn't know what to say. I'd been anticipating meeting Tyrone Addison. I hadn't given it much thought, because it was not imminent, I felt. And anyway, it's not my way: I try not to anticipate too much. But now, what? I felt confused. My mind was suddenly flooded with a million questions, too many to bother with just one, but you have to start with a single step, as I'm sure Books would have told me.

"You never saw Tyrone again? What about the others? Jacobsen?"

Vera stood up and walked across the room. She was a lithe woman, graceful, in excellent physical shape. She cupped one elbow and gazed out the window. "I saw Grootka, several times. But not Janney," she said.

"But . . . didn't you marry him? Aren't you Vera Jacobsen, his wife?"

"I was his wife. Now I am his widow, his relict. Makes me sound as if I still belong to him, doesn't it?" She made a huffing sound that might have been amusement. "If anything, he belongs to me. I have everything he ever had, his name, his money, plus his memory. . . . I'm all that remains of Janney, you might say. I married Janney long before I started living with Tyrone and became *his* true wife, but I never divorced Janney," she said, turning to look at me. "I'm not sure if Grootka knew that, at least not at first. I guess from your expression that if he did know, he didn't tell you."

"I'm just taking a wild guess here," I said, "but from Agge Allyson's appearance, whether you were married to her father or not, she is Tyrone Addison's child."

Vera had turned back to the window, peering down the block. "Still there," she reported. Then she faced me again. "Would you like a cigarette? I smoke ten a day. It's time for number five, already. I may exceed my limit today."

She took a cigarette from a pack on a nearby shelf. She lit it and blew out the smoke. She smiled. "Wrong again, bright boy. About Agge, that is. I wonder if Grootka really knew you very well. Agge isn't Ty's daughter. I had her a couple of years earlier. It was what first caused the split between me and Janney. Agge's dad—and she knows this—is Albert Ayler."

"You're kidding. Another genius."

"Yeah. I liked fucking geniuses. Genii."

She perched on the high bar stool and said, "Dead black genii."

"So, Tyrone is dead."

She clapped her hands in approval, but then the ashes from her cigarette fell and she busied herself putting it out and cleaning it up. Finally, she said, "Well, he's legally dead anyway, not having been heard from for twenty years."

"And Jacobsen? Also dead, then?" When she nodded, I said, "Legally?"

"Yes. A lot of people disappeared in 1975, you know. It was getting like Chile around here. Did you know, one hundred and seventy-six thousand people disappeared in the U.S. that year? Went missing, as the Brits say—I like that phrase. Went missing. I looked it up, the statistic. Heck, thirteen hundred and forty-five disappeared in Michigan!"

"It sounds like a lot," I said. "Did you really look it up?"

"No. I made that up. I wonder how close it is, though."

"So," I said, "Tyrone Addison, Janney Jacobsen—what was his real name, by the way?—and Jimmy Hoffa all disappeared from your view and, I guess, anybody else's, on August 8, 1975?"

"That's right. And many other thousands in the days since, I guess. But everybody's really only interested in Jimmy Hoffa, the famous butt of jokes. It was Janwillem, by the way. He was Dutch. I know Jacobsen isn't a Dutch name, but it was his. I met him in Amsterdam. He was a jazz fan, the way only Europeans are jazz fans. They *adore* jazz musicians. Well, I adored a few myself. Still do."

A telephone rang, or buzzed, somewhere in back. Vera hopped off the stool and darted out of the room, quickly returning with a cordless, which she handed to me. "It's your buddy."

Jimmy had made a quick check with the Ferndale cops. They knew of no reason anybody would be surveilling that house or street. If I wanted, they'd send a cruiser by to roust my nosy parkers. "You get that?" Jimmy exulted. "Nosy parkers. That's pretty good, eh? I told the Ferndale guy—Terry Moser, remember him, from Palmer Park?—that was the best one I'd heard in ages. You want them to come around? Oh, I checked with a couple other guys who might know about drug stuff, but that was just a flying chance. I ran the plates and the car is registered to . . . well, guess."

I hate to guess. I sighed. "Humphrey DiEbola," I said.

"Close," Jimmy said. "It's a company car. Krispee Chips. Still doing business at the same old stand. Want me to send the Ferndale Fuzz around?"

"Yeah, send them by. Ask the guy to get I.D.s on both, if he can."

"You okay? I could send Stanos. He's standing right here. It's on his way home."

"Stanos lives in Ferndale? I thought you said everybody had to live in Detroit."

"Nominally, anyway. No, he lives in Hamtramck. For some reason Hamtramck is deemed to be living in Detroit. Don't ask. He's always lived in Hamtramck. But it's not far to Ferndale."

I thought about it. "I'm in no hurry," I told Jimmy. "If they don't leave before me, I'll give him a call—what's the number?"

I hung up and went to the window. "This could be interesting," I said. "Ferndale is sending a cruiser. While we wait . . ." I glanced over my shoulder, "Do you mind if I make an observation? You don't seem very cracked up about the vanishing of the two men in your life. What did Grootka tell you?"

She came and stood near me, looking over my shoulder. "It's been a long time. A lifetime. I made a life for myself." Her voice was still and collected. The grief must have evaporated long since.

But then she added, "I can still work up a bitch, if you get me started."

We watched the street quietly and her voice curled around my ear. I say that deliberately. It was almost palpable, although I couldn't feel her breath. A woman's voice in a still room on a quiet afternoon. I was very conscious of her standing just inches away.

"I came back to town. Tyrone and I had an apartment in the area below Highland Park, off Hamilton. Agge was at Janney's. She was normally there. He had a very nice woman who looked after her . . . well, you met her."

"Kenty's grandmother?"

"Yes. Sena. I went to Janney's and stayed with Agge and Sena. I thought I'd stay there until the boys returned; it's a much nicer place than the other. But they never returned, and not a word from anyone, of course. I was furious. I told myself that whatever happened, I wasn't living with either of these men anymore. Not Tyrone, who was so obsessed with himself and his music that nothing else really mattered; and definitely not with Janney, who had used his money to keep me around as a link with his darling Tyrone, and an occasional piece of ass. No more."

"You sound like you're still angry," I observed.

"Only when I think about it," she said. "Finally, Grootka came by. He'd been to the apartment first."

I was about to ask what he'd said when the cruiser came slowly down the street. As it passed the driver glanced over at us. He pulled up next to the Continental, a few doors down. Both officers got out, moving cautiously around to either side. No doubt they had already been apprised of the fact that the car belonged to Krispee Chips: it was explicitly a Mobmobile. That means different things to different cops. But it always means caution.

I stepped back to let Vera get a better view. She was intent. The cop on the driver's side approached carefully, his hand on his gun, as if casually resting it there. He leaned over from the rear seat position and said something. The window came down and they talked. Then the cop stepped back as the driver got out. On the other side a similar scene was enacted. Two young men in casual wear stood on either side of the car. They were white, about twenty or twenty-five, seemingly unresisting, even cheerful. They showed their wallets to the officers. They got back in the car. The cruiser backed up to allow them to pull out, then followed them down the block and beyond our vision.

"Where are they going?" Vera asked me.

"Nowhere," I said. "The cops just ran them off. I expect to hear from the cops shortly."

In fact, the cruiser came back down the street within minutes and pulled up in front. The driver got out and came to the door. I greeted him and invited him in. "This is Mrs. Jacobsen," I said to introduce them. He was a nice-looking fellow, white, about six feet tall with that little reddish moustache that so many cops seem to like.

"They're a couple of wise guys," he told us, "right out of the movies. Names on the licenses are . . ." He looked at his notebook. "Michael Arthur Simi and Alessandro Gee-ah-cammo Abb— Abba-bob . . . what do you make of that?" He showed me the name.

"Abbaglione? Something like that. Both from Detroit, hunh? Same address? That's—"

"Krispee Chips," he finished for me. "Must be a finishing school, eh? They have a dormitory, nice gym facilities, I hear . . . swimming pool. Of course, these young men were surprised to learn that they were making the housewives nervous. Sorry ma'am." He nodded to Vera. "I had to tell them something. But I didn't say where the complaint came from."

"Did they ask?" I asked.

"No. No they didn't. They said they were just having a talk and they had parked in a quiet place. Didn't mean to disturb the peace. They were leaving."

"They Americans?" I asked.

"Well sir, they got Michigan driver's licenses, but they don't talk American. European, I'd say. Speak good English, though. Bit of an accent, but not bad."

I thanked him and sent him on his way. He said they'd keep a rolling surveillance on the house and street, to see if the Continental returned, but I could see that his heart wasn't in it, and I didn't think it called for any encouragement. Wouldn't hurt, though, if they cruised by now and again.

When he'd gone I agreed with Vera that her suspicions had been well-founded. Of course, it was possible they were watching some other house . . .

"Oh, don't be ridiculous," she snorted.

"Well, tell me what Grootka said."

"He didn't say much, that's for sure. I was pretty distraught at the time, of course. He just tried to calm me down, while letting me know that Ty and Janney weren't coming back. I don't know." She looked pensive. "I don't suppose it's much different for war widows, or women whose husbands have died in a plane crash. No." She shook her head, matter-of-factly. "It can't really be any different. I'd been worried, but Grootka was pretty straight about it, pretty firm. I suppose I should have been grateful—at least I didn't waste any more time waiting."

"What the hell did he tell you?" I demanded.

"He said it hadn't gone right. He was sorry, but they wouldn't be coming back. He said I shouldn't ask any more questions. There wasn't anything useful he could tell me. He'd brought Tyrone's soprano sax. That was all he could save."

"He said that? All he could save? What does that mean? A fire? A wreck?"

"He wouldn't say. I think he said, All he could save. I can't be positive now. It's what I remember, but maybe I just put it that

way to myself. It was what I had of Tyrone. And I don't have that.
I gave it to Grootka. He was grateful, as I knew he would be."

I was aggravated. I think that's the best I can say. Not quite
angry, because I had no real object for my anger, but more than
peeved. "He never gave you any hint? No word about Hoffa? Did
they meet with Carmine?"

"Nothing. He just gave me some money, a pretty nice amount,
which he said was from Tyrone, and the sax. Said it was all he had
for me. Yeah, I think now that it was, 'All he had.' Not 'saved.' Yeah,
that's it," she said. "He said, 'This is all I have for you.'"

"How much money?"

"It was about ten thousand dollars, in fairly large bills, in a
roll. I knew it wasn't from Tyrone—how could it be?—but must have
been from Janney. He liked to carry a roll, sometimes, though I never
saw one with that much cash. So anyway, I knew Janney was dead,
too. He wouldn't give Grootka any money for me."

"And Grootka didn't say what had happened? Didn't
explain?"

"When I asked him what happened he said, 'Sorry, babe.
Things didn't go right. Nothing went the way it was supposed
to. They ain't comin' back.' And he never would tell me any more
about it."

"That was it?"

"That was it. Once in a while I'd bump into him in a club
where there was some good jazz and we'd talk. Usually, after one of
those times, he'd call me back in a day or two, say how good it was
to see me, and all that. And then if I asked about what had happened, insisted that I deserved to know, he'd say that maybe it would
all come out someday. In the meantime, I should keep my mouth
shut. 'For how long?' I'd asked. And he'd tell me how it was best
left up to his good friend Mulheisen. Old Mulheisen would figure it
all out when the time came.

"Then one day about four or five years ago he called and said he'd like to come by. He brought this notebook. It was all wrapped up, just like that. He said I should keep it in some safe place, maybe even a safe-deposit box. He said you would come for it one of these days. When you needed it. But in the meantime, if I got into a jam, or if I noticed people hanging around, strangers—like those two guys—then I should try to get in touch with you. But he was pretty spooky on this point. He said there were people in your department, or bailiwick, whatever it is, who couldn't be trusted. I shouldn't just go and make a complaint, because then there would be this formal investigation and all kinds of hell might break loose and you would certainly get bumped off the case. He gave me your home phone number, just for emergency, but I lost that a long time ago."

"Where did you keep the notebook?" I asked.

"In the refrigerator. That's why it's in that plastic zip bag. I took it out a couple of days ago, to see if it had been damaged."

"Did you read it?"

"I tried. Well, yeah, I read it. A long time ago. The hand-writing's not bad, though the spelling is bizarre! But I got through it."

"What did you think?"

"It's bullshit." She was firmly dismissive. "It's all Grootka's bull. Something happened, sure, but I'll bet it wasn't what he tells. How much of this stuff have you read?"

"Four books like this," I told her. "I presume this one picks up the story where the last one left off, which is when they are arranging to meet Carmine."

"Do you believe it?"

"Why not?" I asked. "Why don't you tell me your version, so I can compare?"

Here I can confess that the "Prologue," which I've provided as a simple narrative of the events before I was exposed to the note-books, and before Grootka came onto the scene, is a reconstruction of events *as seems likely to me*. This reconstruction needn't be taken as literal truth or fact, but it seems to me to be the most plausible scenario. It is based largely on the story I was now told by Vera Jacobsen. There's no point in repeating her version, which doesn't differ remarkably.

We compared notes, and her major objection was to Grootka's depiction of her doing a striptease to entertain the Mob guys and distract them from searching for Hoffa.

"My God!" she exclaimed. "They came in there, leering and snuffling, eager to find out what was going on. They'd heard something for sure, but I had a feeling that they didn't really know anything. Anyway, what were they gonna do? Look under the bed? Well, if they had, they'd have found Jimmy, because he was under there. But they were mainly just trying to bluff Lonzo into giving the guy up. I got fed up and grabbed my towel and went out back to catch a little sun. We had a nice little sunning place back there, out of the way, but handy so I could hear Tyrone if he wanted me. And then this maniac, Grootka, pops up out of the bushes! He's waving a rod and his eyeballs are popping out, gawking at my tits!"

The image was amusing, with its suggestion of Grootka priapically "waving a rod," especially as Vera unconsciously massaged her left breast (I realized that even at fifty-eight, or whatever she was, she was not beyond seductiveness.) But then I recalled with a start that a man had died.

"Yes," she nodded, sobered herself. "A thug. Never a more apt word," she added, an edge of derision creeping back in. "And, of course, at first we thought Janney'd been shot."

This was a point I hadn't gotten clear from Grootka's text. Had Janney been there all along? Or had he just arrived? With Carmine, for instance?

No, no, she assured me. Janney had been there earlier. A couple of days earlier. He had come up to talk to Tyrone about the recording gig, in L.A. On that occasion, now that she thought about it—"It was all so long ago, it's not easy to remember the exact sequence"—it seemed that Janney had left to go back to town without knowing about Hoffa's presence. Yes, she was pretty sure of it, now. Hoffa had stayed in his bedroom.

"And he had returned when?" I asked.

"Just at that time, just when Carmine and Humphrey had left. I went back in the house and Janney must have come walking up the driveway when that Cooze guy saw him. Cooze would have killed him, but Grootka shot first."

And Lonzo, I wondered? When did Lonzo get wind of Hoffa's presence?

Vera didn't know. He just showed up one night. She thought that he hadn't known about Hoffa being there, beforehand, but somebody had told him that his nephew and his wife were staying in his cabin, and they hadn't asked permission. "Although I thought Tyrone had," she declared. "He said he had. But I'll tell you what," she mused, "Lonzo was always after my ass. If he knew I was up there, he'd be there like a shot. It had happened before, and maybe Tyrone didn't tell him because he knew he'd come sniffing around . . . not that Tyrone paid much attention to other guys' interest in me."

They couldn't hide Hoffa from Lonzo, of course, but she said he was cooperative and he did keep his boys out of the house. In answer to my next question she said she did not think that Lonzo had informed to Carmine. "If he had told them, they wouldn't have been poking around," she said, logically. "They'd have just grabbed Jimmy and probably shot the whole bunch of us on the spot. But they didn't really know."

"So who told?" I asked.

She shrugged. "Janney, of course. Trouble was, he didn't know for sure, and he was too chickenshit to come with them in case it didn't turn out."

It seemed that Jacobsen had long been dealing with the Mob in one way or another. Besides his printing business, he had gotten involved in a nightclub and various other enterprises that had brought him into contact with the Mob. He wasn't exactly a Mobster himself, or even a Mob wannabe, she thought, but more of a guy who was intrigued and excited by Mobsters and liked to hang around them, to pretend that he was "connected." He had a kind of innocence, or perhaps it was his European posture, that may have led him to think that he could flirt with the bad guys and not get dirty.

There was an edge of bitterness in her voice now, and she seemed aware of it. "Grootka," she said, as if clearing her throat. "If only he hadn't stuck his big nose into all this. What did *we* do wrong?" She looked at me, but I had no answer for her. I knew Grootka. "We didn't do any wrong," she insisted. "We were just trying to help. If Grootka hadn't come along, maybe Hoffa would have gone home, eventually, and everything would have been all right. He'd probably be alive today, and so would Tyrone, and Janney.

"But," she said, crossing her arms and assuming a firm, no-nonsense expression, "it didn't happen that way. Now I've gone on to other things, a different life. I'm not unhappy with it. But I can't help feeling that Grootka screwed everything up, and I just wish I had him here right now to give him a piece of my mind. You knew him, you were his friend." She looked at me with a curious expression.

"I wasn't exactly his friend," I protested.

"Exactly," she agreed. "You couldn't be his friend. He chose you. Like he chose Books, or Tyrone. He decided you were somebody worth wasting his time on and so he imposed himself on you. He used to reconstruct my sentences, when I spoke to him. 'What you mean is,' he'd say, and come up with something I would never say. But it was close enough to what I meant that it wasn't worth struggling against him to correct it. He was always doing shit like that. The guy was oblivious to other people, in a way. All he knew was his own point of view, which he assumed everybody else was interested in and would naturally accede to."

"You put it so well," I said.

"No, I don't." She sighed. "He was a complex man. He liked people, like you and Tyrone, Books. I think he liked me, too. And those he liked he tended to think a little too highly of, if you know what I mean. Maybe it's an extension of his egotism: if you were his friend you must be great, or if he was going to waste time on you, you must be something."

I was interested in her analysis and quite in agreement. "Did he choose you?" I asked.

"I suppose so. He used to praise me, not just to my face, but to other people. It could be embarrassing."

"I know that one," I said.

"And then he'd hit on me."

"Hit you?" That didn't sound like Grootka, brutal as he could be.

"No, no—hit *on* me. He'd want to fuck."

"And did you?"

"Oh, sure. You want to know what it was like? No? Well, it was . . . vigorous. Yes, that's it. It wasn't bad. Very vigorous and I had my pleasure, which I think he liked the idea of, although he acted like he didn't care if I got off or not." She shook her head, not quite ruefully.

"But eventually you left Detroit," I said. "You started producing records. How did you get into that?"

"It was a natural development form Janney's business. Not the printing business, which I sold, but he had independently produced jazz recordings before, in Holland and here. I knew something about it, I was well acquainted with the jazz scene . . . it was natural. I've done well with it." She was matter-of-fact, but you could see she was proud of the accomplishment.

"Where did you get this name, Hastily Improvised Productions?" I asked.

"It makes sense," she explained. "I specialize in Free jazz, improvised music."

"Does that sell? I mean, do you make a living at it?"

"It's all right," she said. "I don't think you can get rich producing art in America, but if you work hard you can do all right. Anyway, I have plenty of money, enough for me anyway, and I can help out Agge, but she never needs help." She said this with an edge of pride.

"She seems quite competent," I agreed.

"Oh, she'll do well. She always has. She's one of those kids who just . . ." And I was treated to a long and happy exposition of the merits of Agge Allyson. I wondered if my mother had ever bored her friends with my triumphs.

11

Kiss Your Axe
Good-bye

Grootka's Notebook, #5

We pulled outta Nigger Heaven about 11 P.M., a little over a week after Hoffa dropped outta sight. We was gonna drive up north, and it wasn't a good idea driving in daytime on the interstate, 'cause somebody could of recognized Hoffa. So we took two cars, with Hoffa and Jacobsen and Lonzo in Lonzo's car, and me and Tyrone in my car. We stayed pretty close together, but not acting like we was together, and in a couple hours we were driving through Clare, which is a nice little town up where the woods begin. It's off the interstate, and from here we hadda drive about forty miles to find another back road.

[*Here Grootka provides a map, which is of questionable value and not worth reproducing. It is possible to pinpoint the exact location of the cabin, however, using the map and internal evidence of the notebooks.—M.*]

The way we set up the deal was, Carmine and the Fat Man [*Humphrey DiEbola.—M.*] would go to a motel in Cadillac that Hoffa knew about, that same night. When we were ready we would call the motel and tell them where to meet us. My plan was we would get into the hunting cabin, look the terrain over, and some-

time the next day we'd call and it would only take them about a
half hour, maybe a little more, to come out and meet. But I sure as
hell didn't want them showing up with a bunch of goons, and I
didn't want 'em coming before we was ready.

The cabin was all right, if you don't mind being out in the
middle of a goddamn wilderness, which ain't my idea of paradise. It
was down a dirt road, about a quarter of a mile from a county
blacktop. It was completely in the trees, not on a lake or nothing,
so there wasn't no neighbors. Cess Morgan must of been a complete
pig, Sister Mary Herman would have straightened him out, but we
got the place cleaned up. Anyways, it's down this road, which is
almost roofed over with trees, which are these hardwoods, I don't
know what kind, but a lot of leaves and it's cool, although later,
when it got hot, there wasn't a lot of breeze around the cabin. But it
never got too hot.

It's just a hunting cabin, pretty primitive. One room with a
sink and a table and cupboards on one end. The sink has a hand
pump, so you got running water, more or less, right in the house.
Pretty modern for ol' Cess and his hunting buddies, I guess. And he
even built a bathroom on the back, instead of the old shitter, which
was still over by the edge of the clearing. The toilet you gotta pour a
bucket of water in the cistern to flush. But it works okay. Better
than a outhouse, anyway. And there's a propane tank for the
kitchen range, which is pretty nice, and a space heater that would
run you out of there in below-zero temperatures. But it's a hunting
cabin, so it has to have a little stone fireplace and, naturally, Mr.
Jimmy Hoffa loves a fuckin' fire, so we gotta make a fire because it's
a little cool at night, and anyway, a fire is always nice. With a little
Jim Beam, naturally.

Oh yeah. No electricity. No phone. He had these kerosene
lamps with glass chimneys that I kinda liked. Kind of a nice light
and it gives off a faint odor that ain't actually too bad.

This clearing is about, oh, the size of a couple of house lots in town, and then the woods start. The road makes a couple jinks, so you can't see very far down it. In the morning, me and Lonzo took a long walk around the woods. There wasn't much to see. It was just woods, pretty big trees. From driving around and all, it looked to me that this was the only house in about a square mile. There was a farmhouse further down, near a crossroads, but too far away to be any concern. The cabin sat in a state forest, there wasn't any logging going on, no farming, no ponds or lakes to attract summer folks. Only good for one thing, and that was for about two weeks in November when guys come up from Detroit to hunt deer. It was probably not even legally Cess's, was my guess. [*It belonged to a relative of Morgan's, who was apparently unaware that the cabin still stood and was in use for hunting.—M.*]

It looked pretty simple to me. I figured Carmine and the Fat Man would drive out with a stooge or two, to meet Jacobsen, who would be waiting at the end of the road. They would not know that I was even anywhere around. I would of sent Lonzo to meet them, but I thought him being a Negro it might attract attention from passersby, in case there was any, which you never know. Anyways, Jacobsen would hail them down when they come down the black-top and get in the car with them to ride back on the dirt road. About halfway to the cabin, which is a furlong, if I remember my days at Hazel Park raceway—about halfway down the backstretch. You can't see the road or the house from there and I would have Lonzo's car parked across the road, so nobody could drive right up to the cabin.

Lonzo would be there, at the car. Carmine or the Fat Man could go up to the cabin on foot. Whichever. Lonzo and Jacobsen would let the guys know that the woods was full of Hoffa people, but they didn't want no trouble. Course, they don't know I'm even there. Tyrone I didn't want to get in no trouble, so I had him take my car and drive to a little town, I think it's called Faraway, and make the call to the motel in Cadillac that would start the show. Then, if everything is on, he should make sure the tank is full of gas and drive back to let us know. I'd wait for him by the road. Then he should go on down the blacktop, not toward Cadillac, the other direction—toward Faraway, and then at noon (or whatever time we agree on) he should turn around and drive back. By that time Carmine and them should be there. If there was nobody at the cabin drive, that meant Carmine and them had already gone up and he should park in a place we found about a hundred feet down the road, but off where you wouldn't notice the car unless you was looking for it. From there he could watch the road to make sure there wasn't no surprise reinforcements coming along five minutes behind. If somebody did show, or it didn't look right for some reason, he should blow his horn—his car horn, not the soprano sax he brung along.

If he heard trouble—I mean shooting—I told him to wait right there by the car for fifteen minutes. Don't come in to look around. If I or somebody didn't come along by then to tell him it was all right, there wasn't anything he could do to help us. He should take off and just keep going.

"To where?" he asks me.

"To San Francisco," I told him. " 'Cause if this don't go right, they're gonna be looking for Tyrone Addison for a long, long time. They won't quit."

But I didn't expect nothing to go wrong, really. Carmine or the Fat Man would play it cool on this first visit. They'd want to get a good look at the situation. Then, the second trip would be the dangerous one. Which is why I told Hoffa to do his best to not blow his top, to keep his cool and just talk it out with them. I didn't want no second meeting.

"Talk *at* Carmine," I told him, "but remember that you're talking *to* the Fat Man. He's the one you gotta convince."

"I thought just one of them would come up to the cabin," he says.

"That's what we say, but they'll say no, they both gotta talk to you, and Carmine ain't going up there by hisself. So we give in, but no hoods. Just them two. Anyways, maybe you should come down from the cabin, to greet them."

"Won't that be dangerous?" he says. "I'm not scared, but what if—"

I knew he wasn't scared and I told him so, and it was damn dangerous. One a them hoods might have a fucking tommy gun or something and start chopping wood. But I didn't think so. Anyways, they didn't have no reason to be afraid of us, I figured, so they wouldn't be throwing too much muscle around when they didn't know the lay of the land. I thought it would be all right if he came down from the cabin, but stopped just where they could see him. That'd be a few hundred feet maybe, too far for a decent pistol shot, but close enough to yell hello and wave for them to come up. And wait for them.

That seemed okay to Hoffa. "I'll hold my hands up, waving," he says, "but showing 'em that I ain't armed. I'm welcoming them. And don't worry, I won't lose my temper. This is important for me, for my family, and for the union."

"That's the stuff," I said. But I was bullshitting. It didn't look good to me at all. I figured it would all go wrong, every fuckin' step. Something stupid would happen and everybody would get killed. But, what the fuck, it looked like an interestin' mornin'. Hell, maybe we'd get lucky and it'd go at least half-right, which is: they come, they look the place over, maybe even get far enough to see Jimmy waving hello, and then for some reason say they gotta come back.

I'm figuring on that, at least. They'll want to control the play, not let Jimmy set the table. There was a good chance that they wouldn't even be at the motel, or only the Fat Man would be there. In other words, stall for time, try to figure out where this was all going down, see if they couldn't load the dice somehow.

If they wasn't at the motel, or didn't wanta drive out and meet, wanted Jimmy to come to them, or one of us, probably Lonzo, to come and set up a "more convenient" meeting—maybe one of them is sick, say—then Tyrone would tell 'em politely he'd have to check and would call back later that afternoon. Then he should come back and we'd figure the next stage.

So we had a nice night. I had Lonzo checking around outside, on guard duty, then I took over. Tyrone and Jacobsen alternated taking a long walk around, but keeping out of sight, in case anybody came along. They were armed, but what was the point? Neither one a them had ever fired a gun in their lives, they admitted, but it might help if they at least showed a gun. I gave them each a .32 auto, little throw-down guns that I'd picked up here and there, over the years, which they could carry in their pockets without too much trouble.

But me and Lonzo were heeled. I offered him a .45 auto, but he comes up with a Llama 9 mm, which he likes. He's got some extra clips for it. Plus he brung a 12-gauge pump from home. Me, I've got the Old Cat plus a few other miscellaneous pieces. So I figure we're okay for a first meeting, anyway. I offered a piece to Hoffa, but he says, "No way. This is s'posta be a peace conference, not a war council."

We was sitting around the fire, having a snort of bourbon, smoking a coupla stogies, and I axed him what he's gonna tell Carmine and the Fat Man. He's gonna have this all talked out by afternoon, he says. He's gonna stay clear of the details of any kind of deal they got with Fitz, but he wants them to know that he's got nothing against 'em, they always been able to work together and he wants to go on working together, but he knows in his heart that Fitz is not doing the union any good. The membership is disillusioned when they see the kind of shit Fitz pulls, and he don't blame nobody, but when the membership starts droppin' everybody has got a problem, 'cause pretty soon you ain't got no union. So they gotta work out their differences, but he thinks they'll see that it's worth their while to have a strong leadership back, and he'll go on TV and tell the fucking world that he's okay, no problem, nothing to do with the Mob, he just had to get away and try to figure out, for himself and for the union, what the future needed, and he decided that it needed him to be back running the Teamsters. Amen.

"Good luck," I told him.

Later I went out with Tyrone and he brung along his soprano. We both played on it, in the woods, but it seemed a little eerie and I got thinking that maybe it would attract attention, so we quit. It was dark as hell in them woods, so we walked down the drive to the blacktop, where at least you could see the sky, which was crawling with stars, I never seen so many.

I'd been thinking about Tyrone, where he fit into all this. I told him that no matter what happened tomorrow he hadda get the hell outta this. He and Vera fucked up the minute they picked up Hoffa. I knew they had got some idea that somehow they was gonna make something out of this, some money, big money, which would help them get a record out or something. But that was bullshit. There was no way that getting involved could do anything but screw him and Vera. My advice, I said, was to just take off, once he done what I asked him to do.

"You mean just split?" he says. "But what about you, what if you and the guys need help, need a car?"

"We got a car," I said. "The only reason I insisted on bringing two cars was for this. I told you the plan there, in front of everybody, but that was bullshit. You split. Once you come back and let me know that the deal is running, you split. You ain't no use to us after that, anyways. If everything goes fine I'll ride back to the city with Jim and Lonzo and Janney. They'll be a little pissed at you taking off, but I'll explain to them what I'm telling you now, that I told you to go. Not only that, I gave you the money."

"Hoffa's money?"

"Yeah. I took it out of his bag, a few days ago. There's two hundred thousand dollars. I left him with two grand, wrapped around some funny money that Books got for me. You take it."

He argued, but he was just a kid. What could he say against me? Then I told him the toughest part. He hadda forget about Vera. I knew it was hard, I said, but it had to be.

"There's no way out of it," I told him. "You guys fucked up. No matter what happens now, Tyrone Addison is dead. You seen too much and you don't have no power, nothing to protect you, nothing to offer. You can be dead dead, or you can be fake dead, but after tomorrow there ain't gonna be no Tyrone Addison no more, so you can forget about that part of your life."

"What about you?" he says. "You blew that guy away, that Cooze."

"I'm Grootka," I said. "They don't fuck with Grootka. I'm more trouble than I'm worth. Plus, they think they know me. They figure they can deal with me. I'm in their world, part of their plans. You ain't. You're a jive-ass nigger bopper, no offense. You ain't nothing to them but danger. So at best, if everything goes down like good grits, you don't have no future. And Vera don't have no future with you."

This was what he really couldn't take, and you can't blame him. But he must of known, they both must of known. If he cut loose from her they prob'ly wouldn't bother her. The Mob don't take chicks seriously. If she became a problem, sure, they'd zip her shut in a heartbeat. But if Tyrone fades and she steers clear, keeps her mouth shut . . . they might survive. I explained it to him, over and over. He wouldn't buy it.

But I insisted. We were standing in the middle of a empty road in a fucking forest in northern fucking Michigan and owls are hooting whenever we quit yelling and I'll tell ya, Mul, I was a little bit, I don't know, not scared, but I'm not so great in the fucking woods at night, it ain't my scene. I'd rather be on Dexter Avenue at four in the morning with a bunch of drunk spades who think I been hiding the bottle. But I put the heat on the kid until he finally broke down and said, "All right, if the deal goes bad, *then* I'll split."

"And don't go near Vera," I said. "Don't even call her. She'll figure it out. She ain't a infant. If I get out of this, I'll talk to her. But you and she are done. Got it?"

"Unless everything's cool," Tyrone says.

He's still got this idea that if Hoffa can pull this off then he and Vera can go back to their old life and he'll play music and make a hit record and they'll get rich . . . and it just goes on and on. Bullshit.

The next morning me and Lonzo and the others took our walk and figured out the system, like I said, and I sent Tyrone off about eleven. Eleven-thirty he's back, says he talked to Carmine, who agreed to everything and they'd be here in about a half hour. So I sent him off down the road and I take up my spot, which is near the dirt track, in the woods. I can keep an eye on the road, see if there's any other vehicles, make sure Tyrone is in place so he can watch and blow his horn.

High noon and here comes Tyrone, cruising slowly up the county road, but no Carmine. Tyrone eases by, looking at Janney, who shrugs and waves. As Tyrone gets near me, I step out of the woods and wave him on, but Tyrone just proceeds up the road and pulls into the hiding spot we found. I see he's gonna play it that way, so I sigh and move back into my observation spot.

It's another full half hour before Carmine's limo shows. I
can't say I was surprised. Another fifteen or twenty minutes and I'd
of called it off, 'cause it meant they was setting something up. But a
half hour is not enough to bitch about. Anyways, here they come,
tooling up the blacktop in a Town Car, or whatever them things
are, but it's all tinted windows and I can't see shit. It ain't like when
they came in at Nigger Heaven. Jacobsen hails them and they pull
over and the window comes down, a little. Jacobsen says his piece,
pointing up the road, then the back door opens and he gets in. I'm
watching from inside the woods, not fifty feet away, but they'd
never spot me. Still, it makes me nervous, the car just sitting there
like that, half on the blacktop and half into the drive, the seconds
ticking by like minutes. I'm starting to get interested, wondering
what they got to talk so long with Janney for?

But, finally, just when I'm about to go back and signal Hoffa to
get lost, the deal's not gonna happen, the car eases into the dirt track
and begins to trundle up toward the cabin. I wait a few seconds and
step out to the road. From where he's parked, Tyrone should be able
to see me. I signal "okay," with a clenched fist, and for the last time
I motion to him to hit the road, waving him off, but there's no
response. I look around. I don't see no other cars, nothing.

Oh well, I think, it's his funeral. And I hustle back on up
through the woods. I make pretty good time and I'm there to see
Lonzo standing behind his car, which is parked across the dirt track,
the shotgun out of sight but his right hand is hanging down, and I
figure he's got the gun in it. The limo is standing there, twenty feet
from him, and Jacobsen is standing outside the open back door. It
looks like he's relaying messages back and forth from the guys inside
to Lonzo. I hear him yell out, "They want to see your weapon!"

Lonzo hoists the 12-gauge with one hand, then sets it down.
"Ain't nobody gon' get hurt!" he yells back. "We all be cool. You
tell him, Jake! They cool, we cool!"

And then, lo and behold, Carmine and the Fat Man get out on either side. The Fat Man is wearing a black suit, in August. It must be like a fucking oven, I figure, except of course they got air-conditioning. But outside it ain't air-conditioned. It's at least eighty-five and not a breath. Humid. It's shady, though, so I ain't sweating, but I ain't wearing no black suit, just my light summer gray, and anyway I never sweat. The Fat Man has also got on shades and a hat. He looks like a fucking cartoon Mobster. Carmine is wearing a pale green jumpsuit kind of leisure outfit, with brown-and-white shoes. On his head he's got some kind of fucking golf hat, and shades, of course.

A couple of goons get out of the back, too. Young guys in dark slacks, sport coats, sport shirts. Shades, natch. And they got Uzis. Holding 'em muzzle up, like the Secret Service guys do, as if they wanta keep the fucking BBs from falling outta the barrel.

Which leaves at least an armed driver and another armed man in the front seat, but you can't see them, it's tinted. That's a lotta firepower, but no more than I expected, and if nobody else comes to the party I guess we can play. Anyway, Lonzo knows what to do.

By now he's got the 12-gauge in his hands, resting the barrel on the roof of his car. But he's friendly, he ain't pointing it at no one, just showing it. "Only one comes forward! You other guys, get back in the car. Don't want no trouble!"

The goons look at Carmine. The Fat Man says something I can't hear, and then the goons get back in the car, but they leave the door open, not wide open, but ajar. Lonzo yells to shut the doors, and they do. Which leaves Carmine and the Fat One, plus Janney, standing. That ain't one man, but Lonzo shrugs. "Okay!" he yells, over his shoulder.

Mr. Jimmy Hoffa comes down the path. He stops and waves. He's got on a shirt that's too big for him, must be one a Lonzo's, a

Hawaiian shirt with the tails out. "Hey, Carmine!" he yells. "Humphrey! Where's Tony?"

Carmine says something to the Fat Man, who has strolled around the car and now is standing next to him. Then Carmine yells out, "Tony wouldn't come. He's chickenshit. He's scared of you and"—he points around to the woods—"your fucking trucker buddies! He thinks you're gonna beat him up!" He laughs, very loudly. The Fat Man laughs too, but he's looking around. Jimmy laughs.

"Hey, Jimbo!" Carmine yells out. "How you doing? They treating you all right up here? Whatta you got, some bimbos back in the woods? What izzit, Indian squaws or something?"

They all laugh.

Jimmy comes down a little closer. "Nah, it's just a cabin. You been here, ain't you? It's Cess Morgan's old place. C'mon up. We can talk. C'mon. There's nobody out there." He half-turns, waiting, waving his hand at the woods to indicate that it's empty.

"You sure?" Carmine yells, gawking around, almost clowning—he's got his hand up to the bill of his golf cap, like a Indian scout. But you know, Mul, even here in the middle of the fucking North Woods, Carmine looks like a million bucks. Even in that stupid suit, which it looks like a fag put on him. He's lean, not old, not young, got that steel-wool hair that looks like it's ironed on his neat little skull—Perry Como hair. But even with those Italian designer glasses on, I can see he's nervous. He mutters something over his shoulder to the Fat Man, then he calls out, "I think I'll stay here, Jimbo! I don't feel too good. I had a shitty breakfast. These shitkickers up here, they don't know how to make a breakfast— fucking pancakes like lead. I'm gonna stay in the car. You and Umberto can settle this."

Carmine looks yearningly at Hoffa. You can tell he don't wanta be out here in this bullshit woods. He wants to be on a golf course, or on his yacht in the Detroit River, or in Hawaii.

Hoffa stands there, his fists on his hips, shaking his head. Then he shrugs and waves the Fat Man on. Carmine steps back to the car and opens the door to get in.

That's when I seen the first guy. I don't know how many there was. Not many, I guess. Maybe only two or three. They were in the woods, between the car and the cabin. They must of come the back way, but they must of known where they was going. There was no sound from the road, so maybe they got Tyrone first. But I think they knew where they was going.

The guy I seen was beyond Jimmy, just stepping out of the woods. He was maybe twenty feet from Hoffa and he had a rifle, which he had brought up to his cheek, aiming. I shot him clean with the Swedish K I'd parked in the woods for myself. He went flying back, arms wide, the rifle tossed, and he lay there. Just a single shot. But I switched to auto right away.

The Fat Man whirls around. He's got a revolver, nickel-plated. He shoots Jacobsen right in the face. The two punks bounce out. One shoves Carmine into the back, the other grabs at the Fat Man, trying to wrestle him into the car and in the bustle knocking the gun out of his hand, which it gets kicked under the car. Then the two kids slam the doors and jump out of the way so the car can back up at very high, dirt-throwing speed, and they're crouched in that movie position, both hands on the Uzi, blowing away the bark off the trees on either side. Obviously they got no idea where I am.

I ran out one clip on them, and believe me, that goddamn K is a cannon, though of course there's so many trees, you're not gonna hit anything like that. But it puts the kids back out of the way, retreating back down the track. So I run to help out Jimmy, slapping a new clip into the K. Lonzo has disappeared, I notice, lying half under the car and not moving. I stop on the edge of the road to hose the boys back and I see that the limo has got away.

Then I look up the other way and there's Jimmy blazing away with a revolver at the trees.

I don't know where that gun came from, but it didn't help Mr. James R. Hoffa. Because a second later he was pert-near cut in two by a hell of a fucking cannon, from somewhere not too far back in the woods. I mean, that was ordnance. I don't mean like a law, but like artillery, except this kind of ordnance is laying down the law. It sounded too big to be portable and it actually made everybody stop firing when it quit, because you didn't want to be on the same field with that kind of shit.

Anyway, it didn't speak again and there was Jimmy Hoffa splattered all over the drive. And pretty soon you could hear the little birds calling. Be a good place to take your mother some time, Mul. Maybe she could tell me what that bird is that goes *witchety-witchety*.

12

Lonzo's Blues

I think it frequently happens that a person about whom we have been thinking is soon enough thrust upon our attention for other reasons. In this case, I had been anxious, after talking to Vera Jacobsen, to interview Lonzo Butterfield and Books Meldrim. The former for whatever information he could give me regarding Vera and Tyrone, as well as Grootka and Hoffa and Jacobsen, of course. The latter because I felt now that he was the silent partner in this entire episode, as well as its aftermath.

First things first. Earlier, I had tracked down Lonzo Butterfield. It wasn't difficult. He wasn't in hiding or anything. He was in a rest home and not in very good shape. The home was off Davison, near Van Dyke, not far from Forest Lawn cemetery, and not more than twenty minutes from Vera's place in Ferndale. It wasn't a bad place, as these places go, but it wouldn't have made much difference if it had been. Lonzo wasn't paying too much attention; he was kind of self-absorbed.

He was just a shadow of the Lonzo I used to know. Instead of looming about six feet, six inches or more, and weighing three hundred plus, he seemed to be about five-ten, and he sure didn't weigh any more than a hundred and fifty pounds. He harbored an incredible mélange of disorders, from diabetes to a cirrhotic liver, including various tumors, some of them malignant; he had suffered at least one mild stroke, partial renal failure, a cardiac arrest or two, you name it. The resident doctor (or perhaps he was only an occasional visitor, it wasn't clear) was a young man of thirty who seemed almost proud of Lonzo, as a kind of catalog of disease and decrepitude. "The man's a walkin' Dorland's Cyclopedia," he declared.

"Walking?" I gaped at Lonzo, who was admittedly mobile, but bent over and pushing a wheeled walker that also carried a couple of bottles of fluids that were tubed into his arms, as well as sacs that were receptacles for tubes issuing from his legs and abdomen.

"Shufflin', then," the doctor conceded. "But, what the heck, he's breathing."

He was breathing, but barely, and he wasn't talking much. I had remembered him as a dark-skinned man, but he seemed faded into a khaki color, except for around his eyes, which were as dark as the old tenor man Ben Webster's. His mind seemed in gear. He appeared to recognize me and he certainly lit up when I mentioned Grootka.

"Saymalie," he breathed. We had made it back to his bed in his little room. The room was plastered with old posters of Coltrane and Miles Davis, and there was a safe on the floor, a square green metal box of heavy gauge steel that was not only padlocked but was actually secured to the floor with heavy chains that led from welded rings in the steel box to steel rings or loops mounted onto the floor with heavy lag bolts.

He repeated the word or phrase until I grasped the meaning: he meant that Grootka had saved his life. I supposed that part of the problem in understanding him was the bullet that had taken a chunk of his tongue and broken his jaw. Now that I thought about it, the two or three times that I had met Lonzo he had been a little inarticulate, but I had attributed that to alcohol. And I recalled another thing: that in each case it was Grootka who had brought us together. So now I saw that Grootka had meant for me to meet Lonzo, to get to know him.

"Grootka saved your life?" I said. "When they killed Hoffa, you mean?"

His eyes grew round as saucers. "Whirjoogeddat?" he croaked.

"Grootka's notes. He left me his notebooks." I showed one of them to him. "Tells the whole story. You, Grootka, Tyrone, Janney Jacobsen."

He shook his head, his withered lips in a grimace. "Jake," he said. "Asso."

"Jake was an asshole?"

Lonzo nodded. "Tole." He nodded more. "Jake tole."

"Told who?"

"Ca-mine." Lonzo squeezed his eyes tightly. "Gruuk, Gruu-ook, Grrk. Grrka," he shook his head slowly.

"Grootka didn't know? He didn't know that Jacobsen was the one who told Carmine where Hoffa was?" Lonzo nodded. "He thought it was you, didn't he?" Lonzo nodded more. "Did you know? At the time?" He shrugged. "You suspected, but you didn't know?" He shrugged. So it seemed that he hadn't known, probably not at the time, anyway, but later came to know. I put it to him and he nodded. "Did you ever tell Grootka?"

Lonzo shook his head. "Try . . . b'na."

He had tried, but Grootka either didn't believe him, or had ignored him. The information was coming from the wrong person. When somebody asks who killed Cock Robin, that bird with the bow and arrow can deny it until his breath fails, as this one was doing.

At this rate, I thought, I'll get all the information I need by the turn of the century, if Lonzo holds out, which seems doubtful. I wanted to ask him why Jacobsen would betray Hoffa to Carmine, but it seemed too complex to answer, and anyway, would he know?

A few possibilities occurred to me. Assuming that Jacobsen already had a relationship of some sort with Carmine, which he must have had, one could infer a motive of fear: if Carmine discovered that you knew and hadn't told him, he'd be murderously angry. Or greed: there would be a variety of rewards for whoever helped the Mob out of this potentially disastrous jam. And don't forget jealousy. I wasn't so sure about that one. Was Jacobsen jealous of Tyrone? Or Vera? I didn't know, and when I phrased it to Lonzo he wasn't much help.

"Get Hoffa 'way," was the best Lonzo could provide, meaning that he thought—he signified with shrugs and so forth his not very strong feelings or knowledge—that Jacobsen simply wanted Hoffa out of the way, possibly that he felt that Hoffa's presence was too dangerous for Tyrone's good health, or his own plans for Tyrone. Something like that.

I had a feeling that this was probably the case. It had that foolish, almost heartbreaking air of validity that human actions sometimes have when the inconsequential leads to desperate acts. We think at first, *Oh no*; but something deep inside says, *Oh yeah*.

"What about Vera?" I asked.

His shoulders and chest heaved, simulating laughter, and he attempted a grin, but his last ministroke had made only a smirk possible. Still, he was clearly cheerful as he hoisted his open palms before his midriff to evoke heavy breasts, and he shook his head admiringly. "Helva woom. Peesass. Helva woom. Golotta-lotta guts. Got guts. Hard, *hard*," he emphasized sternly, "hard wook . . . sh' hardwook'n. Fuck'n Ty, leff'r."

That seemed understandable, with some effort. His condemnation of Tyrone for leaving her was not severe, it would seem, at least on conventional grounds, but rather he thought it foolish. Perhaps he thought Tyrone should have taken her with him when he vanished, assuming that he vanished on his own and wasn't, rather, *disappeared* as the Argentinans have it. But Grootka was fairly convincing on that topic, I thought. An obscure young jazz musician might be able to disappear—indeed, he certainly had—but probably not with a sexy white wife or mistress.

I asked him what he thought of Tyrone taking off, otherwise. He smiled. Then his face lit up and he had an idea. He gestured me to be patient and he got painfully off his iron bedstead and knelt on the floor to unlock the strongbox, as he called it—"Dass my strawn-box"—from which he took a plastic-encased audiocassette tape. It was not a professional commercially produced recording but one made by someone who had recorded from another source. He popped it into a little portable cassette player, which he also got from the strongbox. It was the kind that joggers use, which had flimsy earphones attached, and he listened for a few seconds before handing the earphones to me. He watched me expectantly as I put on the headset.

I was surprised by the quality of the sound, not audiophile quality obviously, but certainly not bad. A terrific jazz group was playing, evidently a live concert. It sounded familiar, especially the baritone sax, which was crisp and authoritative, full of amazing leaps of intervals. It was M'Zee Kinanda, of course. I recognized the sound, if not the tune, which seemed to be more of an up-tempo bop blowing vehicle than one of Kinanda's wild Free pieces. I thought the recording must date from a period before his more recent, esoteric stuff. This was furious fingering to a driving bass and drums, more consciously swinging, rooted in the chords.

"Is this old stuff?" I asked Lonzo.

"Na, na." He shook his head. "New. Live. Dee-troit. Two, three." He gestured with fingers. "Juss . . . juss now. Live."

So, it was recently recorded, live. A friend or somebody, he didn't say, had taped it and brought it. Good stuff. Great music. But I could see that Lonzo was exhausted by my visit. He flopped back on the bed and gratefully allowed me to drape the headset on his shrunken noggin. He closed his eyes and listened and I walked away.

A very heavy dark woman of middle age, wearing slacks and

a vaguely medical smocklike overshirt, was pushing a cart of medicines and drinks in the corridor. She had a name tag that identified her as Mrs. LoRhetta Butler, Nurse's Aide. I asked her who had brought Mr. Butterfield a new tape.

"He got a new tape? Oh, I'm so glad. That poor man, he didn't have but two or three tapes," she chattered as she bustled in and out of rooms, dropping off glasses of apple juice or shaking out an aspirin onto her broad hand and offering it to a patient with a paper cup of water, or waiting while another swallowed his medicine. "And somebody stold one and then he dropped another one and I"—she giggled embarrassedly and covered her mouth with her hand— "stepped on one and broke it! So he didn't have nothing to listen to on that little old Pakman, or whatever it is. Here, honey." She stood over an ancient old lady with perhaps ten strands of white hair on her shriveled black head, her face an absolute raisin of wrinkles, while the old lady drank some pink fluid from a tiny paper cup. "It must have been Miss Vera brought it," the aide concluded.

I was pleased to think of the austere Mrs. Jacobsen visiting an old reprobate like Lonzo. According to the aide she didn't come often, or rather she came frequently and then wouldn't come for weeks, but then she'd reappear regularly again, every other day. I thought it must have to do with her movement in and out of Detroit. Not very many other people came, just an occasional, very occasional old acquaintance.

"Mostly trash," was the aide's contemptuous dismissal. "Jailbirds, they look like. Course I know he was a bail bondsman. But 'cept for that other po-liceman, Miss Vera the only white person who comes."

"What other policeman?"

"You a po-lice, ain't you? Unh-hunh, well, there you are. He come a few days ago. He didn't even talk to Lonzo, just looked at the visitor book and axed me about who come to see him. I knew it was some po-lice business, so I didn't say nothing."

"You mean you didn't tell the policeman anything, or you didn't say anything to Lonzo about it?"

"Wasn't anything to tell. I ain't got no business tellin' no police about Miss Vera. So I didn't say nothin' to him and I didn't say nothin' to Lonzo."

I was a little puzzled. "Well, why are you saying something to me?" I asked. "I mean, if I'm a po—"

"You a *real* po-lice," she interrupted.

"You mean the other guy wasn't a real policeman? What was he?"

"He was almost a po-lice," Mrs. Butler said, "but I didn't trust him. He was the insurance po-lice. He called hisself a 'vestigator!" She laughed, a genuine mirthful laugh. "He some kind of 'gator, that's for sure! Asking about Lonzo's visitors! What's it to him? And then he axed if I knowed Mr. Meldrim. Hah! That's what he was really innarested in."

"And do you know Mr. Meldrim?" I asked.

"Sho' I knows him. I see Books Meldrim come visit Lonzo every month, also he pays the bills. Least, he signs the bills. I think they go to a bank. But I knew Books when he had a little business on Dexter Avenue." She laughed, remembering and not unfondly. "I useta buy my dream books from Books Meldrim. And he useta play piano at the Liberry Bar, oncet in a while."

"I thought you said only trash came to visit Lonzo."

"'Cept for Mr. Meldrim and Miss Vera," Mrs. Butler corrected herself. "And you." She looked at me with a cocked eyebrow, as if to suggest that she might be willing to change her mind about my status if I wasn't careful.

"But you didn't tell any of this to the other policeman. Did he show any identification? A name?"

"He didn't show nothing. He said he was from the Conda-mental 'Surance Comp'ny. But one of the other girls, she from over on Mack? She tole me she seen him at the Ninth Precink. That's way over on Chalmers, ain't it? Choichnya, I calls it, so many houses been flattened, like that place in Russia, Garage-nee. He didn't give no name. Little fellow, real nice suit. He might of been a po-lice oncet, but that was some time ago. Vonda says he is the chief of po-lice over there."

"Very neat?" I asked. "Patent-leather hair?"

"That's him."

I told her I thought she was a very acute observer. She didn't know what to make of that. I assured her it was a compliment.

"Compliments are nice, but I'll tell you about that little rat and it ain't no compliment. He is a nasty little rat."

If the man she was talking about was indeed Captain Buchanan, commander of the Ninth, who fit her description per-fectly, I quite agreed with her assessment. But I didn't say so. I started to leave, but I thought of something. "How long has Lonzo been like this?" I asked Mrs. Butler.

"Like what?"

"Well, he's very infirm. Has he been here long?" I wanted to get an opinion from her about his prospects, but didn't want to just come out and say, How long would you guess that he's got?

"This prob'ly just one of his bad days," she said. "I don't know, I ain't hardly looked at him." We were standing by his door and she peered in. "Well, he don't sound so bad to me."

Lonzo was asleep, his mouth open, the headset still on his head, and snoring loudly.

"Drunk," she said. "He been in the strongbox again. Miss Vera must of brought him something besides a tape." She sniffed. "Didn't you smell that?"

I stuck my head in and sniffed. Now that she mentioned it, there was a faint whiff of vodka.

"Was he chewing gum?" she asked.

I had noticed his jaws moving around, but I hadn't imagined that he was chewing gum.

"When he chews that Cloves gum he sho' been in the strong-box," she said.

On the way out I bumped into the young doctor again. "Would you say Mr. Butterfield's actually in pretty fair health?" I asked.

"That man's got about twenty serious problems," the doctor said, "but he's got a very strong constitution. When you consider the abuse he's heaped on that body . . . whew! He's been here for a couple years, off and on. This time he might be here for good. He came here from Detroit General, after he recovered from a little stroke. But he'll be around for a while, I imagine."

"Does he always talk like that?" I asked.

"Like what? Hard to understand? Well, he had some oral problems a few years ago, but they're pretty much healed up. If you found him incoherent it's probably because he's drunk." He smiled gently. "At this stage, we don't say much about drinking, as long as it doesn't cause problems for others. It gives him a little purpose, a game, hiding it from the nurse, fighting for the right to drink at least secretly . . . and it cuts down on the narcotics we have to supply."

"Is he ever sober? Coherent?"

"Once in a while, if there's some purpose to it. Are you from the insurance company, too?"

"Who me? No." I showed him my identification. "I'm trying to close up an old case in which Butterfield can maybe give me some leads. Has somebody else been asking about him?"

It was the small man, as the nurse had described.

I was now fairly anxious about Books Meldrim. I had no idea what Buchanan was up to, but obviously he hadn't been investigating Lonzo Butterfield on genuine police business, not that he had ever been a detective, anyway. But for many years I had known that he had strong ties to Carmine Busoni, though it wasn't anything that I or anyone else could prove to his discredit. For him to be making these kinds of practically open inquiries, however, he must be under some pressure. It seemed to me that the Mob was showing way too much interest.

I drove back into the city on Woodward Avenue, past all the miserable degradation of that street. It looked like hell. This was Detroit's Main Street, the proud avenue that old Judge Woodward had laid out almost two whole centuries ago, ridiculously wide, and which he had insisted was not so much named after himself but was the road to the woods, to the great forest of the north and hence, wood-ward. Now it was a wretched cavalcade of broken windows, hideous graffiti, trashed stores, and abandoned buildings. But when in my memory, I asked myself, had it actually been pretty? I mean between McNichols and the G.M. Center? It had only been at best a discouraging sweep of ugly stores and dull brick buildings, with occasional bursts of attractiveness, a park, a school.

It wasn't unfamiliar Detroit scenery. In this town you can bet that industrial and commercial interests are always uppermost. There might be occasional, sporadic eruptions of civic pride and cultural values that are familiar to other cities, many of them much younger than old Detroit. But Detroit says, Outta the way! We're busy here! Go play with your trees and cathedrals and museums and landscapes somewhere else. We got work to do and when we're through with this job, you can trash it and we'll build something else.

But now, strangely, as I cut across on neighborhood streets, avoiding the freeways, my thoughts of Vera and Lonzo were interrupted by the realization that Detroit was actually looking a little better these days. Many neighborhoods had been devastated, but many of them, perhaps most, had been landscaped as a consequence. A brutal landscaping, to be sure, since it was perfunctory and carried out in response to fire and to prevent further conflagrations, but still, it had opened up the city. Maybe this was a normal, natural thing for cities, something that should have happened less violently, but was inevitable.

As I drove, I thought of all the things that I'd forgotten to ask Vera. Like, why *she* had sought to entice me into this case, if her daughter was in more or less daily contact with me? Somehow, I'd left her daughter out of this, forgotten her, or perhaps it had been some unconscious desire to not involve her. But now that I was thinking about it, I began to wonder just what was the grant that Agge had garnered to research her project. I'd been assuming that it wasn't a total scam, I realized. But who was behind it?

And another question that I needed to pursue was the degree of Books Meldrim's involvement. From what I'd read so far, it wasn't clear that he'd been more than peripherally aware that something was going on at Lonzo's, at Turtle Lake. Did he know more? Did he know the whole story? And what had been his position in the aftermath, in the years since? I was certain that he wasn't telling me everything, but how much was he holding back? I had to get hold of him, soon.

I was driving through some old, partially bulldozed neighborhoods, in the Grand Boulevard–Mount Elliott vicinity, not far from the old Packard plant, which was still functioning as some sort of warehouse complex, when I saw a billboard that advertised housing units in a newly constructed, or reconstructed, residential project. It was jointly sponsored by some citizen's group, it seemed, and a Detroit bank. The offices were not far. I parked the Checker and went into the storefront offices.

I was asking the pleasant fat woman at the front desk about the available units when a lean and Mephistophelian figure issued from a back office, a man of his youthful forties, with tremendous

Italian optics, a beautiful silk suit, and splendidly handsome black shoes. He started to pass me by, but stopped and said, "Say . . . my *man*! Mul! What in the dim-dam-diddly brings you in here? You arrestin' the sister, here? She didn't do it! Hah, hah!"

He held up his hand, a long, slender palm and extralong fingers, so I could slap it.

"Gregory!" I slapped the hand. "What are you doing here?" We both asked it. He was here because he was the man who had gotten the bank behind this rebuilding project. He was interested in my need for a place to live.

"In a project like this, they always like to have a cop," he said. "But I don't know . . . Fang of the Ninth. It might be too much. But yeah, come on, I'll show you what we got."

We hopped into his Chrysler to take a tour. Gregory and I went back to a year or two I had spent at Wayne State, right after I got out of the air force. I thought we had taken biology and German together, but he thought it was political science, with his mentor, Dr. Ravitz. "And that creative-writing course, with the poet, what's his name?" Gregory snapped his fingers as we sped into a newly graded and sodded block. "Levine! Levin. Something like that. 'They feed they lions.'"

I had no idea what he was talking about. He talked very fast. It was generally nice to be around Gregory because his mind and his mouth ran so fast that he did all the thinking and talking for both of you. All you had to do was smile and nod and occasionally interject a name, or a number, or point out a direction.

He drove toward downtown and showed me a block in which there were seven large old brick houses, all of them either totally remodeled, or nearly so, to provide apartments for four families in each.

"The brilliant new cultural center"—Gregory used phrases like that, which obviously came from a written description—"is only six blocks that way." He pointed from the front yard of one of the brick multiplexes, across the boulevard. You could see the gleaming dome of a new building in the distance. "Lot of new building in town," he said.

It was true. There was a lot going on. He finally found me a place, a four-room apartment on the top floor of a three-story renovated building, with a back porch that gave a view of Canada to the south. It was pretty cheap, too. Gregory was sure he could get me in. I was very pleased and excited, almost enough to forget what had just been occupying my mind. I had visions of moving in within a few days. The apartment was all done, even to the painting.

"You can walk to the Opera House," he said. He snapped his fingers suddenly, reminded of something. "I saw you! You were walking with some chick, just a few days ago. Young sister." His eyebrow waved approvingly.

"Oh yeah," I said. I hadn't seen him, but he must have been at the M'Zee Kinanda concert.

"I thought you were a moldy fig," he said, accusingly.

"A moldy fig?" I had to laugh. I hadn't heard the phrase in years; it used to mean a retro jazz fan, in the bop era. "You mean like Tommy Dorsey and that stuff?" I said, climbing back into his huge car. "Well, it's all right. But I'm into much wilder stuff these days. I even dig Sun Ra."

He laughed. "Well, M'Zee is pretty heavy shit—too free for me. It's like Charles Gayle and all that stuff, everybody blowin' like mad—I keep expecting to see their teeth come flying out the bell of the horn. I like to hear some chords. But I'm glad to see you pickin' up on somethin' like that. You know what I mean?"

I did know what he meant. It was a curious thing, I felt, to have discovered this whole vein of music, a world of music, you might say that was so obviously outside the mainstream, but still was so alive and fresh and had an entire audience of enthusiasts that I had not dreamed existed. I managed to get a few words of this notion out before Gregory whipped it away to play with it like a stolen basketball, spinning it on his fingertips and flipping it over his back and through his legs.

"I know! I know, man! It's so damn hip! I mean, here all these cats"—he waved his hand across his huge windshield, indicating a mass audience of the unhip—"who don't even know it exists! It's like here is this cat over here, all he digs is Mahalia Jackson and the Original Raspberry Boys of Alabama. Then you got this babe, she digs . . . I don't know, Dusty Fucking Springfield. This cat over here, he won't listen to nothing but Poop Doggy Do, and this chick has only got ears for Miles. That's all right! It's great! But the industry, see . . . the industry hates this shit! It's too many goddamn different kinds of fucking music, you understand, my man? What they want is maybe three kinds. Three!"

He brandished three fingers as he wheeled the big Chrysler off the freeway. "The industry wants to make seventy million CDs of Michael Jackson and fuck the rest! So they pretend that they ain't nobody else out there. Oh, they throw in Wynton Marsalis for the fogies and some redneck country-and-western shit for the crackers. They blow the rest of them away with overwhelming advertising for Michael. But you know what?" His voice fell to a dramatic whisper. "Nobody gives a shit. They go on supporting their favorites. They buy the records, the CDs, go to the concerts. It's cool. It fucks the Man! Which is what we got to do. Always." He looked at me over his photosensitive Italian spectacles. "Begging your pardon, Mul baby."

"I'm not the Man," I said.

"Naw," he laughed in agreement. "You too fucking poor. But you know what, I'm glad you're into this Free Jazz. It's the wildest, most innovative stuff going, and you just know that fifteen, twenty years from now—hell, it's going on right now!—the whole music world is going to be built on what M'Zee and Albert and Horace are doing right now. Well, not Albert, he's dead, but Horace and M'Zee. And to think that M'Zee is a homeboy!"

"He is?" I was startled. Then I saw. It was so obvious that I wondered for a moment if I hadn't known all along. A case of willful blindness—a state not altogether unknown to me.

"Hell yes," Gregory said. "We went to school together. You knew him. He was in that German class, with Barry and Donna and Ruth and all them cats."

"Are we thinking of the same guy?" I was having doubts now.

"Hell yeah! Tyrone. Tyrone Addison. He sat right up front. He put the moves on Ruth, the Jewish bombshell! You remember!"

"Tyrone? Tyrone who went out with Ruth?" I remembered him clearly. I realized that I had never really known his last name. A skinny, mysterious-looking guy. I'd thought he was on dope. "I didn't even know he was a musician," I said.

"Man, where you been, Mul? The cat was gigging on Dexter Avenue while we were in school! He played with Miles and Woody Shaw! Fool!"

"And that's M'Zee Kinanda?"

"Hell yes!"

"What did he . . . become a Muslim, or something?"

"Aw man, he ran away from some white chick. He was always prowling on them white babes. Blondes with big tits. He didn't chase them, they chased him. He had to beat them back! Then one of them, a married bitch, married to some rich dude, she flipped and ran away from her old man, some kind of foreign dude, maybe he was a Syrian or an Ay-rab, who knows? Lotsa money involved, see? So her old man comes after Tyrone with a sword, is the way I heard it. Anyways, Tyrone, he splits for L.A., changes his name to M'Zee K. Best thing that ever happened to him. He wasn't going nowhere here. But he got into that bag out there, the John Carter and Horace Tapscott scene. They dug him, helped him out. Best thing that ever happened."

"But everybody knows he is really Tyrone?"

Gregory looked at me and laughed. "Course, they do! How come you didn't know? Oh," he said, amused. "Yeah, well, it's like everybody knows, but it ain't something that people talk about to the Man, you understand. It's *known,* but don't go 'round quackin' about it. And the press, they don't know, of course—they never know shit. So it ain't like it's gonna show up on the record jacket, you dig."

"It's an 'in' thing," I said.

Gregory shrugged. "Here we are. This your car? Man, you are poor. Maybe you ain't the Man. I ain't so sure, now, they gonna let you into that fancy new pad."

I found Agge Allyson at the archives. "I was just talking to your mom," I said. She was sitting on a low stool, poking through a cardboard box of files, covered with dust. She looked pretty beautiful. She sat back for a moment and looked at me, then shrugged.

"So?" She went back to the box.

"So how come you fill me full of crap with all that stuff about a grant and writing a history of the department?" I squatted down next to her.

"It's no crap," she said. She didn't look at me, still pretending to page through some files.

"It's crap," I said. "A history of the force! What a joke! I should have known better. I *did* know better, but I let myself be persuaded. What was the name of that foundation again? The one that gave you the grant?"

"I don't believe I said." She stood up. "It's the Alpha/Alpha Foundation. The director is a Mr. Toscano."

"Where is this Alpha/Alpha Foundation located?" I asked. "How did you hear about it?"

"I didn't hear about it. They heard about me. You don't apply for one of their grants. They have a network of academics, to whom they pay a stipend to keep an eye out for likely candidates for their grants. They're in Grosse Pointe, but I was interviewed at Wayne."

It sounded interesting. I had never heard of such an arrangement, unless it was in le Carré novels about the recruitment of spies from Cambridge. Agge assured me that it was not unusual. She didn't seem very upset by my anger at her behavior.

"What did I do? I didn't send you any computer warnings of cries of 'wolf.' I told Ma not to do that. I told her it was nonsense."

"So you're sticking with the story that contacting me was just an accident, that you are really working on a history of the force?"

"Of course. Really, Mul. . . . I suppose I shouldn't have mentioned to Ma that I ran into someone who knew Grootka. She was always obsessed about that old Grootka. I hardly remember him, myself, though he seems much more interesting now."

I could hardly believe this. I had made a policy out of not accepting coincidence, especially where a murder had been committed. But what could I say in the face of this practically cheerful declaration?

"Ah, tell me again how you happened to get onto this notion of focusing on Grootka's activities," I asked her, "as a lens on history, so to speak."

She dusted off her hands and placed them on her hips. She was very young, I saw, as if for the first time. Perhaps it was having met her mother, but I was conscious of her being so very much younger than me that I lost all interest in her, in a romantic way, as it were. Especially when she popped her forefinger into her mouth, girlishly, thinking for a moment.

"You know," she said, after a suitable time, "it really wasn't my idea. It was suggested to me, by Mr. Toscano."

"This is the director of the Alpha/Alpha Foundation? He's the one who came to interview you at the university? What's he like?"

"He's very pleasant, though I'd say he isn't very used to these interviews. Most of the questions were asked by his assistant, Miss Sedgelock. Mr. Toscano just occasionally interjected. But it was he who suggested the Grootka approach."

"That's interesting," I said. "Grootka is pretty well known in police circles, although not so much anymore, but I'd say he was practically unknown otherwise."

"Oh, I wouldn't say that," Agge said. "He's still pretty well known on the Street, as you guys like to put it, and in a certain milieu."

"Well, yes, I see what you mean. But the director of a foundation hardly belongs to that milieu. How often do you see Toscano?"

"I haven't seen him since our one interview. They send a check to my bank account every month, so I don't even see that. It's pretty nice." She smiled.

"How much?"

"Five thousand?" She almost winced, looking at me as if for approval. She knew it was a pretty hefty figure.

"They're paying you five thousand dollars a month to research and write this history! For how long?"

"They only promised a year, but hinted that it could be renewed."

"A foundation is paying a gi— a newly graduated student sixty thousand dollars for—"

"I'm not exactly buying a house, or even a Buick, on these wages," she said, somewhat indignantly. "You know, I've put in years of study. I'm a Ph.D.!"

"Sure, sure," I said. "I didn't say you weren't worth it. But how often do you hear of it? Young lawyers do better than that, I know."

"So do M.B.A.s, and what do they know?" she retorted.

Indeed, I thought. "Well, what do you plan to do?" I asked.

"Do? What are you so angry about?"

"Me? I'm not angry, I . . ." I shut my mouth. What was I angry about? I guess I was angry at being used, for being misled, for having interests in this young woman that I suddenly saw—with the same suddenness with which I saw that Kinanda was Tyrone Addison—were not only futile but absurd. She was at least twenty years younger than me. I was disappointed and felt a little abused. But what the hell, I was a big boy.

"I'm not angry," I said. I made an effort to smile. Not a Fang smile, but a genuine one. This young woman didn't owe me anything and the best I could see, she had simply been misled herself. But she was also, I saw, the contact with whoever was trying to manipulate me.

"You must report on your progress from time to time," I said. "Who is this Miss Sedgelock? How do you contact her?"

Agge crossed her arms, rather like her mother had when confronted by me. "Why do you want to know?" she asked.

I explained to her that I thought that her project was not a bona fide project, that it was really more in the way of a fishing expedition. But I had to admit I didn't know what kind of fish the Alpha/Alpha Foundation was fishing for. Possibly, they simply wanted to assess how much was known, particularly by me, about the death of Hoffa and Grootka's role in it.

Agge was a little hard to convince. No researcher or scholar wants to think that her project is false, that it's really somebody else's stalking-horse. But she was compelled to realize that once such suspicions were aired and allegations were made, they had to be resolved before she could continue. She agreed to approach Alpha/Alpha, with me.

Her contact with Miss Sedgelock was not very encouraging. Miss Sedgelock, who was not to be found at the number she had provided—it turned out to be an answering service—finally rang back to say that Mr. Toscano was unavailable, but that she would be willing to meet with Agge the following week. She did not wish to meet with Sergeant Mulheisen of the Detroit police. She was fairly curt in declaring that Miss Allyson's relations with the department were her own lookout, that the foundation could not be involved. She hinted a little nastily that Miss Allyson might find her grant rather abbreviated if she were unable to carry out her stipulated research and report. I was unable to monitor this conversation, but Agge's account of it seemed unsettling. I could tell that Agge was deeply upset.

The prospect of a meeting next week didn't satisfy my sense of urgency, but what could we do? I told Agge to go ahead and meet, and we'd see if something more immediate could be arranged. As we parted I remembered something.

"How long have you known M'Zee Kinanda?" I asked.

"Known him? I don't know him. He asked me for a date, but I kind of brushed him off. These old guys are always hitting on me."

"He asked you out?" I was shocked. Well, as shocked as I get. Startled, anyway.

"He asked me to come over."

"You didn't know that he is really Tyrone Addison?"

"That's Tyrone? You mean Mama's old boyfriend?" She was genuinely intrigued, I could tell. "You mean he isn't dead, he just changed his name? I wonder if Mama knows that."

I wondered, too.

13

Meeny, Miny, and Mo

Grootka's Notebook, #6

I ran back through the woods, looking for anybody, but whoever had been there was gone. At least I hope they was. I didn't wanta stand toe-to-toe with whoever was cranking that fucking cannon and, anyways, I had work to do and I knew it hadda be done in a hurry. I heard some cars, probably the limo and what-ever other vehicle they brought with them, but by the time I got to the county road it was empty and you wouldn't of thought nobody'd been there. I hiked up the road to where Tyrone had taken my car and it was still there, but no sign of Tyrone and no sign of the money. I looked around but not much, 'cause I figured that cannon might of been heard, even out here in the woods, and I didn't wanta be around when somebody came to check. The keys was still in my rig, so I pulled out and drove back to the dirt track and up to where Janney Jacobsen lay in the road.

Janney was dead forever. It was too bad about Janney, I thought. He got in the way. But, what the hell, he might be some use, after all. I searched him and found a roll of bills, quite a good roll, ten thou at least, which I hadda figger was pretty goddamn useful. He didn't have no gun, though. I'd given him a H&R .32

earlier, 'cause he wasn't armed, so where the hell was it? I found it
on the side of the road, actually all but covered up in the leaves.
Whadidhe, try to get rid of it? Or maybe it just flew outta his hands
when the Fat Man shot him? I didn't know, but I wrapped it up
careful in his shirt, which I had stripped from his body, real quick.
He'd been shot in the face, just below the left eye, a small entry but
no exit wound, which with a .32 didn't surprise me none. Too bad
for Janney, but just as well for me, I thought, since I wasn't gonna
have to screw around hauling a half-dead body or a whole-dead
body away.

Lonzo was alive, though, hiding under his car. It wasn't a
good hiding place, but he didn't have much of a chance to go
someplace else. I guess he figured when I drove up that I was the
Mob, coming back to mop up. He thought I'd been taken out, he
said, when he heard that big cannon, and now he figured they'd just
blast his ass. But no, it was me, although he wished I hadn't wasted
so much time fussing with Janney, who was a dead rat.

Anyways, I dragged him out from under the car. He was a
long ways from dead, but he wasn't exactly whistling "Zippety-doo-
dah." He'd taken a shot in the mouth, which it was one hell of a
piece of luck. It removed a coupla teeth and broke his jaw, but
didn't kill him, though it burned his tongue a little so he couldn't
talk for shit, which wasn't nothing to complain about from my
view. I told him it was because his fucking mouth was so fucking big
that when they shot at him that was all they could hit. But he
showed me he had gotten another shot in the shoulder which
knocked him down, but otherwise just took a little chunk of meat
out of him.

"You're better off than the white meat," I told him, but he
just glared like he didn't get the joke.

I axed him if he could drive and he said he could, though his
jaw was starting to hurt awful bad. But I told him we hadda get the

hell outta there. He nodded, and then he pointed to Jimmy and looked at me kind of questioning. I went to look, but I knew it didn't mean nothing. Jimmy and Janney could be comparing notes somewheres, but they wasn't anyplace local. I never seen such a mess as those shells made of Hoffa. I picked up the revolver he'd been waving and wrapped it in his Hawaiian shirt, which luckily wasn't too bloody, it being loose and open, so he didn't lay on it and bleed too much. It could come in handy, too, you never know.

The guy in the bushes that I'd popped, I checked just to make sure. It was sure. So that left Janney. Lonzo was sittin' in the passenger seat of his own car, I don't know what he was thinking. I wasn't gonna drive both cars. I pointed that out to him and told him to follow me, in case he got too bad to drive.

I couldn't take Janney with me, even if I wanted to, and I sure as hell wasn't gonna waste no time and effort on Hoffa, who as far as I was concerned was to blame for all this shit in the first place. Well, that ain't right—Carmine and the Fat Man were to blame, but I wasn't in no mood to argue it out in my mind. The trouble was that Janney was a connection between me and Lonzo and Tyrone and Vera and the Mob. Hoffa was dead and folks expected him to be dead. There was also a dead Mob guy in the bushes. Okay. And the cabin belonged to somebody that Hoffa knew but none of us knew. Okay. So there really wasn't nothing to connect us to the Mob and to Hoffa, except Janney.

I hustled up to the cabin and looked it over, making sure there wasn't nothing to connect me and the others to this sorry scene. I was tempted to burn the fucker down, but that don't always get rid of the evidence and anyway it just attracts attention and I wanted time to get the hell out of this part of the country. I hadda figger the Mob would be back to clean up their part of the mess. I couldn't do everything, I didn't have a lotta time, but I tried to wipe down the place to remove as much of the fingerprints as I could.

Though I never had much confidence in fingerprints. If you know whose you're looking for in the first place, it's fine, but if you're just prospecting, good luck.

So, that was it. Me and Lonzo drove outta there in good time, no interruptions. I stopped in Faraway, at a outfit called Fred's that is a butcher who makes great venison sausage and stuff. I had Fred make up a couple sammidges for me and Lonzo, plus he wrapped up some sausage for when I got home, and we managed to get the two cars back to Detroit, no sweat. I began thinking that my weekend in the country hadn't been too unprofitable. The sausages was real good.

Tyrone Addison has disappeared. I don't know what happened to him. After a few days, when she didn't hear nothing about Hoffa or Tyrone, Vera called me at Homicide. I went out to see her. She was living at Jacobsen's, taking care of the kid. Turns out she was married to Jacobsen! They had this kid, Agge. Nice little girl, except she ain't Jacobsen's kid if Vera is s'posta be the mother. Anyways, I give Vera the roll I took off Janney and Tyrone's soprano sax, but she insisted that I keep the sax, so finally I took it.

I guess we both figured Tyrone had been snapped up by the boys who done the number on Hoffa. I heard that they cleaned up Cess's place, although I never went back. But I ain't heard nothing and it's been a few weeks, so I don't expect to.

[*Here there is a piece of notepaper taped onto the original text, as before, with some observations by Grootka that obviously date from somewhat later.—M.*]

Mul, by now there ain't gonna be no sign of Jimmy, unless a miracle occurs. Maybe he's in a iceberg somewhere in Alaska, that'd be the only way we're gonna see Jim again. But I don't think so. I since found out that the cabin in the woods was burned down and the new owners (guess who?) had the site bulldozed and landscaped. Yeah, the new owner is the Krispee Chips Corporation. They built a fancy lodge there. I guess for the employees, you can guess which ones. Hint: it ain't the secretaries. [*End of note.—M.*]

Except for Tyrone disappearing, everything has worked out pretty well. Anyways, about as good as you could hope. The trouble with these things though is that they never do stay under the ground. Somebody has got to dig, it's human nature, especially when it's such a big-time guy like Hoffa. I may be gone by the time you're reading this, otherwise I guess you wouldn't be reading it, I'd be telling you it. But if you are reading it, prob'ly it's because something has happened. What could it be? They found Jimmy? I doubt it. No, I bet it's because Carmine or the Fat Man has decided that enough ain't enough. One of them, maybe both, has got to thinking that you can never bury nothing deep enough. They prob'ly got to poking around and decided that ol' Grootka must of been involved and he prob'ly left some evidence that will hang them.

Is that it? Did I guess right? Or did they guess right?

Well, I don't know how right I was, but they were right on. The guy to talk to is Books. I left everything with him. Even some of the sausages.

Yr pal Grootka.

Well, that was about it. That was about all the "help" I was going to get from Grootka, I guessed.

14

No Mister
Nice

There was no
answer at Books Meldrim's number. This was more than a little unsettling. I had a strong desire to march into Buchanan's office and
confront him. But what would I say? Why were you poking around
Lonzo Butterfield? What's your interest here? That wasn't going to
get anybody anywhere. Nor could I descend on Humphrey DiEbola,
the erstwhile Fat Man. For one thing, I couldn't approach him on
my own; I needed the backing of the department, at least. Which
meant Jimmy Marshall, my lieutenant, not to say the support of
my captain, Buchanan. But really, it needed the authority of the
F.B.I., the U.S. marshall, the county prosecutor. All of these people.

Of course, if you are Grootka you don't need any of these
people. You just strap on the Old Cat and go to work. But that was
just the problem, wasn't it? Grootka had interfered, deeply, in the
lives of several people and then when it had come to a small war,
had grinned and waved and walked off, kind of like Ronald Reagan
getting on Air Force One. "Oh, Mulheisen will take care of it." He
had more or less said just that.

But this wasn't looking after Books. And I had a feeling that
someone ought to, if only to warn him that sleeping dogs were up
and about.

I didn't need any help to do this. I could drive down to Books's Lake Erie hideaway and be there in an hour, maybe less. It took less.

Books's car was parked in the drive, which was a treacherous little lane that led down from the road toward the lake, very narrow, with no way to turn around. It brought one to a point below the house, actually, and then one had to climb stairs to the deck. I peered into the house from the sliding glass door and realized immediately that there was trouble. All the books were thrown on the floor. Many other things had been tossed on the floor, as well, including flour, houseplants, clothes. Somebody had done a job.

The door was ajar and although I hadn't noticed any other cars about, nor any signs of other people—the neighbors were weekend and summer folk, not regular residents—I drew my gun and entered. I stepped away from the framing doorway and listened. What I heard was that well-known silence that says, *Nobody home.* I called for Books. No response. Then I moved through the house, carefully.

I'm not an admirer of the two-handed-squat approach when searching room to room. I like to be alert, but erect, not planted. I keep my hat in one hand and my gun in the other, close to my waist, where it can't be batted away and possibly lost. The hat can always be waved or tossed as a distraction. Stillness is helpful, listening. Move quickly, stop, listen. There was nothing to hear.

Room to room and the whole house had been tossed. Trashed. It was a mess. They had even thrown jars of mustard into the open box of the grand piano. That kind of violence evokes fear for the inhabitant. But no sign of Books, no nice Mr. Meldrim. Finally, I went back on the deck.

I stood there amid the disarray—I hadn't noticed when I came up that the deck itself had been savaged, chairs kicked over and a railing splintered—and felt . . . well, I started to say depressed, but it felt more like despair. I had failed in the one thing that was essential: to protect. It didn't matter that I was still almost totally baffled by this case. (Note that I said "still," as if I were confident that the case would yield its meaning eventually, if not its solution. This is true arrogance.)

It was not a bad day. I sighed and stood there on the deck, in this great silence broken only by a faraway gull and the gentle lapping of water against the shore and the pilings of the dock. Unconsciously, I took out a cigar and lit it. The sun was not shining, but the sky was light, a familiar kind of pearly lakeside luminescence that made it impossible to see a true horizon. The lake was slaty gray and gently undulating, cold and grave. The air wasn't really cold, just that dull, breezeless chill that can seem almost unnoticeable until your nose and fingers get numb.

I had an incongruous thought: the Red Wings were playing the Blues tonight. I actually considered trying to attend. What an amazing thing the human mind is! It crawls out of a depression to take refuge on the ice of a hockey rink! Or maybe it was only the well-known salutary effect of the H. Upmann's tobacco.

I descended the steps to the little dock and walked out to the end, noticing a freighter seemingly motionless at the very limits of visibility. I looked down at the little boat tethered at the end of the dock. The blue canvas of the protective cover was drawn over the boat, but not over the outboard motor, which was in the upright position, with the propeller in the water. Evidently, Books had been fishing but hadn't restored the motor to its horizontal position. And then I noticed that the cover wasn't really tightly drawn about the boat. A brisk wind would strip it off, exposing the interior. It wasn't like Books to leave it like that. I clambered down the two or three steps of the wooden ladder to the point where the soles of my shoes were just above the water and leaned out. With the cigar clenched in my jaw and clinging to the ladder with my free hand, I flipped back the loose canvas with the snub-nose of my .38 Chiefs Special, fearful of what might be underneath.

Books Meldrim lay there, on his back. His brown eyes were open and he held an old long-barreled revolver on his breast. He looked up into my eyes and said, "I was hoping it was you, Mul."

I swear I could have kissed the old bastard. Instead, I said, softly, "You bastard. Just taking a little nap on the bosom of the deep, Books?"

His eyes were pretty bleak, but he smiled. He clambered up and I helped him onto the dock. He stood next to me and looked up at the deck and the house. "You left my door open," he said. "That's no good for my piano." He pronounced it "pee-yaner."

Books had gotten a good look at the two young men who had come to the house. He'd seen them drive up, noticed the Michigan plates and their manner, and had spent an hour of terrified hiding. His last resort was the boat. I knew from his description that the two men were almost certainly the two I'd seen outside Vera's house in Ferndale. I called the border patrol and put a watch on the tunnel and the bridge, but the men had had plenty of time to get back to Detroit, so I didn't expect too much.

I helped Books straighten up much of the mess and encouraged him to notify the police, but he brushed that notion aside. He made coffee and we each had a hard jolt of brandy. His fear, anxiety, and then anger were yielding to depression, I could tell, but he was tough and fought it down. He looked about, at the stains on his rugs and walls—he had thoroughly cleaned the mess out of his piano.

"The gen'amens did a number on me, didn't they?" he said, mildly. "I'm surprised they didn't take a dump on the davenport."

"You'll get it all straightened out," I said. "I'll help you." I sounded agreeable, and I meant to be supportive—the man had been through a hell of a deal—but my depression had long since changed to fear, then to relief, followed by a rising anger. I recognized the signs; it was nothing unusual. I remembered a very pretty little cousin of mine, Sarah, who used to come visit me in the summers from California. One day she was dancing in the kitchen while my mother was making cookies. My father had gone down into the basement, which at that time was really only a root cellar, reached by a trapdoor. The trap was open and Sarah, dancing about, singing merrily, had heedlessly tumbled into the hole. I remember my mother's shouts of horror and then relief when my father issued out of the cellar holding the little blond girl, who was dazed but then laughed to see my mother's fright. My mother had struck the little girl, not very hard and not across the face, but then she'd tried to cover up her violent reaction with a justified anger, raging about Sarah's thoughtlessness. It was soon apparent that the slap had only been a frightened reaction, a kind of release of tension.

I felt some of my mother's anger now, listening to Books prattle away. I knew he was just working off his own excess anger and fear, but still.

"Thank you. Yeah, we can fix it up, but it'll always be there, a little faint stain. Well . . . it is time to wind this up. Time to quit playing games, playing Grootka's game. You remember the last time you were out here and I said you should cook a little fish as you would rule the empire?"

"Yeah, yeah. Lao-tse, wasn't it? Govern an empire as you would cook a little fish?" I wondered if he was going to slow down anytime soon.

"It works both ways," Books said. "But that's a concept that wouldn't make a lick of sense to Grootka. If a .38'd kill you, why not use an elephant gun and be sure? That'd be Grootka. Well, I'm ready."

And now it was my turn. "You're ready? Well, I'm glad. What the hell do you people think is going on here, anyway? You saw those guys—they didn't drive all the way down here to trash your house and scare you. If they'd found your ass it'd be floating in Lake Erie now. Don't you know that?"

"What's got you so goosey?" he said, eyeing me curiously. "Wasn't nobody trying to shoot your ass."

"How do you know?" I retorted. "I get my ass shot at twice a week. Part of the job. How come you didn't tell me that M'Zee Kinanda was really Tyrone Addison?" That was what was bugging me.

"Ah, so that's it," Books said. Then he assumed an annoyingly pious expression and offered, "If the man wants to be known as M'Zee Kinanda, that's his right. It ain't my business." He started muttering and putting things away, pretending to ignore me.

"Don't give me that crap. This whole thing's been a put-up job from the start, leading me around by the nose, feeding me a little info here, withholding it there, 'here read this notebook, here's a tape' . . . it won't do. Not anymore. I've had it." And I had. I was angry.

"All right, all right," the old man said, holding up his large, slender hands placatingly. "I'm sorry about that. I just didn't know how to go about it, how much you should know, what I was supposed to reveal . . . Grootka said—"

"Oh, don't give me any more of that Grootka crap," I interrupted. "Give me the goods. I want to hear it. What do you know? I know you weren't up north with those guys—or do I? All I know is what I read in Grootka's notebooks. Which reminds me, are there any more of them? I want them, right now."

"That's what those fellas were after, I expect," he said. He'd dropped the philosopher cloak, I saw, although I suspected it was one that he would prefer to wear as closely as his skin from now until he croaked.

I was momentarily arrested. "Did they get it?"

"I don't have any more," he said. "Course, they don't know that."

I waited a beat or two. "Well, that might be something," I said. "Now tell me a story."

I sat back and lit a cigar. Forty-five minutes later we were en route to Detroit. His story was not vastly different from the one that had slowly accreted in my mind. Books, naturally, played down his role when it was likely to appear criminal, but played it up when it looked admirable, particularly if it seemed wise and sagacious. I didn't mind. It was a good story. You know it.

He had not gone to Faraway, or wherever we should call the cabin in the north, he said. I believe him. Grootka had returned and told him the whole story. Books had helped him write it up. "Except that he wouldn't let me actually write it, and the man couldn't spell 'hockey,'" Books lamented. "Had to be in his writing and in his spelling. Otherwise, it was no good."

"But what," I said, and then repeated, with menace, "*what in hell* was the point?"

"Grootka didn't give a damn about Hoffa," Books said. "So in a way, you had to ask, why not just let it drop? Him and Lonzo got out okay, Tyrone and Vera got out okay, I stayed clear right along. . . . Sure, a couple of guys died, but people dying every day."

"Not all of them are Hoffa," I said.

"That's right," Books readily agreed. "Nobody gives a rat's ass about ol' Janney, he was a foreigner and a oddball, anyway. Who gives a hoot for some jive greaser like Cusumano? I don't believe I ever even saw the guy before and he sure was a killer, hisself. But there's Hoffa. Hoffa is like Pharoah." He pronounced it "Fay-row."

"Pharoah? What the hell are you talking about?" We were fast approaching Windsor, and I was looking for the tunnel exit.

"Pha-roah don't ever die alone. When Pha-roah dies, a lot of people got to die. He ain't going into that pyramid alone. Pha-roah ain't taking the sun boat without company."

"Don't get philosophical on me, Books," I warned him.

"I ain't being philosophical. That's the truth. That's just the way it is. Pha-roah don't die alone. We all are just lucky it was as few as it was."

I had called ahead, and Customs waved us through. Stanos was waiting for me on the other side. We pulled into the parking lot and he stood up from lounging on the trunk of his Olds Ciera. He was tall and rangy, with a raw face that was all nose and chin and bumps but had somehow weathered from ugly, acned youth into a cruel but not wholly awful maturity. He looked meaner than two dogs tied back to front.

"My good Lord," Books breathed, looking at him. He'd heard me calling for Stanos to meet us. "It's like a young Grootka. Ain't it? I never thought to see anything like that again."

"The world is round, Books. He's not as smart as Grootka, but he's got time."

Stanos leaned into the car. He was wearing a gray suit that looked like he'd stolen it from Grootka's closet. It flapped open to reveal a shoulder holster that carried a gun as big as the Old Cat. "You must be Books Meldrim," he said. He extended his arm across me to shake Books's hand. He had a husky, gravelly voice that still carried an element of youth in it, kind of cocky, but sort of indifferently happy with the day. "Glad to meetcha."

He stood up and rocked on his heels, swinging his long arms restlessly and smacking a fist against an open palm. "Well," he said, "nice day for somethin'. You ready to go knock some fucking wop heads?"

I let him stand there for a while until he came down off his high horse. Then I looked up. "It's not like that, Stanos. I just want to go by Krispee Chips and talk to Humphrey."

Stanos grinned. "And you need a little backup? That's great! Maybe they'll get out of line." He gestured with his thumb at Books, and said, "Is the spoo—, is he goin'? Yeah? Great! That's just great. Okay!" He slapped his hands like a pistol shot and turned toward his car. "Le's go!"

I looked at Books. He was looking me in the face. He shook his head slightly, his lips pursed to whistle softly. I gave him my best Fang grin. "Le's go!"

* * *

Humphrey DiEbola was not the Fat Man, not the man I had met many years ago with Grootka in the halls of 1300 Beaubien. Nobody today would think to nickname him the Fat Man. I had seen him several times in the interim years, and not more than a couple of weeks earlier, but each time he looked leaner. He was almost handsome these days. He was standing behind his desk in the old office that had been Carmine's. It still had the fascinating sculpture in the corner: a man-size figure of a rat in a pin-striped suit and a fedora, carrying a shotgun. It was a great piece by the legendary sculptor Jabe.

It was a pleasure to meet the nice Ms. Soteri again. She ushered us into DiEbola's office and I was taken by surprise. There stood Ms. Helen Sedlacek, sometime paramour and associate of my old nemesis, Joe Service, standing behind the boss in her own pinstripes.

Ms. Soteri brought coffee, along with a tray of brandy. Humphrey leaned back in his padded leather and teak chair and patted the hand of his assistant, Helen. "What can I do for you, Mul? This isn't about Ortega, is it? I'm afraid I haven't heard any more from the fellow."

He basically ignored Stanos and Books. Stanos had slammed back the brandy and set the glass down on a bookshelf, near his coffee cup. He lounged with one hand idly scratching at his midriff, comfortably close to his shoulder holster, and smiled at nothing at all. Books sat as silent as Buddha, merging with the soft leather chair.

I had been thinking carefully about what I was going to say to Humphrey all the way down here. I wanted to get it right. "Mr. DiEbola, I didn't come here with any kind of wish list, or demands, or to hassle you—"

"Mul, it's Humphrey," he interrupted.

"Sure, sure. We've had some problems in the past . . . I don't want to go into all that. The police have problems of one sort or another with anyone, any organization. Yours is a little different. No, no, I'm not going to get into that."

Humphrey nodded. I noticed Helen step a little closer to him and then I saw his hand slip down behind the desk. *What the hell,* I thought, *is he actually going for a gun?* But then, no, I saw Helen's hips move slightly and I thought, *What the hell! He's feeling her ass!* I couldn't believe it. Humphrey DiEbola was feeling Helen Sedlacek's ass right in front of us. *They have a relationship!*

"You know, sometimes I can feel the earth tremble," I said.

"What?" Helen said, echoed by Humphrey.

"I was just going to say a few words about you've got your agenda and I've got mine and I'm sorry, but when your agenda crosses mine the one that takes precedence is . . ." I paused, tapping my chest. "But then I felt the earth tremble. I can see it doesn't make much sense talking. Just let me say this, Humphrey. I know where the bodies are buried."

Helen spoke quickly. "People often say that, but then when they go to dig them up . . ." She lifted a hand and opened it, palm up, then tipped it over as if pouring out dirt or something, "Nothing there."

I decided to ignore that. "I've got a case that would be—how shall I put it?—*difficult* to make," I said, talking not to Helen but to Humphrey. "But it'll make."

Humphrey leaned forward, both hands in view on his desk, clearly interested. "This is about Pepe, isn't it?" he said.

I shook my head. "We're nowhere on that, Humphrey. I don't think I'm giving away department secrets if I tell you I don't think we're going to get anywhere on that. This goes way back." I looked at Helen then and tried a little smile, one that I hoped would look rueful. "I was hoping you and me could talk privately," I said. I glanced at my two companions and said, "I'm sure Stanos and Mr. Meldrim would excuse us."

Helen did not like this, at all. "Sergeant Mulheisen, I've had to deal with you before," she said. "So has Umb—, Mr. DiEbola. The problem with dealing with you is that you speak for yourself, and whether you're genuinely candid or not, you don't necessarily speak for the police department. So there's no point in speaking to you at all, is there?"

"Well, Helen," I said, "I know you have the ear of various police, uh, *figures*. I daresay some of them are pretty significant. But this, what I have to say to Humphrey, is just between him and me. He and I. Him and me." We all smiled at that verbal clumsiness. It's amazing how nicely that works.

I walked outside with Humphrey and we strolled down the graveled parking lot toward the loading docks. I looked back and saw Helen standing in front of the building with her arms crossed, watching us. Stanos stood nearby. Books was drinking from a fountain.

"How long has this been going on, Humphrey?" I asked him, looking back at Helen.

He glanced over his shoulder and grinned. "Can't sneak the sun past the rooster, can I?" he said. "I've known Helen since she was a baby, Mul, but by God . . ."

He really was happy. I hated to spoil his day. "You ever hear of a guy named Cusumano, Humphrey?" He shook his head. He looked serious now. "No? Well, it doesn't matter. As far as I know his body doesn't exist. And it wouldn't matter if it did. I think he got to be part of a Buick, or maybe a Ford, though even that would have been junked by now. But the name should evoke some memories. A place, a time? A guy? How about a guy named Jacobsen?"

Humphrey turned away from me. He was an intelligent man. He didn't like games. But right now his mind wasn't on my needs. He was watching Helen. She had sauntered over to Stanos and was talking to him, her back to us, hands on her hips, feet boldly apart.

She was a good-looking woman, young. Stanos was laughing, lighting a cigarette, his own legs widespread like hers. She laughed at something he said.

"Janwillem Jacobsen," I said.

"Never heard of him," Humphrey said, over his shoulder. He turned back to me. "What is it you want, Mul? I want to get along, you know that. Carmine, he was old-fashioned, but that's all gone. We can get along. Just tell me what it is." He wanted me to name my price, I could see, and get out of his hair. He had his hands full. I could feel the earth tremble.

"I have the gun that killed Jacobsen," I said. "It has your fingerprints on it. Like I say, it would be a hard case to make, but it'll make."

I'll give the man credit. He didn't blink. He just looked at me, not a muscle moving. "Okay. You have a gun. All God's chillun got guns, Mul. What do you want for yours?"

Now, that was the question. What did I want?

"I want the guy who took down Hoffa," I said.

He glanced away, at Helen again. She was talking fairly animatedly with Stanos, her hands gesturing, her short skirt swinging. She had pretty nice legs. She and Stanos were getting along like a quarterback and a cheerleader, it seemed.

"What do you want with him?" Humphrey said. He could hardly attend to what he was doing. I almost felt sorry for him.

"What do I want with him? Humphrey, I'll be famous. I'll be the dick who broke the Hoffa case. I want to send him to prison, for murder, to avenge the death of one of our greatest union leaders. What do you mean, 'What'?"

"What if he's dead?" he asked.

"Is he dead?"

"A long time ago. But . . . I could find a guy . . . a guy who was there, anyway. He didn't pull the trigger, but he's still . . . you know, what is it? Culpable."

"What's his name?"

"Bring me the gun. I'll bring the guy."

I stared off into the sky. It was a little sunny here, not like down on the lake. I thought for a minute about what was implied by that "I'll bring the guy" statement. It could mean a lot of things, such as: DiEbola would find someone to take the fall, he'd provide a corpse . . . I wasn't sure what other permutations were conceivable. So I tossed in my kicker, as if I'd simply overlooked it: "There's one other thing."

DiEbola restrained a sigh of impatience. "What now?" he asked. He wanted me to leave and take my tall, skinny detective with me.

"Buchanan," I said.

He looked at me sharply. But after a moment he snorted. "Sure. Why not? He's a goddamn liability, anyway. I'll send you some material on him. Where do I send it?"

I held up my hands in horror. "Don't send anything to me! I'm not your pal. You got something on Buchanan, send it to someone who can use it. Or let me make that clear: someone who *will* use it. The papers, maybe."

He smiled. "I'll do it today. It's a pleasure to serve the community, Sergeant."

Driving away, Books said, "Stanos and Helen kinda hit it off."

"I saw that. What was it all about?"

"They went to Denby High School together. She remembered him, he was in the band."

"Yeah? I guess I heard that. From Jimmy Marshall. They used to be partners, in the patrol car."

Books chuckled. "Man, I bet he was a mess in high school. But she was sure flashing the pussy in his eyes. Now why do you think she did that?"

I looked at Books. "You know why she did that, Books."

It wasn't far to the Renaissance Center hotel, where M'Zee Kinanda was staying. I pulled into the underground parking and as we took the elevator up, I observed, "You know, Books, I thought I was taking Stanos along to DiEbola's for muscle, but the muscle wasn't needed. Still, he did all right, didn't he?"

"Oh, it was the muscle that she responded to, all right," Books said.

Kinanda had a top-floor suite. It gave him a terrific view of Canada and much of Detroit. He was dressed in sweatpants and a kind of Russian-looking belted smock that had a cadet collar. He wore Persian slippers and a brocade skullcap. He was very happy to see Books, clearly. To me he said, "Well, Sergeant, we meet again, but without the pretty girl. Too bad."

I tried to imagine this robust, self-confident man of the world as the skinny, self-absorbed Tyrone that I'd pictured from Grootka's and Vera's accounts. It was a different man, to be sure, though not completely different. One was soon conscious of a kind of restrained impatience, which may be what we notice when we remark patience, of a man who would rather be at work.

"The pretty girl," I said, "was Vera Jacobsen's daughter, Agge. Did you know that?"

He shook his head. "No, but I'm not surprised. I knew there was something familiar about her. In this life—in the show-biz side of it, anyway—you meet so many people. You get used to people seeming familiar, even if you're in Paris, or Moscow. Well, the musician's life is pretty cosmopolitan, especially nowadays."

"M'Zee, lets forget Agge. I want to talk to you about the Hoffa case." He nodded. I sketched briefly the extent of my knowledge and its sources. "You can see my situation," I said. "I don't have any kind of case, and yet I have a duty and an obligation. On top of that, I'm more or less hopelessly compromised here."

He nodded and observed, thoughtfully, "It's a tough one, I agree. And yet . . . I can't help feeling that the real stickler is the ethical and moral issue. Right? If, for instance, you had simply been told these things, not as a police officer, but as an interested citizen, a bystander, you wouldn't have the same problem. Or at least, you wouldn't feel such a bind. Am I right?"

"Possibly," I said. "As long as we remember that what's important is not what I feel, but what was done."

"Oh, yeah, sure." He picked up a soprano sax and took the mouthpiece cover off, placing his lips around the mouthpiece and fingering the keys lightly. "I'd like to play you something," he said.

I wasn't really in the mood, but what can you say? "Great," I said and stood with my hands clasped behind my back, gazing over his shoulder, out the windows.

I didn't know what the tune was, but he played an absolutely heart-wrenching three or four minutes of pure, soaring melody. It made one want to weep. A haunting blues in such a beautiful, pure tone . . . I saw it, floating like a pear in midair, and enclosed within it the sunny field and the orchard, the woods, the little birds gaily calling in the flickering shadows . . . and then their sudden haunted silence when the hawk arrives and their tentative but waxing joy when he leaves. I stared through misted eyes out through the big, tinted windows at the river and beyond it to the flatness of Canada in the spring. From up here I could see that the haze on Lake Erie, which had made it such a pearly day of terror for Books, was just a local thing . . . in reality, the sun was shining everywhere.

"That's wonderful," I told him. My voice was a little husky. "What's it called?"

"I call it . . . 'Faraway.'"

I didn't quite take it in. I said, "It's beautiful."

"Yeah, but is it catchin' crooks?" He laughed. He set the sax on its stand, next to a gleaming baritone. "For a long time I called it 'Blues in G,' but that didn't seem quite, ah . . . quite it. So where we at? Oh yeah, you're trying to figure out how to reach that final note, that resolving G. Well, everybody knows—in the key of G, you only got that one sharp, F. Unless," he muttered in an aside, "you're in G minor." "Now," he went on "what would I tell Grootka? Probably something like, 'Don't strain for the note, be free.'"

"F-sharp minor, hunh?" I said. "How do I get to G from F-sharp?" Suddenly, it struck me. "Faraway?"

He lifted his right middle finger. "Just lift this finger," he said. "F-sharp. G."

"What's in Faraway?"

"A man named Fred. He runs a little butcher shop, skins out deer for hunters, makes some nice sausage. If he's still alive, he can tell you about Grootka."

In the car, Books said, "Do I have to go?"

"Did you know about this Fred?"

"I heard of him. I ate his sausages. Grootka used to go up there every deer season, and he'd bring back some sausages."

"I never knew Grootka was a deer hunter," I said.

"I don't know that he ever shot a deer," Books said, "but he'd bring back some sausages, every year."

"What do you think's up there?"

Books shook his head dolefully. "I don't know," he said.

"Well, we better get started."

He sighed. "I'll put on a tape. You still got that Kinanda?"

15

Outtake

I think his
name was Fred Miner, but in the way of things, in a small town,
or maybe it was in the can—he'd spent some time in Jacktown, courtesy of some people who wanted him to serve it for them, and were
willing to pay—folks called him Major. Not Fred Major. Major Fred,
I guess. If you didn't know him too well, as with Kinanda, you could
call him Fred. If you were a pal, you called him Maje.

He'd spent more years at Jackson than he'd planned. There
was some violence, and he wasn't protected. So he spent the time
and came out and got his payoff, and retired to fish and hunt and
support himself. But in one of those crappy little ironies of life, he'd
found himself going blind. He could still fly-fish, after a fashion, on
the Manistee and the Au Sable—"Sort of like night fishing, you
know?" He laughed. A low, rumbling laugh.

He had a round, grizzled head with a curly beard and he wore
a wool cap indoors and out, along with a red-and-black-check wool
hunting shirt that had the sleeves rolled up to reveal long johns.
He wore wool military pants and felt-lined rubber and leather boots.
His eyebrows had gotten shaggy and he hid behind them, it looked
like.

When Books and I showed up it was quite late. But he said he'd just been sitting in the dark, listening to the radio, to the hockey game. The Red Wings were beating the Blues. So we had something to talk about. I fumbled through my introduction until finally he said, "You're Mul."

"That's right."

"And you." He turned to Meldrim. "You'd be Books. C'mon in. Grootka said you'd be along, one of these days. It's taken you a while." He turned on some lights. He had a small shop with a couple of refrigerated meat counters, not presently showing a lot of goods and all of it wrapped and put down for the night, of course. "You'll want some of my venison sausage. I'll give you some to take with you, but I just cooked some up a while ago."

He led the way into a very messy bachelor apartment in the back. That's where he'd been sitting, in a chair surrounded with duck decoys, carving gear, shotguns, implements like that. He'd been carving a decoy head. It was unpainted, so I had no idea what it was supposed to be. There was a smell of sausage in the air, all right. He turned the burner on under a skillet and began to warm up the remains of a thick sausage or two, which he had sliced into discs. He sawed off a couple of large chunks of home-baked bread— "Neighbor lady bakes it," he said. "It's just farm bread, but good." He slapped some sausage onto the bread and shoved the plates at us. The wine was jug wine in jelly glasses. It was delicious.

"I guess you come to get Grootka's package," he said.

"That's right," I said, glancing at Books. He smiled slightly and gave his head a tiny shake, as if to marvel at my luck.

Fred found his key ring and a big dry-cell lantern. He pulled on his hunting coat and led us through the shop and out the back. "I want you to know that I never opened that box," he told us as he showed the light for us to follow, "and I know that Grootka never did. I don't know what's in it and I don't want to know. I'd appreciate it if you could just take it with you and whatever happens from there, let it happen there."

He led us along a path that went back along a creek, which we had to cross on a mossy two-by-twelve plank, and into a little thicket, which shortly gave way to a clearing. While he unlocked a padlock on a rough wooden shed door, I told him I'd do what I could, but I couldn't promise anything.

"Grootka brought it by one afternoon and asked me if I could keep it for him. It was all wrapped up, already, but he got me to wrap the box again and put it in another box. 'Just for safekeeping,' he told me. He said you'd be along and to tell you everything I knew about it."

He opened the door and turned on a light as we followed him in. The interior of the shed belied its rustic exterior. It was really a well-made place, with thick, obviously superinsulated walls and a concrete floor with a drain. Sinks, good lighting, and lots of counter space, heavy chopping-block counters, with knives and saws and cleavers ranged against the back wall. A Dewalt bandsaw, a slicer, a grinder—all these and more modern power tools and appliances were available and obviously in regular use. And beyond this work area, the heavy doors of two walk-in coolers. Fred explained that many of his customers brought in animals that needed to be processed in privacy. "A farmer raises more than beef, you know," he said, "and sometimes the critters aren't tame. They have to be processed out of season. They make good sausage."

They did indeed. Or rather, Major Miner made good sausage. But I was interested in whether Grootka had actually said I would be around, and when he'd said it. The Maje cleared that up. Grootka had brought the box to him to be stored indefinitely on August 10, 1975. He had paid a year's storage in advance, but the Maje couldn't remember how much that was. The last time he'd been by, about five years ago, he had paid a thousand dollars, which the Maje had accepted as sufficient payment for "eternity."

"I got the feeling he didn't expect to be coming back," the Maje said. "He looked about the same to me, but I figgered he knew best. Anyways, the first time he mentioned your name was about 1980, somewhere in there. He said you'd be coming for the box and to just give it to ya. So here it is."

He had unstacked some other boxes in the cooler, all of them, like this one, sealed containers of supplies like plastic wrap. This one was about the size of a liquor carton. It was neatly wrapped in clear plastic, heat-sealed by the Maje's device. I'm not good at this, but I estimated it to weigh about ten or fifteen pounds.

The Maje insisted that we take a box just as large, filled with frozen sausage. He had a lot of it, he said, gesturing at the three deer carcasses still hanging in the cooler, waiting their turn to be made into breakfast. We put them in the trunk of the Checker and drove away. It took ten minutes or more to find a lonely country road. In the light of the headlamps, I cut open the plastic and opened the box, with Books looking on.

Perched on top, just beneath some newspapers from 1975, was the revolver. "Yes," I said, relieved. Grootka had not let me down. It was a Harrington & Richardson .32. It was wrapped in ordinary kitchen plastic wrap, and I'm sure that the fingerprints of Humphrey DiEbola were undisturbed. The technology these days is so much better than in Grootka's day, that Forensics shouldn't have too much trouble making a positive identification.

I was a little curious, however. Was this the gun that Grootka had given to Jacobsen? I thought it might be. If so, it suggested a scenario in which DiEbola had obtained the gun from Jacobsen, either by force or plan. It didn't make any difference; the crucial thing was that the gun carried DiEbola's prints. Of course, without

Jacobsen's corpse, without the fatal bullet, none of this meant much.
But DiEbola would know the importance of this gun, and he had
shown that he knew.

I delved down into the package to see what other goodies
Grootka had provided—blood-soaked clothing, no doubt. I could
see a stained shirt. I peeled it back.

Janney Jacobsen's cloudy blue eyes stared up at me.

We had dis-
cussed it from every angle as we drove through the night. Neither
of us had slept, although Books may have nodded. But now he was
sitting as silently as I in the morning traffic jam north of Detroit.
An accident had cars backed up beyond Sashabaw Road. I turned
on the radio.

Books had grumbled, finally, "If you're gonna chop folks'
heads off, seems like you'd chop the important heads." He thought
that Grootka should have preserved Hoffa's head. But I pointed out
that Grootka was not interested in Hoffa. Grootka knew that the
telltale bullet was in Jacobsen's head. He'd have preferred to pre-
serve Jacobsen's body, no doubt, but that wasn't feasible. He'd had
no idea how soon the Mob cleanup squad would arrive, but arrive
they would. He'd taken what he could take.

"Trouble with you cops," Books said, "is all you think about
is the forensics. You got no respect for the human side."

"Pha-roah, you mean?"

"All right, make fun." He fell silent then.

But we both perked up when the newscaster informed us:
"Detroit organized-crime figure Humphrey DiEbola was slain last
night. Security personnel at his Grosse Pointe estate reported that
an unknown assailant apparently shot and killed the elusive Mobster as he walked on the grounds. Details are sketchy, but a body
was removed to the Wayne County morgue this morning. Specula-

tion has already begun about who will succeed DiEbola, who many have credited with vastly improving the scope and profitability of organized-crime activity in the Detroit area following the assassination of his predecessor, Carmine Busoni, some three years ago. The FBI is noncommittal on that score, but they do not rule out the possibility that DiEbola was removed by disaffected loyalists of the Busoni faction. More on this story as it develops."

The traffic began to move. Books said, "I wonder if they *would* tolerate a woman don?" He had read my mind.